Tom Holt was born _____ uch given to brooding _____ at Westminster School, _____ and the College of Law. He produced his first book, *Poems by Tom Holt*, at the age of thirteen, and was immediately hailed as an infant prodigy, to his horror. At Oxford, Holt discovered bar billiards and at once changed from poetry to comic fiction, beginning with two sequels to E F Benson's Lucia series, and continuing with his own distinctive brand of comic fantasy in *Expecting Someone Taller, Who's Afraid of Beowulf?, Flying Dutch, Ye Gods!, Overtime, Here Comes the Sun, Grailblazers, Faust Among Equals, Odds and Gods, Djinn Rummy* and *My Hero*. He has also written two historical novels set in the fifth century BC, the well-received *Goatsong* and *The Walled Orchard*, and has collaborated with Steve Nallon on *I, Margaret*, the (unauthorised) autobiography of Margaret Thatcher. Thinner and more cheerful than in his youth, Tom Holt is now married, and lives in Somerset.

MY HERO
ODDS AND GODS
FAUST AMONG EQUALS
GRAILBLAZERS
HERE COMES THE SUN
OVERTIME
YE GODS!
FLYING DUTCH
WHO'S AFRAID OF BEOWULF?
EXPECTING SOMEONE TALLER

I, MARGARET
THE WALLED ORCHARD
GOATSONG

LUCIA TRIUMPHANT
LUCIA IN WARTIME

DJINN RUMMY

Tom Holt

ORBIT

An *Orbit* Book

First published in Great Britain by Orbit in 1995

This edition published by Orbit in 1996

Copyright © Tom Holt 1995

The moral right of the author has been asserted.

A CIP catalogue record for this book
is available from the British Library.

ISBN 1 85723 363 8

Printed and bound in Great Britain
by Clays Ltd, St Ives plc

Orbit
A Division of
Little, Brown and Company (UK)
Brettenham House
Lancaster Place
London WC2E 7EN

For James Spartacus Hale
and Colin Wilberforce Lincoln Murray,
who, on 1 October 1994,
abolished slavery in south Somerset.

ONE

6 *7,811 pints today please, milkman.*

Rule one in the licensed victualling trade: Know Your Clientele. Ignore it, and you might as well keep the doors locked.

Mr D. Jones had been in the business for a very long time, and he had long since learned everything there is to know about running a hotel, bar and bistro catering exclusively for drowned sailors.

It is, in fact, fairly straightforward. Good plain food; *never* under any circumstances allow the bar to run dry; strong tea with lashings of milk and sugar. And, of course, ensure that all tables are secured to the floor with half-inch carriage bolts.

He glanced up through the glass roof. Light never quite made it down as far as The Locker, but the water overhead was turning the precise shade of muggy dark olive that implied daybreak. Time to roll up the shutters, take the towels off the pumps and start a new day.

D. Jones folded the scrap of paper, pushed it into the bottle and rammed home the cork. Then he opened Number Six airlock.

A message in a bottle.

Having decided to kill herself, Jane went into the nearest chemist's shop.

'I'd like a large bottle of aspirins, please,' she said to the man behind the counter. He looked at her. In fact, as far as Jane was concerned, he made an unnecessarily thorough job of it, as if he was planning on doing an autopsy without the tedious business of cutting her up first.

'Aspirins?' he asked, making it sound as if she'd asked for the elixir of eternal youth.

'Aspirins,' Jane replied. 'Please. And could you hurry it up? I'm on my lunch break.'

The man, who was white-haired and very tall, sniffed. 'Any particular sort?' he asked. 'Or just aspirins?'

'Just aspirins.'

The man smiled. 'Not sure we've got any of those in stock, just aspirins. I'll have to look out the back. Don't go away.'

Before Jane could say anything, the man had darted away into the stockroom. She felt a strong inclination to make her escape while he was gone, but the voice of logic inside her head dissuaded her. *Come off it, girl*, it said, *you've made up your mind to commit suicide and you're afraid something bad might happen to you? In a chemist's?*

The man reappeared.

'You're in luck,' he said, extending a hand containing a big brown bottle. 'Just the one left. Directions on the label, that'll be two pounds seventy.'

It was, Jane couldn't help observing, a very old bottle. It had cobwebs on it. She'd read somewhere that out-of-date medicines could be very bad for you.

'Thanks,' she said. 'Just what I wanted. Keep the change.'

Now then; where? Did it matter? Anywhere she could be sure of a little bit of peace and quiet. Her flat. No, not her flat; they wouldn't find her for days (who would they be, she wondered) and by then she probably wouldn't be very nice ... A hotel? She looked in her purse, which contained three pounds and seventeen pence, and no cheque book or credit card. She'd left them at home, on the basis that you can't take it with you. This, she muttered to herself, is getting tiresome.

A railway station. Yes. She was, after all, about to embark on a very long journey.

There was a station; and the station had one of those waiting rooms that make you decide to wait on the platform instead. Guaranteed privacy. She sat down, opened her bag and took out the bottle.

Note. Should she write a note? It was traditional, yes, but when you looked at it objectively, what the hell was the point? She had no family or other human associates to whom she owed an explanation; what made her think that the coroner was going to be interested in her tawdry little problems? They have a hard life, coroners; long hours, calls out in the middle of the night, constant association with lawyers, policemen and dead bodies. Boredom would probably be the last straw; and besides, she didn't have a pen with her, and a suicide note written in eyebrow pencil smacked of undue frivolity.

Goodbye, cruel world. She unscrewed the bottle ...

WHOOSH!

'Thank goodness for that,' said the genie. 'For a moment there I was beginning to get worried.'

He hung in the air like a cloud of gunsmoke on a still, bright day; and as each second passed he became more substantial and more brain-wrenchingly incredible. There was a tinkle as the bottle hit the concrete floor and disintegrated into small, sharp brown fragments.

'You'd think,' he went on, 'I'd have had more sense, particularly in my line of business. First thing they teach you in genie school, if a strange man comes up to you, offers you sweets and asks you to get into his bottle, walk away, or better still, rip his head off and swallow it.' He sighed, and the effort made his component molecules sway in the air. 'Fourteen years this Tuesday fortnight I've been in that sodding bottle, and the sanitary arrangements left something to be desired, I'm telling you.'

He was no longer transparent; scarcely translucent. A shaft of light nudging its way through the dusty window hit the back of his head and, knowing what was good for it, refracted violently.

Genies are designed to be useful rather than ornamental, and this one was a masterpiece of the genre. There was enough ivory in its tusks to make cue balls for all the snooker tables in Europe.

'Who are you?' Jane said.

The genie frowned. 'Are you serious?' it demanded. 'Or just extremely sceptical?'

'You're a *genie*?'

'Hole in one.'

'A real genie?'

The genie clicked its tongue. 'No,' it replied. 'I'm a fake, you can tell by the lack of hallmarks. Of course I'm a real genie. What do you want, a certificate of authenticity?'

'What ...?' Jane felt her vocabulary clot. On the one hand, she had made up her mind to put an end to her pointless life, the existence of genies wasn't really germane to the various issues that had influenced her in making that decision, and time was getting on. If she didn't get a move on, she'd arrive in Heaven too late for dinner. On the other hand ...

'Admit it,' she said, 'you're my imagination, aren't you? I've taken the pills and I'm hallucinating.'

'Thank you very much,' replied the genie, offended. 'Do I look like a hallucination?'

Jane considered. 'Frankly,' she said, 'yes.'

The genie considered this. 'Fair enough,' it replied. 'Maybe that wasn't the most intelligent rhetorical question

I've ever posed. Do I take it, by the way, that you were planning on eating the pills?'

Jane nodded.

'Headache? Sore throat?'

'Bad dose of life,' Jane replied. 'Fortunately, the remedy is available over the counter without a prescription.'

The genie shook its head. 'Bad attitude you've got there, if I may make so bold,' it said. 'There's lots of things worse than life, believe you me.'

'Oh yes? Such as?'

'Such as death, for one,' the genie replied, 'spending a lot of time in bottles coming in close behind to clinch silver. Mind if I sit down, by the way? Cramp.' Like a closely packed swarm of bees it drifted down and hovered an inch or so above the bench opposite Jane. 'Mug's game, death is. All that standing about in queues and filling in forms. Compared to death, life is just a bowl of cherries.'

'Ah,' Jane replied, with a strong trace of ice in her voice, 'I wasn't planning on dying, I was planning on being reincarnated. So put that in your pipe and smoke it, Mister Clever.'

The genie nodded. 'Don't get me wrong,' it said, 'there's nothing bad about reincarnation *per se*, it's basically a very good system, cost-effective and ecologically friendly. It's just that, until they iron out the technical glitches …'

Jane frowned. 'I don't think you're a genie at all,' she said. 'I think you're actually the imaginary friend I had when I was five, only grown-up. You're just as irritating as he was, and you've got the same knack of poking your finger in your ear and wiggling it about when you're talking.'

'Do I do that?' The genie looked at its hand. 'Really?'

'Really.'

'Have you seen the length of my claws? How come I don't lacerate my eardrums?'

Jane shrugged. 'That's your problem, surely. Look if you

really are a genie and you've been sent to make me change my mind—'

'Sent? Who by?'

'Search me. Is there anybody who sends genies, or do they just turn up? No, forget it, no offence but I'm really not interested. It's been lovely meeting you, really it has, but it's time I wasn't here.'

'Sure?'

'Positive.' Jane looked at the floor. 'I take it,' she said, 'the bottle was empty. Apart from you, of course.'

The genie nodded; or at least, it shimmered up and then down again, like an indecisive smoke signal. 'You want some aspirins, I take it?'

'Please.'

'Your wish is my—'

'Hold it.'

'Shit.' An expression of disgust flitted across the genie's face. 'I thought you'd say that,' it muttered. 'Perceptive, aren't I?'

Jane leant forward, her chin cupped in her hand. 'My wish is your command?'

The genie winced. 'Bloody marvellous,' it said. 'Humans, all they're interested in is one thing. My mother was right, it's wishes, wishes, wishes all the time with you people. Makes me sick.'

'Three wishes?'

'Absolutely correct. Still, since you're absolutely dead set on killing yourself, there really isn't much point, is there? Unless you want a hand getting the job done, that is.' The genie grinned toothily. 'In which case,' it said, 'absolutely delighted to oblige. Fourteen years in an empty bottle, one thing you do get is decidedly peckish.'

Jane shook her head. 'That,' she said, 'was before I had three wishes from a genuine genie. You've got to admit, it alters things.'

'Up to a point,' the genie said. 'I mean, we're talking parameters of the possible here. There are very strict rules about what we are and are not allowed to do for clients.'

'I'll bet.'

'So strict,' the genie went on, shimmering persuasively, 'as to make the wishes virtually worthless, in my opinion. Not worth the hassle. Forget all about it if I were you.'

'I think I'll give them a try, thanks all the same.'

'Gosh, there's a train just coming in, if you're quick you could jump under it and—'

'Three wishes,' Jane said firmly. 'Agreed?'

The genie sighed. 'In which case,' it said, 'you'd better have one of these.'

There was a rustle of pages, and a book appeared in Jane's lap. She picked it up and squinted at the spine:

OWNER'S MANUAL

'Demeaning, I call it,' the genie muttered. 'I mean, owner, for God's sake. Makes me sound like a blasted lawn-mower.'

Congratulations! You are now the owner of a Model M27 'Gentle Giant' general service domestic and industrial genie. Provided it is properly maintained and only genuine replacement parts are used (N.B. use of non-standard parts may invalidate your warranty) your genie should provide you and your civilisation with a lifetime of cheerful and near omnipotent service—

'Gentle giant my arse,' the genie interrupted. 'Well, giant maybe, but gentle …'

Jane read on for a while, and then closed the book. 'Three wishes,' she said.

'That's right. You saw the bit about the "Wish By" date, by the way? Very important, that.'

'Very well,' Jane went on, 'I'll have the first one now, please.'

'Fire away.'

'I'd like,' Jane said, 'another twelve million wishes.'

The genie's head jerked upright. 'Now just a cotton-picking minute,' it complained, 'that's not fair. There's no way …'

'Why not?' Jane smirked. 'Completely legitimate request, according to this book.'

'Rubbish. Like I said, there are strict rules.'

Jane nodded. 'I agree,' she said. 'Here they are on page four, paragraph two, three lines up from the bottom. Want to have a look?'

'I know the rules, thank you,' said the genie icily.

'As follows,' Jane continued. 'One, no wishes that change the very fabric of reality. Well, that's OK, if I can have three wishes I can have three billion, it's all the same in principle.'

'Matter of opinion,' grunted the genie.

'Two,' Jane said firmly, 'no wishes beyond the genie's power to fulfil. Obviously no worries on that score.'

'I've got a bad back, mind,' the genie interjected. 'Gives me one hell of a lot of jip in the winter months, my back does.'

'And finally,' Jane said, 'rule three, all wishes to be used within three hundred years of first acquiring the genie.' Jane glanced at her watch. 'By my reckoning that gives me till half past twelve on the sixteenth of June 2295. Agreed?'

'Twenty past twelve, I make it.'

'Then twenty past twelve it shall be.' Jane closed the book. 'Nothing in there that says I can't wish for more wishes. And if with my next wish I wish for another nine trillion and four wishes, there's absolutely nothing you can do about it. Is there?'

The genie scowled. 'I think this is probably something of a grey area, interpretation-wise,' it said. 'However, as a gesture of goodwill, would you accept six wishes in full and final settlement?'

'No.'

'You're not a lawyer by any chance, are you?'

'That's a horrible thing to say about anybody.'

'True.' The genie scratched the back of its head, and for a few moments bright sunlight seeped through the gashes made by its claws in the glittering air. 'All right then, tell you what I'll do. All the wishes you want for three years, how about that?'

Jane shook her head. 'For life,' she replied. 'But I promise I won't wish for anything too yuk, provided there's not an emergency or something.'

'God, you drive a hard bargain.'

'I know.'

'Can I go now?' The genie lifted its arm and sniffed. 'I mean, I'll be there as soon as you call, word of honour, but I'd really appreciate it if you'd just spare me a few minutes. You know, to freshen up, brush my teeth, that sort of thing. I won't be long.'

'That's all right.' Jane considered. 'What's your name, by the way?'

The genie looked embarrassed; that is, the million billion minuscule points of light of which it was composed flickered red, one after the other, all in the space of a fraction of a second. 'Just call me Genie,' it said quickly. 'That's what everybody else does, and it's much—'

'Name.'

The genie dimmed. 'Kawaguchiya Integrated Circuits III,' it mumbled.

'Kawaguchiya Integrated Circuits?'

'Fraid so.' The genie nodded stroboscopically. 'Commercial sponsorship, you see. Pays for all the running repairs, plus a twice-yearly check-up and insurance. People call me Goochie for short. If they dare,' it added. 'And even then, never more than twice. Myself, I prefer the acronym. It's more me.'

'Kick?'

'Kiss,' Kiss replied. 'The C is soft as in coelacanth, certain and celery. Like I said, though, just plain Genie does me absolutely fine.'

'With the light brown hair, huh?'

Kiss sighed and gathered together his photons with all the dignity he could muster. 'All things considered, I was a fool to leave the bottle. Be seeing you.'

He said; and vanished.

Much to Jane's surprise, he came back twenty minutes later.

'Would you like a cup of tea?' she asked.

'Thank you,' Kiss replied. 'Nice place you've got here, by the way.'

Jane raised an eyebrow. 'You like it?' she said. 'Personally, I think it's a dump.'

'Objectively speaking, it probably is. Sure beats an aspirin bottle, though.'

'I'll take that as a compliment,' Jane replied. 'Milk and sugar?'

Kiss shook his head – he was, Jane noticed, considerably more together than he had been; the gaps between the little points of light and shadow that comprised him were much smaller, and unless he stood with his back to the window you'd almost imagine he was solid. 'A slice of lemon, if you've got it.'

'Sorry.' Jane frowned. 'Hey, who's doing the wishes around here, anyway?'

Let there be lemon; and there was lemon. She handed him his cup (it was disconcerting to say the least to push one of her grandmother's Crown Derby teacups into a glistening dustcloud, but there was no crash) and bade him sit down. He repeated the hovering manoeuvre she'd witnessed before.

'I wasn't expecting you,' she said.

Kiss's eyebrows flickered sceptically. 'You usually lay out the best china just for yourself, do you?' he enquired.

'I don't remember giving you my address,' Jane replied.

Kiss snorted. 'Give me some credit,' he said huffily. 'I am, or was, one of the marshals of the hosts of heaven, rider of the tempest, companion of the cherubim. Looking someone up in the phone book is scarcely taxing my powers to the limit.'

'So how did you find out my name?'

'You write your name inside your handbag; evidently a throw-back to your schooldays. Rather endearing, I thought. Mind if I smoke?'

Jane frowned. 'Actually,' she said, 'I'm allergic to tobacco.'

'Who said anything about tobacco?'

Jane shrugged. 'Please yourself.'

A second or so later she became aware of the most delicious perfume; attar of roses or something like that. Two hundred quid for a tiny bottle sort of thing. She nodded approval.

'Actually,' said the genie, 'it's woodbines. Well, this is all very pleasant. So far, anyway.'

'Let's hope it stays that way,' Jane replied. She pushed her hair back up out of her eyes, and put on a serious face. 'I think it's time we did a little basic ground-work, don't you?'

The genie looked at her. 'Ground-work? You mean ploughing or something?'

'I mean,' Jane replied, 'I want you to tell me something about yourself. You see, I haven't got the faintest idea what a genie is, or where they come from, anything like that. Except that they come in bottles and grant you three wishes,' she added lamely.

'I see.' Kiss scratched the bridge of his nose. 'That's a bit like saying all you know about America is Eggs Benedict and the date of Groundhog Day. Not enough, in other words.'

'That's what I'd assumed.'

'Right, then,' the genie said. 'Now, where shall I start?'

Genies (Kiss explained) are fallen angels. That is to say, in the beginning they were created out of the Mind of God, to do the things for which angels are necessary. All I can say about that is, He's got one hell of a warped imagination.

Most genies got to be genies by backing the wrong side in the civil war between the archangel Michael and Lucifer, Son of the Morning. Not me, though; I was on the right side in that lot, albeit in the Pay Corps. As I remember, I spent the duration of the war either playing cards or wandering around with a clipboard trying to keep out of the way of the officers. Which suited me fine, by the way. Never saw a thunderbolt thrown in anger, and I play a really mean game of djinn rummy.

No, my departure from Heaven was the result of an unfortunate misunderstanding about a lorryload of black market stardust somehow going missing en route to HQ from King Solomon's Mines. I was, of course, framed, but would they believe me? Would they hell.

Well, after that I bummed around for a bit, doing the things genies generally do – You don't? Well, all sorts of things, really: raising storms, necromancy, digging up pots of gold at the ends of rainbows, riding the moon, changing princes into frogs, a few real estate deals, anything to pass the time and put a few dinars in your pocket. It's a good life if you like that sort of thing, though you do tend to end up mixing with heroes and grand viziers and a lot of other low-lifes, and you're really only ever as good as your last job. Particularly these days, with all the science and stuff. In fact, quite a few of the lads I used to hang out with have packed in the road and settled down as lift operators. No, not lift attendants, lift operators. You don't seriously think lifts go up and down all day with just a bit of wire and a few pulleys, do you?

And the movies, of course; special effects. You've heard of George Lucas, I take it? Now that's one genie who really did make the big time.

Anyway, there I was, just sort of pottering about, minding my own business; and then, wham! Lamp time. It happens to all of us sooner or later, of course, it's genetic programming or something, like lemmings. Doesn't stop you feeling a right idiot when the stopper goes down, though.

Well, I was out of circulation for, what, five hundred years, five and a bit, and then – Sorry? Look, do I have to, because it really is very embarrassing? All right, if you insist.

I was at this party (Kiss said, cringing slightly) and there was this djinn, right? Tall, slim, blonde, pair of fangs on her like a sabre-tooth tiger; I mean, we're talking serious chemistry here and, besides, I may have been drinking. Alcohol has a bad effect on my metabolism, it has to be admitted. All I have to do is sniff a bottle of cough medicine and somebody has to take me home in a wheelbarrow.

Anyway, there we were and one thing led to another, and she said, 'Your place or mine?' and the next thing I remember was waking up in this lamp thing with a splitting headache and the lid coming off and me being shot out like someone had just shot a hole through the cabin wall at fifty thousand feet; and there's this magician type in a big pointy hat staring at me and saying, 'Hold on a minute, you're not the usual fiend, what's become of Mabel?'

Mabel, needless to say, was the looker with the luxury dentures, and she'd lured me back to her lamp, done a runner and left me there. I tried explaining, but it didn't do any good. '*Never mind, you'll just have to do instead,*' was all the sympathy and understanding I got out of him, the bastard.

Now here's a word of advice, from someone who's been there; if ever you get yourself indentured to a black magician, try to make sure it's not a black magician who's into the financial services stuff. It's bad enough as it is with the hurtling backwards and forwards through time and space, I-hear-and-obey-oh-mastering twenty-four hours a day, doing evil and getting yourself thoroughly disliked all the time. When you've got all that, plus you have to play snakes and ladders with the international currency markets, it can get to be a serious drag. You can imagine the sort of thing I mean: go sink a few of So-and-so's ships so I can mount a hostile takeover of his company. Oh look, the Samarkandi dirham's risen in early trading, go and raze their walls to the ground and eat their finance minister. I mean, where's the self-respect in that?

(At which point Jane interrupted to say it sounded awful. Kiss nodded sadly.

'It was,' he said. 'And you know what the worst part of it was? All this inside information floating around and me without a dinar to my name. A few lousy coppers in the right place and I could have been taken seriously rich, you know? As it was …'

'I see,' Jane said coldly. 'Do please go on.')

Anyway (said Kiss) eventually the Securities Commission caught up and it was a case of into the sack and off to the Bosphorus for him, and bloody good riddance too. Not, however, much fun for me, because I was in the lamp at the time. And in the lamp I stayed. For five hundred years, with nothing to do except play I Spy. Something, I need hardly tell you, beginning with L.

Just when I was starting to go lamp-crazy, though, off comes the lid and there's this bloke in a sort of fawn safari suit peering in at me and saying something about typical thirteenth-century Bokhara ware, probably indicative of developing commercial links with the Ummayads. That's right, a blasted archaeologist. There are times when you don't know when you're well off.

You'll never guess what his three wishes were. Well, if you know anything about archaeology, maybe you can. As I understand it, in order to become an archaeologist you have to spend your youth stuck in some dusty old library reading books about bits of broken pot. You don't have time for going to parties, or girls. By the time you do have time, it's generally too late – unless, that is, you suddenly find yourself with a virtually omnipotent spiritual assistant and three wishes.

Anyway, after that I needed a year at the bottom of a disused mine-shaft just to recover and get over the embarrassment; after which I got a job as a clerk in a shipping office. It was the least exciting thing I could think of. I was right.

And then, just when I was thinking about what I was going to do next and how much fun I could have with superhuman powers and absolutely no social conscience, I got stuck in the bottle you so kindly extracted me from. No, I'm not prepared to go into details; and if you want any co-operation at all from me in the course of what promises to be a long and interesting working relationship, you'll respect my privacy on that one. OK?

'Superhuman powers?' Jane queried.

Kiss nodded. 'Pretty superhuman,' he replied, 'and I don't have to dash into the nearest phone box and change first, either. Although,' he added, 'all that stuff was a front. He didn't need to change at all, it was just part of the act.'

Jane's eyes widened. 'You mean Superman—?'

'No names,' Kiss replied, 'no pack drill. But it's true, there's more of us about than people think. We've sort of rehabilitated ourselves in the community, if you like to look at it that way.'

'I see.' Jane was staring out of the window. 'You know,' she said, 'I'm so confused about all of this that I almost believe in you. Am I going mad, do you think?'

Kiss paused before answering. 'You're still alive, aren't you?' he said. 'Seems to me that you're that much ahead of the game, so don't knock it. That reminds me. The suicide thing. Why?'

Jane shook her head. 'We'd better respect each other's privacy,' she said. 'Fair enough?'

'Your wish, etcetera. Right,' said the genie, 'what's it to be? Shall we kick off with the wealth beyond the dreams of avarice, get that out of the way before the banks close?'

'That's possible, is it?'

'Piece of duff.' Kiss yawned and picked a stray morsel of fluff out of his hair. It turned into a two-headed snake, burst into flames and vanished. 'Swiss francs are what we usually recommend, although gold bullion has a lot going for it. Up to you, really.'

Jane shook her head. 'Later,' she said. 'Let's just have a look at this book and see what it has to say.'

She opened the manual.

1.1 Getting To Know Your Genie

'Gosh,' Jane said.

'You're probably way ahead of me,' Kiss was saying, 'but just in case you were tempted to, don't look down. Or at least, not straight down. Vertigo is one of the things I can't do anything about, oddly enough.'

Below them, on Nevsky Prospekt, the traffic roared; so far below them that all Jane could see was one continuous stream of white light and another of red. Further away, the absurd spire of the Cathedral of St Peter and St Paul loomed up into the night sky, like a spear aimed at the moon …

'For God's sake look where you're going. We nearly flew straight into that pointy thing.'

'Sorry,' Kiss replied. 'I'm a touch out of practice at flying two up. It's a bit like riding a motorbike with a sidecar, really, you have to remember to compensate—'

'Look,' Jane interrupted, as they flashed past the Admiralty Tower with at least six thousandths of an inch to spare, 'where the hell are we?'

'St Petersburg.'

'*St Petersburg?*'

Kiss shrugged – under the circumstances, an act of carelessness verging on criminal recklessness. 'You said take me somewhere foreign,' he said, as Jane hauled herself back up between the base of his wings. 'St Petersburg's foreign. Can't get much more foreign than St Petersburg, if you ask me. That down there, by the way, is the Prospekt Stachek, and that impressive-looking thing with the crinkly walls is in fact a processed meat plant, would you believe. Designed by Rubanchik and Barutchev in 1929—'

'Put me *down*.'

'As you wish. Anywhere in particular?'

'Yes. The ground. Quickly!'

The ground selected by Kiss for a landing strip turned out to be a pelican crossing on the Ulitsa Zodchevo Rossi, much to the chagrin of the driver of a lorryload of Brussels sprouts who was just about to drive over it. For the record, the lightning-fast swerve by which he managed to avoid running Jane and her invisible companion over was witnessed by no less a person than the acting secretary of the local bus-driver's co-operative, who offered him a job as soon as he was released from hospital.

'No offence,' Kiss said, as they crossed the road, 'but you're a lousy passenger. You may think that screaming *Oh God, we're going to die!* and grabbing hold of my left wing just when I'm doing the tricky part of the landing process is being helpful, but in actual fact …'

Jane sat down on the steps of a building and closed her eyes. 'I think,' she said, 'I'll take the train back, if it's all the same to you.'

Kiss was offended. 'I'd just like to remind you,' he said, 'that if you'd had your way, you'd have killed yourself by now. When it comes to a total disregard for the value of human life, I think you're the one who's into melanistic kettle spotting.'

Jane looked up at him angrily. 'To recap,' she said. 'Any wish I like, so long as it's physically possible?'

'That's right. OUCH!'

'Thank you.'

'There was no call,' Kiss said, rubbing the place on the side of his head where he had just thumped himself very hard, 'for that. If you're not happy about something, all you have to do is say. Remember that, and we'll get on just fine.'

Jane got to her feet. 'Now then,' she said. 'Yes, I'm convinced. You are a genie, and you exist. I think I'd like to go home. Slowly.'

'Your wish is my—'

'And peacefully. Straight and level. You think you can manage that?'

'I'll give it,' Kiss replied, 'my best shot.'

'Is that it?'

Kiss made no reply; he just took off his pinny, folded it neatly and put it back behind the door. Then he started the washing-up.

'And these little bits of grey grisly stuff,' Jane went on. 'You're sure they're really necessary?'

'Quails' guts Marengo,' Kiss replied. 'Where I come from, that's about as haut as cuisine can get. Fried in butter, or served as a crudité with a simple green salad ...'

Jane put down her fork and folded her arms. 'No thanks,' she said. 'Just take it away and bring me a boiled egg. A hen's egg,' she added quickly; but not quickly enough.

'To hear is to obey,' Kiss explained smugly. 'Come on, eat it up before it hatches.'

Jane shook her head; and a moment later there as a faint tapping sound, like Ginger Rogers trapped inside a fire-proof vault. A hairline crack appeared in the side of the egg.

'People think,' Kiss said, removing the plate, 'that these little chaps became extinct because of severe climactic changes at the close of the Cretaceous period. Truth is, nothing stupid enough to taste that good in an omelette deserves to survive. Oh look, here he comes. Whoosa pretty boy, then?'

A small, scaly head with three tiny bumps on its skull poked out through the shell and blinked moistly. Kiss clicked his tongue at it fondly a few times, and then vanished. When he reappeared, he was carrying a plastic tray and a styrofoam cup with a straw.

'More your style,' he said contemptuously. 'Still, it's early days yet. Next week we'll start you on ammonite cocktails and honey-roast mammoth.'

'Want to bet?'

'Your wish is my—'

'Oh, shut up.'

1.2 Setting Up Basic Routines

'For pity's sake,' Jane croaked, rolling over and peering at her clock. 'It's half past three in the morning.'

Over the end of the bed, a cloud of photons glistened

cheerfully. 'Up bright and early, you said,' Kiss replied. 'Here, catch hold.'

To her disgust, Jane received a tray with a plate on it. On the plate was a hedgehog, curled up in a nest of dry leaves. There were cubes of cheese and pineapple impaled on its spikes. It was, Jane noted with relief, asleep rather than dead.

'You did say you wanted your breakfast still in its bed,' Kiss explained, 'so I didn't wake it up. Besides, hedgehogs are usually flambéd at the table, so if you'll pass me that box of matches ...'

'Are you being stupid on purpose, or are you just—?'

'There's no need to be rude.'

1.3 Margins

'Right,' Jane said. 'Today we're going to set the world to rights.'

Kiss looked up from the sink. 'Fine,' he said. 'Is that before or after I do the washing-up?'

Jane blinked. 'I was being facetious,' she replied. 'Were you?'

'No,' the genie answered, squeezing the entire contents of the washing-up liquid bottle into the sink and turning both taps to full power. 'I'm never facetious where wishes are concerned, it's part of being a pro. You want the world set to rights, I'm your sprite.'

'I see.' Jane sat down and drank some tea. It was quite unlike any other tea she had ever tasted, while at the same time being unmistakably tea. She found out later that this was because Kiss made tea by uprooting a tea plant and dumping it in the pressure cooker for half an hour. 'And how do you propose going about it?'

'Easy.' The words *easy, no worries, piece of cake* had come to ring loud warning bells in Jane's mind; it usually meant that the genie was contemplating doing something so extreme as to boil the brain. 'The way I see it, all the misery and unhappiness in the world today is caused by governments, people like that. Just give me five minutes to get this baked-on grease off this grill-pan and I'll nip out and deal with them.'

'Deal with?'

Kiss made an unambiguous gesture with his forefinger and his throat. 'They've got it coming,' he said cheerfully. 'It'll be a pleasure.'

Jane spilt her tea. 'One,' she said, 'you'll do no such thing.'

'Oh, come on …'

'Two,' she continued, 'I thought there were rules about that sort of thing. I mean, what you can and can't do.'

Kiss shook his head. 'There are,' he replied. 'But topping a few politicians is entirely legitimate. It's only impossible things that I'm not supposed to do; you know, things that'd bend the nature of physics. There's nothing in the book of rules about criminal irresponsibility.'

'Ah.'

'I take it you're not keen on the idea?'

'I have to admit,' Jane replied, 'I'd prefer a more organic approach.'

The genie's massive brow wrinkled over. 'What, you mean bury them alive? Can do, just say the—'

'No.'

'All right, then, how about bury them alive in compost? You can't get more organic than compost.'

'I meant,' Jane said firmly, 'something a bit more constructive. Something that doesn't involve lots of people getting killed.'

The genie stared for a moment, then started to laugh. 'Set the world to rights and nobody gets killed? Hey, lady, where have you been all your life?'

★

Few compilers of folk-tale anthologies have recorded the fact, but all genies, regardless of the terms of their indenture or the nature of their employment, have an indefeasible right to one night off a week. Kiss had explained this to Jane in great detail, and had even taken the trouble of marking the whole of the relevant page of the manual in extra-fluorescent yellow marker pen.

Where, then, do genies go on their night off? There is, of course, only one place: Saheed's, in downtown Samarkand (turn left opposite the dye works till you come to a corrugated iron door, knock four times and ask for Ali). There, the stressed-out supernatural entity can relax, unwind and talk over the past week with other genies over a nice glass of cool goat's milk. Or so the theory runs. In practice, Ali the proprietor has had to have an annexe built into another dimension, because the fights on Quiz Nights threaten to upset the Earth's placement on its axis.

'It's amazing, it really is,' Kiss maintained, swilling the contents of his glass round to revive the head. 'The woman is completely weird. What exactly she wants out of life is beyond me entirely.'

His companion nodded sympathetically. 'Europeans,' he grunted. 'No more idea than next door's cat, the lot of them. I remember once, I was in this oiling can over France way, and—'

'Three weeks I've been with her now,' Kiss continued, absent-mindedly finishing off his companion's peanuts, 'and what have we done? Go on, guess. You'll never guess what we've done.'

'Probably not.'

'Nothing.' Kiss scowled. 'Absolutely bugger-all. Not proper genie stuff, anyway. It's all been ironing and shampooing the carpets and would you mind just running a duster over the sitting-room table? The score so far: ruby eyes of gods stolen, nil. Spirits of the dead raised, nil. Tail-feathers of firebirds plucked, nil. Hairs from the beard of the Great Cham abstracted, nil. Ankle-socks paired, fourteen. Potatoes peeled, thirty-two. Any more of this and I'm going to appeal to the Tribunal, because it really isn't on. Have another?'

His companion glanced at his wrist (genies don't need watches but are nevertheless creatures of habit). 'Since you're offering,' he replied. 'Just the one, mind, because I've got wealth beyond the dreams of avarice to fetch tomorrow, and you've got to keep a clear head for these fiddly little jobs.'

Kiss nodded and went to the bar.

'Two large djinns and tonic,' he said, 'ice and lemon in one.'

The bottle on the counter rocked backwards and forwards as if nodding, unstoppered itself and poured liquor into two glasses. Please note: customers who find they've left their money at home when dining at Saheed's don't just get away with doing the washing-up.

'Sounds like you've got yourself a right little ray of sunshine,' his companion observed, as Kiss brought back the drinks. 'What was that bit you said about further wishes?'

Kiss explained, again. His companion shook his head.

'I'm not sure about that,' he said, 'not sure at all. You should get the union rep to have a look at that for you. I mean, there must be something wrong with it, or else we'd all be in the smelly.'

'Lousy precedent,' Kiss agreed.

'Diabolical. They could take it up as a test case.'

'You reckon?'

'Worth a try.' His companion emptied his glass, wiped his mouth on the sleeve of his sixth arm, and stood up. 'Well, be seeing you. Don't steal any glass eyes.'

'Mind how you go,' Kiss replied absently. His companion withdrew, and a few moments later there was a brief outburst of muffled swearing as he discovered that while he'd been inside, some practical jokers had nailed his carpet to the carpet-park floor. (For the record, he arrived back home six hours late, soaking wet and frozen stiff, having had to make the return flight on a borrowed bar towel.)

Kiss lingered on until closing time, playing the video games in a desultory manner and beating the Dragon King of the South three times running at pool. It wasn't just that he was in no hurry to go home; there was something else troubling him, and he needed the noise and smashed-crockery sounds of his own kind about him in order to concentrate his mind. There was, he felt, something very odd going on, and in some way he couldn't work out he was involved in it, indirectly and at several removes. Whatever it was, it remained shadowy and obscure, with the result that he was too preoccupied to notice that he had just beaten the Dragon King a fourth time; which is to pushing one's luck as closing one's eyes and taking both hands off the wheel is to motorway driving. Not very long afterwards, he was rescued in the nick of time by the bouncer and deposited outside among the dustbins, where he passed a quiet night dreaming of jacket potatoes.

'What's it like,' Jane demanded, 'being a genie?'

They were digesting a leisurely picnic, a hundred feet or so up in the air directly above a spectacularly active volcano in the back lots of Hawaii. The venue had been Kiss's suggestion; it would save them having to take the empty fruit-juice cartons and boiled-egg shells home with them, he'd argued, if they could simply drop them into the most spectacular waste-disposal system on the planet. They were sitting on Kiss's own personal flying carpet (a three-ply Wilton Sportster with Hydra-Shock jute backing and a go-faster Paisley recurring motif) and Jane had just finished off the cold chicken.

'Dodgy,' Kiss replied, after some thought. 'You never really know where you are. I mean,' he continued, jettisoning an empty Perrier bottle, which liquefied twelve feet above the meniscus of the lava, 'potentially it's a really great lifestyle, if you can hack it and stay out of trouble. You've got eternal life and eternal youth, there's practically nothing this side of Ursa Major that can attack you without coming a very poor second, you can fly, you can materialise pretty well anything you like so long as it actually exists somewhere in the cosmos, and best of all you have absolutely no moral constraints whatsoever. I guess the nearest you could come in human terms would be a seven-foot-tall, extremely muscular movie star with a good agent and an even better lawyer. That's when the times are good, of course,' he added.

'And when they're not?'

Kiss shook his head. 'Bottles,' he said. 'Also lamps. Very bad news, both of them. I knew a genie once, in fact, got mixed up with one of those raffia-covered Chianti bottles made into a lamp. Poor bugger didn't know whether he was coming or going.'

'Confusing?'

'Just plain nasty,' Kiss replied. 'Take another mate of mine, Big Nick. I told him at the time – this was some years ago, mind – Nick, I said, stripping the lead off the Vatican roof is going to land you in very real grief, you mark my words. He didn't, of course, and look at him now.'

Jane squinted. 'I've heard of him, have I?'

Kiss nodded gloomily. 'I expect so. Big chap, white beard, red dressing-gown, reindeer, sack – thought you'd probably come across him.'

Jane's eyes widened. 'He's a *genie*?'

'There's more of us about,' Kiss said, 'than people realise.'

'And it's a punishment? All the delivering presents and happy smiling faces …'

'You try it and see how you enjoy it. I'm telling you, twelve thousand years in an oil-lamp would be paradise in comparison.' Kiss shuddered reflexively. 'And if that wasn't bad enough, the other three hundred and sixty-four days each year it's not just a bottle the poor sod's banged up in, it's one of those paperweights; you know, the sort you shake and it snows? I think you'd have to have a pretty warped mind to come up with something like that.'

Jane agreed.

'And it's getting worse, you know,' Kiss went on. 'Generally, that is. In the business. Admittedly in my young days there were more of the bad guys about – sorcerers and mages and the like – but at least they hadn't invented the unbreakable plastic bottle or the child-proof bottle-top. Makes my blood run cold, that does.'

Jane tried to imagine what it was like, being a genie, and found that she couldn't. Hardly surprising, she decided, but a trifle disappointing nevertheless. She dropped a paper plate over the side and watched it drift down and blossom, first into fire, then fine white ash, then nothing at all.

'And what about you?' Kiss said. 'Since we're obviously into a heavyweight experience-swapping trip, how about you telling me why the suicide thing? I have this feeling that it's something I ought to know, purely on a business level.'

Jane sighed. 'Why not?' she said. 'I expect you could find out if you wanted to.'

'No problem,' Kiss agreed. 'I could read your thoughts, for a start.'

'Could you?'

The genie nodded. 'It's frowned upon, of course,' he added. 'Not quite the done thing and so forth, especially within the parameters of the model genie/mortal relationship. But entirely feasible.'

'Hang on,' Jane objected. 'What happened to no moral constraints whatsoever?'

'It's not moral constraints, just peer group machismo. And we're drifting away from the subject rather, aren't we?'

'I suppose we are. Go on, then. Guess.'

'Guess why you wanted to kill yourself?'

'Mphm.'

Kiss frowned, and changed himself into a tree. Trees, as is well known, spend their entire lives trying to decide what they're going to do next, and therefore possess tremendous powers of concentration. It's only the lack of an effective central nervous system that keeps them from sweeping the board at chess tournaments.

'Unrequited love,' he said. 'Close?'

Jane scowled. 'Spot on,' she replied. 'Is it that obvious?'

'No,' replied the genie, with a hint of smugness. 'In fact, you've concealed it terribly well. I have the advantage, however, of superhuman intelligence. Not,' he added, 'that I use it much. Gives me a headache.'

'Me too.'

Kiss changed back into his customary shape: a nine-foot-tall clown, complete with red nose and a woolly ginger wig. 'Tell me about it,' he said.

'Nothing to tell, really.' Jane leaned over and stared at the seething flames below until her eyes hurt. 'His name was Vince, and he had the desk opposite mine at the Bank. In his spare time he played a lot of volleyball, his favourite food was pizza and he was saving up for one of those overland adventure holidays where you cross some desert or other in an open-topped truck. What I ever saw in him I can't for the life of me imagine, but there it is.'

Kiss nodded. 'It's the same with us and bottles,' he said. 'Only, of course, we eventually get out of the bottles, even if it does mean waiting till they biodegrade. As I understand it, your lot don't have that guarantee.'

'I don't know.' Jane sniffed. 'If you ask me, it's all a case of misunderstood biology. In fact, as an example of a very big hammer to crack a very small nut, it's hard to beat.'

Kiss rolled over on to his back and materialised a bottle of cold milk. He took a long pull, wiped the top of the bottle on the palm of his hand and offered it to Jane, who declined it.

'If you like,' he said, 'we can see what we can do about this Vince character. If you really want me to, that is.'

Jane shook her head. 'I don't honestly think it's something you can interfere with,' she replied. 'I thought you were only allowed to do the possible.'

Kiss shrugged. 'There would have to be an element of compromise,' he replied, 'and certainly you can't compel one mortal to love another. On the other hand, you can suggest to a mortal that he act affectionately towards another mortal if he doesn't want his ears ripped off and shoved up his nose. That'd be no bother whatsoever.'

'No, thank you.'

'Sure? The more I think about it, the more I warm to the—'

'Really,' Jane said. 'No thanks.'

'Suit yourself.' The genie yawned. 'So, what exactly do you want? I don't want to seem pushy or anything, but it's time you made your mind up about that. Most people have a shopping-list ready formulated before the cork's out of the bottleneck.'

'Well, I don't,' Jane said. 'Apart from the immediate things, I mean, like not having to clean the kitchen floor or go to work. Grand ambitions really aren't my style.'

'They don't have to be all that grand,' Kiss suggested. 'In fact, something modest but time-consuming would suit me down to the ground. A complete collection of Bing Crosby records, for example; or better still, a determination on your part to have lunch in all the wine-bars in the Southern

Hemisphere. I could handle that, if you could.'

Jane removed the straw from a fruit-juice carton and chewed it thoughtfully. 'Really,' she said, 'I suppose I ought to make the world a better place. Eliminate nuclear weapons, irrigate the deserts of Northern Africa, that sort of—'

'Oh dear, not *again*,' Kiss sighed. 'Sorry, but if I see one more North African desert, I shall probably be sick.'

'Oh.' Jane looked startled. 'You mean you already …?'

'We all have,' Kiss sighed, 'at one time or another. One of humanity's more predictable requests, I'm afraid. Exactly as predictable, in fact, as causing famine, pestilence and floods, which is Mankind's other great preoccupation. That's why we have the Concurrency Agreement. It was worked out by the Union, what, three thousand years ago, and just as well, in my opinion.'

Jane demanded footnotes.

'Simple,' Kiss explained. 'Suppose you have, say, fifty genies. You can bet your life that at any one time twenty-five of them are going to be indentured to do-gooders, let-the-deserts-bloom types; and the other twenty-five will be working for psychotic maniacs. We just set off one against the other, and things remain exactly as they are. Saves a lot of aggravation in the long run, and of course it gives your lot something to do into the bargain. Flag days, jumble sales, fighting wars, that sort of thing.'

'I see. How very depressing.'

'It is, rather. So, if you want me to convert the Nullarbor plain into a swaying forest of Brussels sprouts, just say the word, but you mustn't count on them staying there for more than a fiftieth of a second, if that. The rules are very strict.'

'Fine. I think I'd like to go home now, please.'

'Your wish is my—'

'Do you have to keep saying that?'

'Unfortunately, yes.'

TWO

A hot-air balloon bobbing uncertainly over a desert landscape.

Inside the balloon, a man and a girl, surveying the view with binoculars. There's nothing to be seen except sand and, in the far distance, huge rocky outcrops. No signs of life whatsoever. That suits the man and the girl perfectly.

The girl stoops down and picks up a metal cylinder, like a steel thermos flask. She opens it and rolls into the palm of her hand a single seed, no bigger than a grape pip. It sits, heavy for its size, in the soft skin of her hand. It looks, if anything that small and inert can manage such a feat, smug.

'Well?' asks the man. He has to shout because of the roaring of the wind, but his shout is so full of awe that it sounds like an extremely loud whisper; as if he was talking to a very deaf person in a cathedral.

'Here's as good a place as any,' replies the girl. 'Let's go for it.'

She leans over the side and reels for a second at the sight of so much nothing between her and the ground; then she deliberately opens her palm and lets the seed fall.

The seed falls …

And hits the ground.

WHUMP!

Was it a seed, or was it a bomb? Difficult to tell; there's

a mushroom-shaped cloud standing up from the desert floor ...

But that's not smoke or dust, that's foliage; a huge, thick stem supporting a giant bud –

– which bursts into a hot-flame-yellow flower with a raging red centre. The flower lifts towards the sun – you expect it to roar and shake its head like a lion – and the plant raises its two broad, leathery leaves like wings; and even up in the balloon, a thousand feet overhead, that's a threatening sight.

'Christ,' shouts the man, 'look at that thing grow!'

Look indeed; the plant is twenty feet high and still growing. Fissures run along the desert floor, marking the swift passage of the roots underground like lightning forking across a black sky.

'That,' the girl agreed, 'is one hell of a primrose.'

'Sorry?'

'I said that's one hell of a—'

'Speak up, I can't quite hear what you're—'

'I SAID, THAT'S ONE HELL OF A PRIMROSE.'

'Yes.'

No longer growing; instead, consolidating. The stem swells, to support the weight of the flower. The petals fan out, snatching photons out of the air like a spider's web. Hot chlorophyll pumps through the swelling veins. The roots tear into the dead ground like miners' drills. And stop.

'Hey up,' says the man, 'I think it's on its way.'

The primrose is rocking and bouncing up and down, for all the world as if it's on a trampoline. Now it's swaying backwards and forwards, using all the leverage of its already phenomenal bulk to rip its roots free. In this particular part of the desert, nothing has stirred the ground since the seas evaporated and the wind ground down the rock and stamped it flat as a car park and hard as tarmac; fifty million years or thereabouts of patient landscaping, contouring, making good. A few more millennia, God might be saying, and we'll have a decent tennis court. Unless, of course, some bugger of a psychotic giant primula comes along and starts carving it up …

With a crack like bones breaking and much spraying of sand into the air, the roots come free; and for a few seconds they grope frantically in empty air until they touch ground, and –

– like a monster spider with wings and a huge yellow wind-up gramophone on its back, the plant begins to shuffle, on tip-root, sideways across the sand towards the distant shade of the outcrops.

'Gaw,' mutters the man, as well he might. For the Thing scuttling across the sand below him was his idea, and it was his genius (or his fault) that turned a little yellow wildflower commonly found in the fields and hedgerows of Old England into this: *Primula dinodontica*, the Ninja Primrose; or, to put it another way, one of the three components of the ultimate Green Bomb.

'Well,' says the girl, 'looks like that one works OK. Let's try the others.'

'I'm not absolutely sure about this …'

'Don't be so bloody wet. Here goes.'

From a second flask she takes another seed: flat, beanlike, about the size and shape of a small sycamore pod. Before the man can do anything, she's let it go.

WHUMP!

'… serious misgivings,' the man is saying, 'about the whole project. I mean, I never actually imagined for one moment—'

The primrose stops in its tracks. The tips of its roots, as sensitive as the nose of a bat, have felt the thump of the second seed landing, the explosion as the incredible potential energy contained in its brittle husk is released, the shivering of the earth as another set of iron-hard roots is driven deep under the surface. Like you, Mother Earth has this thing about needles …

'That,' remarks the man, rolling back the frontiers of statement of the stunningly obvious, 'is disgusting.'

A savage flashback into the racial memory – the myth of the hydra, the hundred-headed serpentine guardian of Hell's gate – except that instead of heads, this thing has pale blue flowers. Pale blue flowers writhing and twisting on their stems, petals snapping frenziedly at the empty air. The first Devil's Forget-Me-Not has been spawned.

'Two down,' yells the girl cheerfully, 'one to go. I'm really pleased, aren't you?'

The man says nothing; instead, he grabs for the third flask and hugs it to him. As the girl reaches for it, he backs away; forgetting that backing space in the basket of a balloon is strictly limited. *Safe* backing space, anyway.

'AAAaaaaaaah!' he remarks.

As he hits the ground (at which point, his troubles are definitively over) the flask is jolted out of his hand and flies wide, landing on a rock and smashing to pieces. A tiny, tiny seed, no bigger than a grain of salt, falls on to the flat stone –

WHUMP!

– which explodes into gravel as the third and finest achievement of Operation Urban Renewal springs into instantaneous life. Its roots plough through the compacted sand like a torpedo through water as the single grotesque pod, the like of which hasn't been seen on earth since Hieronymus Bosch's window-box was destroyed by the Inquisition, splits and falls away, revealing a flower –

– You have to call it a flower, because botany is a naïve, trusting science which never for one moment imagined that anything like this could happen. A terrible, hideous flower, with jowls and warts and fangs and a big, purple lolling tongue –

– which tilts backwards towards the sun, and spits.

This is *Viola Aeschrotata*, the Hammerhead Pansy; proof, if any were needed, that the business of Creation is best left to the professionals. With a ghastly sucking noise, it ups roots and lurches at a terrific pace towards the other two flowers –

– who stop dead in their tracks, waggle their stamens and stare. A few seconds before, they had been marching grimly towards each other, with the express intention of pulling each other's leaves off. Now they exchange frightened glances, corolla to corolla. Jesus Christ, they are saying, what the fuck is *that*?

Pull yourself together, for crying out loud, empathises the Primrose. So long as we stick together, the two of us can have it for breakfast. What are you, a flower or a mouse?

But the Forget-Me-Not is backing away, its blossoms peeping out from behind its leaves. The hell with that, it broadcasts, have you seen the hairs on that thing? You want to be a hero, chum, be my guest. I'm—

With a lightning flurry of roots, the Pansy springs; and the Forget-Me-Not discovers, rather too late, just how incredibly quickly it can cover the ground on its enormous scaffolding of roots. There is a sickening plopping noise as, by sheer bulk, it crushes the Forget-Me-Not into the ground. The flower cranes on its stem and darts forward; the petals close; the carcase of the Forget-Me-Not shudders convulsively, and slumps.

In the balloon, the girl nods her head in unbounded satisfaction; and then, just to be on the safe side, has a good long pull on the hot-air burner.

For the Primrose, the desert is suddenly a very big, very open, very lonely place. The Pansy rises to the tips of its roots, swaying slightly; there is sap all round the bell of its flower.

OK. There is an infinity of magnificently pointless

bravado in the vibes thrown out by the Primrose, as it rocks back on its roots and crouches, in a floral version of the classic knife-fighter's stance. Come on, weed, make my day.

No responding vibes from the Pansy; nothing at all. It emanates a vast negative aura, like a lawn-mower or a watering-canful of DDT. Every hair on the Primrose's leaves is standing on end.

Look. We can talk about this. The world's big enough for the two of us.

We're on the same side, you and me. Wildflowers united can never be uprooted.

Il faut cultiver notre jardin.

But from the Pansy, nothing. And now it has begun to move; slowly, rootlet by rootlet, dragging up vast moraines of sand and dust as it comes …

Sod you, then, the Primrose snarls, as its leaves pucker in horror. Go climb a trellis.

Ten or twelve seconds later, when it's all over, the Pansy swivels its flower and looks around, until it is satisfied that there's nothing else alive within the range of its senses. That, as far as it is concerned, is how things ought to be. It ups roots and begins to crawl.

Five hours later, the girl in the balloon watches its dehydrated form wilt into a heap, thrash a last moribund tendril, and die. This, after all, is the Mojave Desert; even the roots of the Hammerhead Pansy can't dig deep enough here to strike water. Deserts have this aggravating knack of always having the last word.

Sow a few of those little white seeds somewhere where there's water, however – in the middle of New York, say, or Moscow or Paris or London, where water either runs in rivers through the middle or swooshes about a few feet under the surface in easy-to-find ceramic arteries – and it would be a very different story. The term 'flower power' would take on a whole new nexus of unpleasant meanings.

The girl smiles. The ultimate Green Bomb was now a reality. (And with friends like her, does the earth really need any enemies?) As the balloon drifts on its lazy course back home, she reflects contentedly on the progress of Operation Urban Renewal ...

(... *Our environment is in deadly peril. The relentless spread of urbanisation threatens to poison and smother every last wild flower and blade of grass on the surface of the planet. Every pollutant, every waste product, every man-made toxin in the world originates in the Cities. The Cities, therefore, have got to go.*

Blasting them off the face of the earth by conventional means, however, would create as many problems as it solves. It has been calculated that a bomb powerful enough to take out, say, Lisbon, would generate enough toxic matter to poison eighty-seven per cent of the lichens and ribbon-form seaweeds in the Iberian peninsula.

How can we solve this dilemma, brothers and sisters of the Green Dawn? How can we cauterise the cancer of urban civilisation without killing the patient in the process?

We believe that we have found a way ...)

It was regrettable, the girl mused, that the prototypes of the other two flowers should have been destroyed; not just because it would have been useful to be able to observe their progress but because it's always a tragedy, on general principles, when a living plant perishes. Would it be excessively animist and sentimental, she wondered, if she returned to the spot a little later and held some sort of brief, modest funeral?

No humans, by request.

The back bar of Saheed's was heaving. It was Karaoke Night.

Genies are, when the chips are down, simple creatures, as

refined as the effluent from the *Torrey Canyon*, but with a strong instinctive sense of rhythm. There is nothing they enjoy more, after six or eight gallons of chilled goat's milk with rennet chasers, than grabbing a microphone in a crowded room and miming to Elvis singing *Heartbreak Hotel*. Since turning himself into a carbon copy of Elvis, correct down to the last detail of the DNA pattern, is child's play to a genie, the effect can be confusing to an uninformed bystander.

If this be offence, Kiss was a hardened recidivist, and on ninety-nine Karaoke Nights out of a hundred you could earn good money betting that he'd be up there, informing the Universe at large that ever since his baby left him he'd found a new place to dwell, if he had to jump queues and break bones to do it. Not, however, tonight.

Instead, Kiss was huddled in a corner with a half-empty plastic jerrycan of Capricorn Old Pasteurised on the surface of which icicles were forming, and a guest.

Of all the bars, he was thinking, in all the world, why did she have to come into mine?

'That one over there,' Jane was saying, 'looks exactly like Elvis Presley. Or was he a ...?'

Kiss shook his head. Although there was no house rule prohibiting mortals, no genie had ever, in the long and illustrious history of the establishment, brought his employer there. The only reason there wasn't a rule against it was that in Saheed's there are no rules whatsoever.

Jane, however, had wanted to come. More than that; she had Wished to come, and accordingly here they were.

The agony had started, as far as Kiss was concerned, when Jane walked up to the bar, grabbed the menu and without looking at it ordered a bacon sandwich.

The barman had stared at her. 'A what?' he demanded incredulously.

'A bacon sandwich,' Jane had replied. 'Don't you know

about bacon sandwiches? Well, it's very easy, you take two
rashers of bacon—'

'Bacon,' replied the barman icily, 'is mortals' food. We
don't serve …'

Without saying a word, Jane had turned to Kiss and
smiled; a smile which could only have one meaning. I see
and obey, oh mistress, your whim is my command. Oh
fuck.

He loomed over the bar. He was good at looming. At
Genie School you could do violin lessons or you could do
looming. If you did the violin, you had to practise three
hours a day in your spare time. Kiss had done looming.

'The lady,' he snarled, 'wants a bacon sandwich. You got
a problem with that?'

'Yes,' the barman said, looming back, so that the two of
them together reminded Jane of Tower Bridge a few
seconds after a tall ship has passed through. 'We don't do
mortals' food here. *Capisce*?'

'You do now.'

And the barman, who was only a Force Three genie with
a maximum internal service pressure of a mere nineteen
tons to the square inch, suddenly found himself cutting off
rind and shovelling sliced bread into the toaster. As he
brought the finished sandwich over to the table, Kiss could
sense a certain degree of hostility in his manner.

After that, things had not improved. Jane's request,
expressed in a loud, clear voice, that he introduce her to
some of his friends, instantaneously made him the most
unpopular person in the house, and genies whom he had
known since Belshazzar was in nappies suddenly found it
difficult to remember who he was, or even see him. So
unnerved was he by this that he allowed Jane to beat him in
two consecutive games of pool; the third he only just
managed to win, on the black, by conjuring up invisible
spirits to stand in the pockets whenever it was Jane's go.

'It is usually as busy as this?' she was asking.

Kiss nodded. 'Why are you doing this to me, by the way?' he continued. 'Was it something I said, or what?'

Jane raised an eyebrow. 'I don't know what you mean,' she said. 'I just thought it would be nice to see where you went on your night off. Part of getting to know each other better, that sort of thing.'

'I see. Well, thanks to you I've been banned for life, so from that point of view you've been wasting your time. This is what I *used* to do on my night off, and therefore of historical interest only.'

'Ah, well,' Jane replied, 'it all helps to build up a general picture.'

Muttering something under his breath, Kiss returned to his goat's milk, while Jane looked around her. Something about her general deportment suggested to Kiss that any minute now she'd be asking when the interesting people were going to arrive.

'Hi, doll,' said a voice seven feet or so above her head. 'Want to dance?'

There is, of course, one in every bar: a nerd vain enough to believe that, contrary to all the teachings of experience, there is a woman somewhere who will one day say 'Yes'; realistic enough to focus his search for such a paragon upon the crippled, half-witted and partially-sighted. Or, in this context, even mortals. Kiss knew him well; a harmless enough genie in other respects, a trifling Force Two, cursed for ever to dance attendance on a small jar used for taking samples from suspected drunk drivers. Wearily he rose to his feet and clenched his fists ...

'How nice of you to ask,' Jane said. 'I'd be delighted.'

The genie, whose name was Acme Better Mousetraps IV, blinked twice. 'You would?'

Jane nodded and smiled.

'Straight up?'

'Absolutely.'

'I can only do the valeta and the military two-step.'

'That's all right, we can learn together.'

She stood up. Acme Better Mousetraps IV leaned forward, picked her up awkwardly by one arm, and placed her on the palm of his hand.

'Right,' he said, as the genie on the stage informed nobody in particular that they weren't nothin' but a hound dog. 'And *one*-two-three-*one*-two-three ...'

Kiss shrugged, lolled back in his chair and drained the last few drops of milk into his glass. There was an outside chance that the two of them would discover how much they had in common, form a mature and lasting relationship and leave him in peace, but he doubted it. In the meantime, he resolved, he would just sit here quietly and hope nobody noticed him.

'Kiss, my man, what's the big idea?'

Kiss turned his head. 'She insisted on coming,' he replied, as Amalgamated Caribbean Breweries IX sat down beside him and filled two glasses with milk. 'Then, when Ambi asked her to dance, she accepted. I accept no responsibility whatsoever for anything that has ever happened ever. Is that clear?'

'Sure.' Acba sipped his milk and wiped his moustache. 'You got yourself one crazy mistress there, man. Rather you than me.'

'Can't fathom her out at all,' Kiss replied. 'So far, all I've done is domestic chores and a little light transportation. She hasn't breathed a word about wealth beyond the dreams of avarice yet.'

'No?' Acba raised an eyebrow. 'Hey, that's weird. Kind of spooky, you know?'

'Don't I just. The only thing I can think of is, her mind's on something else.'

'What?'

Kiss shrugged. 'Who knows?' he said. 'Or cares, come to that? Let's change the subject, shall we.'

'Why not?' Acba grinned. 'Hey, it's too bad you being tied up right now. There's something really heavy going down, and you won't get to have a piece of it.'

'Is that so?'

Acba nodded. 'The word's out,' he whispered, 'for Force Nines and above, excellent package including benefits for hard-working, committed candidate with a total disregard for the value of human life. I'm gonna try and get me a slice of that, no question.'

Kiss sighed. 'Sounds like it could be fun,' he agreed. 'Any idea what it's about?'

Acba shook his head. 'Whatever it is, it's serious men running it,' he said. 'That's all I know. Oh, and it's something to do with the Environment.'

'Oh,' said Kiss. 'That. In that case, it's probably just cleaning something. You're welcome to that. Let me know how it pans out.'

Acba nodded and stood up. 'Stay loose,' he said.

'Chance'd be a fine thing.'

During this time Abmi and Jane had danced two waltzes, one quick-step and a tango, all to the accompaniment of *Blue Suede Shoes*. For his part, Abmi was beginning to have serious misgivings about infringing the rule against impossibles.

'Well, thanks,' he said, lowering Jane gingerly to floor level. 'That was an experience, you know?'

'Oh. Have we finished dancing, then?'

Abmi smiled wanly. The tendons of his left arm were throbbing like wrenched harpstrings, and there were callouses all over his palm where Jane's heels had galled him. 'Hey,' he said, 'have you any idea what the guys will do to me, monopolising the foxiest chick in the joint? No way,' he added, with perhaps a scruple more vehemence than the context could accommodate. '*Ciao*, baby, I gotta fly.' Which he did. In fact, for the record, he put a girdle round the earth in twenty-seven minutes thirteen seconds and hid inside a wardrobe until he was sure Jane hadn't followed him.

Jane returned to Kiss's table and sat down.

'I have enjoyed myself,' she said. 'We must come here again.'

THREE

There was a queue.

You can tell of rationing. You can pontificate about the first day of the January sales. You can boast of your experiences in the line for day-of-performance tickets for *Phantom of the Opera*. But this was a queue to end all queues; so long that it projected sideways into several quite recherché dimensions, so crammed with repressed potential energy that it hovered on the brink of forming a black hole. It was, of course, an auditions queue; and nearly every genie in the Universe was in it.

When you have a queue comprising something in excess of 10^{46} supernatural beings who can flit through time and space with the reckless abandon of a Porsche with diplomatic plates hurrying to a meeting through the Rome rush-hour, queue-jumping ceases to be bad manners and becomes a challenge to the fundamental laws of physics. The Past became a frenzied jumble of genies bashing each other over the head and locking each other in cupboards so as to preclude their presence on the day in question; while a gigantic troll stood with folded arms in the doorway of the Future to keep back the stream of genies who reckoned they'd avoid the crush by fast-forwarding through Time. The Present was under the control of an only slightly less formidable young woman with glasses and a clipboard.

'Next,' she said.

At the back of the queue there was a hard core of genies who hadn't the faintest what the audition was for, but who felt sure that they were right for the part. The general opinion was that God was staging *Aladdin*, with a strong minority faction holding to the view that Springsteen had been taken ill on the eve of the big open-air concert in Central Park, and a stand-in capable of imitating him down to the last chromosome was urgently required. Both versions, although speciously attractive, were wrong.

The door to the small office where the auditions were taking place opened, and a dejected genie slumped out. A voice from inside called out, 'Don't call us, we'll—' as the door closed again.

Next in line was the Dragon King of the South-East. As the girl with the clipboard took his name and nodded him towards the door, he straightened his hair, shot his cuffs, and took a deep breath.

The Big Time beckoned. He strode through the doorway.

'Now is the winter of our discontent/Made glorious summer by this ...' he said. The three men behind the desk gave him a look.

'He's too tall,' said the bald man wearily. 'Next.'

Dragon Kings are nothing if not adaptable. In the time it took for his vast brain to formulate the wish, he had reduced himself by twenty per cent.

'Too short,' muttered the skinny man with the glasses. 'Goddamn time-wasters.'

The Dragon King cleared his throat. ''Scuse me,' he said, 'but stature's not a problem with me. You give me the measurements, I'll come across with the body.'

'Voice too squeaky,' sniffed the freckled man with the cigar. 'OK, Cynthia, let's see the—'

'**The voice needn't be a problem either**,' the Dragon King interrupted, in a pitch that made the foundations of the building quiver. '**Just give me a hint, and I can**—'

The freckled man looked up for the first time. 'Can he dance?' he asked the universe in general.

'Doesn't look like he can,' replied the bald man, raising his voice over the machine-gun cracking of the King's heels on the parquet. 'Two left feet.'

The King, by now rather flustered, took this for a specification, made the necessary modifications, lost his footing and fell over.

'Next,' said the skinny man. The Dragon King got up and silently left the room.

'Hey, Cynthia,' the bald man called out, 'are there many more of these deadbeats out there?'

'Quite a few, Mr Fornaldarsen,' the girl with the clip-board replied.

'Any of them look any good to you?'

'No, Mr Fornaldarsen.'

'OK, send 'em home.' The bald man glanced down. 'Except,' he added quickly, 'for this one. Recommendation from Zip Kortright.' He checked the name. 'Guy by the name of – goddamn stupid names these jerks have – Philadelphia Machinery and Tool Corporation the Ninth. Is he out there?'

'I'll just check for you, Mr Fornaldarsen.'

The door closed. After a moment, the three men looked at each other.

'Waste of time,' said the freckled man. 'Told you it would be.'

'We'll see this Philadelphia guy,' replied the skinny man. 'You never know your luck. Never known Kortright send up a complete turkey.'

The door opened – to be precise, it was virtually blown open by the noise of 10^{46} genies all protesting at once – and a tall, slim figure walked in, sat in the chair and crossed her legs.

There was silence.

'Hey,' said the bald man, 'it's a girl.'

'Correct,' said Philadelphia Machine and Tool Corporation IX. 'You see? Putting your lenses in this morning has already paid dividends.'

'What's Korty thinking of, sending us a girl?' snarled the skinny man. 'We don't need a girl, we need a guy.'

The girl parted her lips and smiled.

'On the other hand,' mumbled the bald man, 'have we actually thought this through? I mean, now I think of it I can see where, if we were to make the hero a girl …'

'It'd beef up the middle,' agreed the freckled man. 'There's that goddamn flat spot between the fight with the chainsaws and the bit where he blows up the Golden Gate Bridge. If we made him a girl, we could put in a bit with her and her kids, you know, mom stuff …'

'Like Cagney and Lacey,' agreed the skinny man.

'Excuse me,' said the girl.

The three men looked at her.

'Could one of you gentlemen possibly tell me what the film's about?'

'Hey,' objected the bald man, 'what's that got to do with you?'

'Well, now,' the girl said, flicking a few microns of cigar ash off her knee, 'if I don't know what the film's about, how do I know whether I want to be in it?'

There was stunned silence; and the genie, who could after all read minds, watched with amused pleasure as the idea began to take shape in all three brains simultaneously.

She wants to know if it's the sort of film *she'd* like to be in.

If we want her, she might not accept.

She *must* be good.

The bald man cleared his throat. 'OK,' he said, 'it's like this. There's this guy—'

'Or girl,' interrupted the skinny man.

'Or girl, yeah, and she's got this brother who was killed in Viet Nam—'

'Big flashback sequence,' explained the freckled man. 'All the footage they couldn't use in *Full Metal Jacket*.'

'Only,' the bald man went on, 'really he wasn't, OK, it was just a dream, and in fact he's hiding out from the Mob—'

'Columbian drug barons.'

'Whatever, and then it turns out that in fact his girl—'

'Her guy—'

'Is working for the CIA, and is actually responsible for a string of serial killings—'

'He turns out,' elucidated the skinny man, 'to be a robot, but that's much later.'

'And then there's this big fight with chainsaws with this psychotic rogue cop—'

'He's a robot, too.'

'And then we have the big chase sequence and that's basically it. That's it, isn't it, guys?'

The other two nodded. 'Except for the bit where she spends three years working with disadvantaged Puerto Rican kids in the barrios of LA, of course,' the skinny man added. 'But that's really still at the concept stage right now. We're working on that.'

The girl frowned slightly. 'That's it, is it?' she asked.

'Yeah,' replied the bald man. 'Plus, of course, she gets killed in the first ten minutes, so all this is her coming back as a ghost.'

'We've already got Connery for God,' added the freckled man. 'Him or Streisand. Or both.'

'Both,' interjected the skinny man, 'and why not Newman as well? Goddammit, the guy's meant to be a trinity, why not really go for it?'

The girl considered, and stood up. 'No, thank you,' she said. 'Good afternoon.'

'We were thinking of calling it *Space Trek 9: The Search For*— What did you say?'

'I said,' said the girl, 'no, thank you. Goodbye.'

The bald man stood up, and then collapsed back into his chair. 'Hey,' he said weakly. 'I don't remember even offering you the goddamn part.'

'That was just as well, then, wasn't it?' said the girl. 'Thank you for your time.'

'Hey, wait a minute …'

Half an hour later, the girl left the office. In her bag she had a signed contract, and a cheque, and the star role in what was now to be called *A Thousand And One Dalmatians II: The Search for Spot.*

Three hundred yards down the street, she stopped, looked carefully around and turned himself back into a man. Well, a genie. Genies, as noted above, have a certain leeway in matters of morphology.

Some of them also have a certain amount of low cunning.

Kiss stood back to admire his handiwork, and saw that it was good. Well, he thought it was good, anyhow. And, since he was a genie and gifted with supernatural good taste in aesthetic matters (not that he ever used it if he could possibly help it; his personal preference when it came to interior decor was plaster ducks and little straw donkeys with 'A Present From Marbella' written on them) he knew that he was right. These matters are, however, essentially subjective …

'No,' Jane sighed, 'it's still not right. God should be older.'

Kiss sighed, and squeezed a big dollop of white on to his palette. 'You're making,' he said, 'a big mistake, I hope you realise that. Generations yet unborn will curse you for this.'

'Older,' she said. 'And more cuddly. Do it.'

Kiss winced, and assumed painting position: flat on his back, hovering eighteen inches from the ceiling. Overhead, the greatest artistic masterpiece ever, the fresco *God Creating Adam And Eve* glowed in a scintillating mélange of colour. He soaked a rag in white spirit, and dissolved God.

'Fine,' he snarled. 'Why don't I just wipe the whole damned lot and do the ceiling over in woodchip and white emulsion?'

'I'm the one who's got to live with it,' Jane replied evenly. 'All I said was, would you help me with decorating the new flat. You were the one who thought it'd look nice with paintings …'

'Or perhaps,' Kiss went on, 'you'd prefer cuddly rabbits and kittens and adorable little puppy-dogs with ribbons round their necks. If so, just say the word. I mean, your wish is my—'

'If you say that just once more,' Jane told him, 'I shall scream.'

Offended, Kiss painted in silence for a while. Under his brush, the splodgy void which had once shown a fierce, jealous, enigmatic God piercing the veil of shadows to lob in the lightning-bolt of Life took form again to reveal the loving, all-compassionate Father of Mankind. Not bad, Kiss had to concede, but the first one was better.

'That's more like it,' Jane called up. 'Much more friendly. The other effort gave me the creeps.'

Gave you the creeps? You silly mare, that was God, it was meant to give you the creeps. I should know, remember. 'Oh, good,' Kiss mumbled through the brush gripped between his teeth. 'Your last chance for a few pink rabbits,' he added. 'Then I'm going to slap on the varnish.'

'No, that'll do fine.' Jane yawned. 'And as soon as you've done that, we can choose the carpets.'

'Carpets.' Carpets weren't what he'd had in mind. What he'd had in mind was eight hundred tons of mirror-polished

Carrara marble, whirlpools of dancing white figures that would make you think you were walking on clouds. 'Anything you say,' he grunted. Women, he thought.

'If I said,' he suggested, floating back to ground level and dunking his brushes in a jam-jar of turps, 'that what you're forcing me to do violates my artistic integrity so much that even looking at it makes me feel like I was walking barefooted over red-hot coals, would it make any difference?'

'No.'

'Fair enough. Now, when you say carpet, obviously what you have in mind is a collection of masterpieces from the golden age of Persian carpet-weaving, featuring works by such immortal masters as—'

'Beige,' Jane interrupted, 'so as not to show spilt tea. And it's got to be hard-wearing, because I don't want little bits of fluff getting everywhere. Ready?'

Let there be carpet, said Kiss. And there was carpet.

'That's fine,' Jane said, as the rolls of beige Wilton unfurled of their own accord and slid smoothly into position. 'Just what I wanted.' Carpet tacks materialised in a bee-like swarm, buzzed angrily for a moment, and flew with devastating velocity to bury themselves in the floor. 'I know it's not what you'd have liked . . .' she added, with a hint of remorse.

Kiss looked up from air-traffic-controlling the tacks. 'Actually,' he said, 'if it was my place we were doing up, it'd be lino. But you said you wanted it to look nice, and I do try to be conscientious. I have trouble, though, with conflicting signals.'

'Nice,' Jane replied, 'as in what I think is nice. Sorry if I didn't make myself clear.'

'Got you,' Kiss muttered. 'You may not know much about art but you know what you like. That sort of thing?'

'That's the general idea.'

Kiss nodded despondently and, out of residual malice,

materialised pink curtains, a pile of lacy cushions and a four-foot teddy bear.

'Yes,' Jane said, nodding. 'Yes, I like that.'

'Fine. I think I was better off inside the bottle.'

'Maybe you were. Let's have some lunch, shall we?'

Kiss nodded, and instantaneously there was a table. It was covered with cloth of gold and laden with dishes of honeydew and jugs of milk of paradise. 'Or would you,' he asked, 'prefer scrambled eggs?'

'No, this looks fine.'

'You're sure?'

'I'm sure. I like yogurt.'

Conversation was slow over lunch; there was still a thin, oil-like smear of resentment over the surface of Kiss's mind, and Jane had her head buried in a furniture catalogue. This didn't do much to improve Kiss's temper (*Formica – anything you like, dear God, but not formica*) and, being dutiful, he resolved to snap himself out of it by being affable.

'Funny bit of gossip going the rounds at the moment,' he said. 'Apparently, there's been some bloke going round trying to recruit genies for some job or other.'

'Oh yes?'

Kiss nodded. 'Offering good money, apparently. Which shows how much whoever it is knows about genies, if you stop to think.'

'Really.'

'If you think about it, I mean,' Kiss went on, trying hard to maintain the affability level. 'I mean, trying to bribe a genie with promises of wealth beyond dreams of avarice is like offering a fish a drink. Still, there's been a lot of interest.'

'Is that so?' Jane said, her face still obscured by the catalogue. 'Well I never.'

Kiss ground his teeth silently. *Small-talk*, said the training manual, *is the mortar that cements together the foundations of the ideal genie/mortal relationship. Talk to your mortal and you will find that empathy inevitably follows.* Something told Kiss that whoever wrote that hadn't been on active service for several thousand years.

'Oh yes,' he ploughed on, 'ever such a lot of interest. I'd probably have put in for it myself if I'd been at a loose end. Whatever it is,' he added lamely.

Jane closed the catalogue. 'Now then,' she said briskly. 'Kitchen worktops.'

The door opened.

Nobody walked through it, and nobody stood in the door-frame. After a moment, it closed itself again. The three people sitting at the table looked at each other.

'Good afternoon.' There was a brief flash of blue light and the genie Philadelphia Machine and Tool Corporation IX materialised in the air, hovering precisely one metre over the table-top. 'Sorry if I'm late, but I had a press conference.'

Better known to millions of cinema-goers as the star of *A Thousand And One Dalmatians II* under the name of Spot (and the corporeal trappings of the cuddliest, most adorable puppy ever) Philly Nine floated gently down and folded his arms. Each of the three members of the interview panel got the impression that he was face to face with the apparition; which wasn't the most comfortable illusion in the universe, not by some way.

'Um,' said the Chair at last. 'Thank you for, er, making the time.'

'No worries,' the genie replied. 'The job sounds interesting.'

'Yes.' The Chair tried to keep the hesitation out of her voice. 'The pay,' she went on, 'is excellent. I expect you want to hear about the money first.'

'Not really,' the genie replied, making his body translucent just to be aggravating. 'Let's see, now, I had one per cent of the gross for making this film I've just done, which at last count came to seventy million dollars, but so what? All I have to do to make seventy million dollars – silver dollars, if I want – is whistle. Like me to show you?'

'Yes,' said the Chair, quickly. 'I mean,' she added, 'if that's all right with you, of course …'

Suddenly it was snowing banknotes. Thousand-dollar bills. Great big coarse sheets of money, drifting and floating in the air, settling in drifts, skittering in the draught from under the door. You didn't need to look to know they were genuine. For a while, the three committee members were a blur of fast-moving arms.

The money vanished.

'Easy come,' sneered the genie, 'easy go. And you reckoned you were going to pay *me*.'

'All right,' panted the Chair, catching her breath. 'Point taken. You are interested in the job, aren't you?'

The genie nodded, like a will-o'-the-wisp dangling from the rear-view mirror of Satan's Cortina. 'It sounds like it might be fun,' he said. 'From what I've heard, that is. Why don't you tell me all about it?'

The second member of the committee took a deep breath. His right hand was tightly closed around a thousand-dollar bill that had somehow failed to dematerialise, and he wanted to divert the genie's attention. 'Our organisation,' he said, 'is a radical group devoted to the cause of ecology. The way we see it, saving the planet is up to us, because nobody else is fit to be trusted with it. OK so far?'

The genie dipped his head.

'As part of our programme,' Number Two went on, 'we intend to destroy all cities with a population in excess of one hundred thousand. The reasons …'

With a slight crease of the lips, the genie waved the

reasons aside. Number Two swallowed hard, and went on.

'In order to do this in an ecologically friendly way,' he said, finding the words strangely hard to expel from his throat, 'we have developed several new strains of . . . of—'

'Wildflowers,' interrupted the Chair. 'Pansies, forget-me-nots, that sort of thing.'

The genie grinned. 'I know,' he said. 'I'll admit, I was impressed. For puny, stunted, pig-ignorant mortals, not bad.'

'Well.' The Chair, too, found that her throat was suddenly dry. 'We need someone to sow the seeds. From the air.'

'Over all the cities simultaneously,' added Number Three, 'so as to create the maximum effect. If all targets are engaged at the same time, they can't come to each other's assistance.'

The genie nodded; a token of respect, the gesture implied, from one thoroughly nasty piece of work to another.

All three committee members suddenly began to wish they were somewhere else.

'And you want me,' drawled the genie, 'to do this little job for you, is that it?'

The Chair nodded. She had a splitting headache, and she felt sick. 'If you'd like to, of course.'

'I'd *love* to.'

'Ah.'

'It would mean,' the genie went on, 'the deaths of countless millions of innocent people. Deaths by the most bizarrely hideous means imaginable. Wanton, barbaric genocide.' The genie smiled pleasantly. 'Sounds like a bit of all right to me.'

Number Two cleared his throat. 'A certain inevitable level of casualties …' he began, and found that he couldn't continue. The genie's eyes seemed to push him back into his chair.

'Smashed into pulp by the petals of a giant primrose,' he said, slowly, with relish. 'Horrific, bizarre, and with that ultimately humiliating soupçon of frivolity that marks the true evil genius. I like it.'

Sweat was pouring down the Chair's cheeks like condensation down an office window. 'It's them or us,' she gasped. 'People or plants. We're talking about the future of the planet. You do see that, don't you?'

The genie frowned thoughtfully. 'I see that you're a bunch of raving lunatics,' he said calmly, 'but so what?' He beamed. 'That makes you my kind of people. Glad to be on the team.'

Number Two tried to stand up, ineffectually. 'Of course,' he said, 'the whole project is still subject to review. We aren't actually committed to anything yet …'

'You are now.'

For a fraction of a second, a very small fraction indeed, Number Two had a vision of what it would be like. For some reason, the city he visualised was Oslo. He vomited.

'These,' the genie went on, holding up a cloth bag the size of a large onion, 'are the seeds of the flowers you so thoughtfully made possible. Anything possible, I'm allowed to do.' The image shimmered and glowed, like the heart of the fire. 'Thanks,' he said, and turned his eyes on the Chair. 'I'm sorry,' he said, 'I didn't quite catch your name.'

'Fuselli,' croaked the Chair. 'Mary Fuselli.'

The genie grew, filling the room. 'Apt,' he said, as the glass in the windows began to creak with the pressure. 'Mary, Mary, quite contrary, how does your garden grow?' The windows exploded and the Chair, Number Two and Number Three blacked out. Two seconds later, the pressure inside the room squashed them as flat as paper.

Philly Nine smiled, wiped human off his sleeve, and soared away into the upper air.

★

Faster than a thought he flew, breaching the Earth's atmosphere in a shower of sparks and soaring in a wide, lazy orbit around the Equator. As he went he amused himself by catching satellites and crumpling them in his fist like foil jam-tart cups. The further away from the planet's gravitational field he flew, the larger he became. A tail of fire flickered behind him, and dry ice knotted his hair.

From this altitude, the planet was mostly white and blue. The genie considered it impassively. It had, he felt, a sort of glazed, ceramic look, like a spun-glass Christmas tree ornament.

Or a very old bottle.

And, like all his kind, he had this problem with bottles. Bottles, in his opinion, were there to be broken.

And if one blue bottle should accidentally fall …

Kiss, genie-handling a huge roll of beige Wilton across the enormous expanse of the living-room floor, hesitated and glanced up through the window.

He swore.

Jane looked up. 'Problem?' she asked.

'Yes.' Kiss nodded. 'At least, there might be. Look,' he said, 'sorry to run out on you in the middle of the job, but could you see your way to managing without me for half an hour? There's something I've got to see to.'

'Can't it wait?'

Kiss shook his head. With a crack the roll of carpet snapped open, flattened itself, hung for a moment six inches above floor level, and started to rise.

'I promise I'll be back as soon as I possibly can,' Kiss shouted. 'Sorry about this,' he added and vaulted into the middle of the carpet which bucked like an unbroken horse, pawed at the windows with its front corners, smashed the glass and shot out into the air with Kiss sitting cross-legged on its back.

*

Philly Nine tutted. He was having trouble with the fiddly little knot the seed-sack was tied up with.

'Hey,' said a voice directly below him. He glanced down, and saw a flat brown rectangle. The slight quivering of its outer seams reminded him of a stingray floating in clear water. He frowned.

'Is that you, Kiss?' he queried.

'Philly!' replied the voice. 'Long time no see! And how's the world been treating you?'

The carpet closed in, drawing level with the hovering figure of Philly Nine, standing in the empty blackness trying to bite through a single strand of cord with teeth the size of office blocks.

'Not so bad,' Philly replied. 'What brings you here, my old mate?'

Kiss shrugged. 'Thought I'd catch a few spacewinds on my new rug. Like her?'

'Not bad,' Philly replied. 'Not bad at all. Like the stabilisers. You any good at knots?'

'I have my moments. Bung it over, whatever it is, and let me have a go.'

Philly Nine hefted the bag, and then checked himself. Coincidence, he thought; there are only seven Force Twelve genies in the whole Universe, and at this crucial moment here's two of them sharing one small, remote postage-stamp of empty space. 'It's OK,' he replied. 'I think I can probably manage. So,' he added nonchalantly, 'where've you been hiding yourself lately?'

Kiss twitched his features into a rueful grin. 'In an aspirin bottle,' he replied, 'of all places. And me, of all people. Well, you know how brown glass gives me a headache.'

'Been out long?'

'Not very. And you?'

Philly Nine shrugged. 'I've been hanging out,' he replied.

'You know, ducking and diving, pulling a few scams. Made a film, would you believe. Boy, that was some experience.'

'Yeah?'

'Yeah. Spooky stuff to be around, film. You hold it up to the light and you're ready to swear blind there's guys trapped inside the stuff.'

Kiss shook his head. 'I think it's just science, Philly,' he said. 'You know, mortal stuff.'

'I suppose so.' Philly Nine folded his hands over the cloth bag. 'Well,' he said, 'nice to see you again, don't let me keep you.'

The carpet continued to hover. 'What've you got in the bag there, Philly?'

'Wildflower seeds,' Philly Nine replied. 'I'm doing my bit for the Green movement. Nothing to interest you.'

'Wildflowers?'

'That's right.'

Kiss raised an eyebrow. 'That's not like you, Philly,' he observed quietly. 'You were always, how can I put this, an evil genie.'

'It's very kind of you to say so, Kiss, my old chum.'

'My pleasure.' There was a moment of silence, disturbed only by the faint sighing of the interstellar winds. 'So why the change of direction?'

'Nah,' Philly answered. 'Me, I'm consistent, always have been. And if I were you, I'd go and fly your doormat someplace else.'

'Think I'll just hang around here for a minute, if it's all the same to you.'

'Suit yourself.' Philly Nine stuffed the cloth bag ostentatiously up one sleeve, and folded his arms across his chest. 'I'm in no hurry. All as broad as it's long, as far as I'm concerned.'

'Good waves, up here,' Kiss said; and, by way of illustration, he let the carpet slip on the spacewinds. A long, slow ripple snaked its way down the length of the carpet. Kiss began to hum:

> 'If everybody had a carpet
> Across the galaxy
> Then everybody would be floatin'
> Like Ursa Minor B ...'

'Cut it out,' Philly urged. 'You know as well as I do you never did like carpeting. Made you space-sick just going out on the ionosphere. What exactly are you doing here, Kiss?'

Kiss smiled. 'Stopping you,' he replied. 'Gosh, from here you can see the big pimple on Orion's nose. Fancy a peppermint?'

'I see.' Inside his sleeves, Philly's fists clenched. 'And why would you want to stop me, Kiss? I never did you any harm.'

'Never said you did, Philly. Always the best of pals, you and me.'

'Quite.'

'What have you got in the bag, Philly?'

Philly Nine smiled; and white lightning snapped out of his eyes, slamming into Kiss with traumatic force and sending him and his carpet spiralling away into emptiness. Philly grinned and took out the bag. A tiny pinch of his fingernails and the knot loosened easily.

He turned the bag over, let go of the neck and shook it ...

... and found himself inside a bubble, bobbing jauntily with the starbreeze. Above him, Kiss looped his Wilton, waved, and ducked behind the Moon.

'Bastard!' Philly yelled. On the floor of the bubble, seeds had landed. He rolled his left fist into a ball and smashed it into the wall of the bubble ...

... which stretched.

Philly Nine noticed with some misgivings the rapidly

thickening carpet of flowers round his ankles. They had already stripped the shoes off his feet (and Philly's shoes were rather special, even by genie standards; hand-stitched gryphonhide uppers, phoenixdown insocks and mono-molecular polysteel soles; the gussets arc-welded in the hottest part of a supernova; the heel reinforced with the enamel from the teeth of a fully-grown snowdragon, the third hardest material in Creation. Imelda Marcos in her wildest dreams never imagined shoes like these ...)

'Hey,' he yelled, 'let me out of here!'

'You'll have to grant me three wishes first.'

Philly began to get impatient. 'Kiss,' he shouted. 'If you don't quit horsing around and let met out of this contraption, I'll kick your arse from here to Jupiter.'

'Three wishes, Philly. You know the score.'

Petals like steel traps were slowly ripping his socks to shreds. Hand-woven from the fibres of firebird feathers (the second hardest material in the Universe) they had been custom-built to withstand the phenomenally corrosive properties of genies' sweaty feet. 'No dice, scumbag,' Philly roared. 'Get me out of here and I might just let you live. Otherwise ...'

The last scrap of sock was digested, and Philly Nine suddenly became acutely aware that the hardest material in the Universe is the petal of a psychotic flower. 'All right,' he screamed. 'One wish. But I'm warning you, you're going to regret—'

The bubble popped; and Philly Nine was falling, help-lessly entwined in roots and leaves, towards the Earth's atmosphere.

'The wish is,' came Kiss's voice from far away, 'that in future ...'

Philly hit the atmosphere like a fly hitting a windscreen. For a fraction of a second the pain of impact paralysed him; and then he was through. Scrabbling frantically he managed

to pull himself up on a handy thermal, and floated agonis-
ingly in the upper air.

He glanced down and breathed a long, slow sigh. All the
wildflowers had burnt up on re-entry – as had his shorts, his
underpants and his impossibly expensive designer Hawaii
shirt.

'... In future,' sighed the winds around his head, 'if
you're going to be evil, make a mess of it. Have a nice day.'

Thirty-six hours later, the hole Philly had made in the
ionosphere was still there. It was closing, but there was still
a gap large enough for, say, a few wildflower seeds to drift
through.

These days, nobody can seriously doubt that plants have
the power to communicate; and the more self-aware the
plant, the greater the power.

Ready? asked the Primrose.

Ready, replied the Forget-Me-Not. *Let's go.*

What about him?

Who?

Him.

Oh, you mean the …

Yes.

You ask him.

GRAAAOOAARR!!!

*I think it's safe to assume he's ready too. OK, chaps, here
goes.*

They dropped in.

FOUR

Jane looked up.

'Where,' she asked, 'have you been?'

'Saving the world,' Kiss replied, materialising just in time to take the weight of the picture Jane was trying to hang straight. 'Bit more left, I think.'

Jane stood back, nodded and made the adjustment. 'What from?'

'Annihilation by overgrown carnivorous plants, if you must know. Has it occurred to you that this one would look much better over there by the alcove?'

'I beg your pardon?'

'Over there,' Kiss repeated, pointing. 'And then you could have the one of the three fluffy kittens playing with the ball of wool over *there*, where nobody would be able to see it, and that'd be verging on the ideal—'

'No,' Jane replied, frowning, 'before that.'

'Overgrown carnivorous plants?'

'Mphm. You are just kidding, aren't you? Only I never seem to know …'

Kiss looked offended. 'I am not kidding,' he replied grumpily. 'I was just looking out of the window when I saw a disturbing fluctuation in the infra-red, which turned out on closer examination to be an old mate of mine heading into orbit with a small cloth bag stuffed up his shirt …'

'You must have remarkably good eyesight.'

'I have, yes. Anyway, when I caught up with him it turned out the bag was full of nightmare carnivorous plant seeds, and he was just working out where to sow them. Fortunately, the silly sod hadn't realised that if you try and drop something through the Earth's atmosphere, it burns up, so as it turns out I needn't have bothered. All right?'

Jane stared. 'Are you serious?' she demanded.

'No,' Kiss said, pointedly not looking at the picture of the three kittens. 'Most of the time I'm aggravatingly frivolous. If you mean am I telling the truth, the answer is yes.'

'A *friend* of yours was trying to destroy the *planet?*'

'Well, sort of.' Kiss yawned, and stretched. 'Actually, he's just this bloke I've known for, oh, donkey's years; and he wasn't planning on destroying the Earth, just all non-vegetable life forms. Or at least I assume that was what he had in mind. My split-second spectroscopic analysis of the plant seeds leads me to believe that that would have been the inevitable result. Bloody great primroses,' he added with a grin. 'With teeth.'

'Hadn't you better tell me what's going on?'

Kiss shook his head. 'Tricky,' he said. 'You remember what I told you about being limited to the possible? However; to start with the primary question, *Is there a God?* we really have to address the …'

Jane asked him to be more specific.

'Guesswork, largely,' Kiss replied, materialising an apple and peeling it with his claws. 'My guess is that somebody hired my old chum to destroy the human race. Somebody a bit funny in the head, I shouldn't be surprised.'

'This chum of yours—'

'A genie,' Kiss explained. 'A Force Twelve, like me. That's pretty hot stuff, actually, though normally I wouldn't dream of saying so. We rank equal and above the Nine Dragon Kings, just below the Great Sage, Equal of Heaven. We get fuel allowance but no pension.'

'And this particular …'

'He goes by the name,' Kiss said, straight-faced by sheer effort of will, 'of Philadelphia Machine and Tool Corporation the Ninth, or Philly Nine for short. Remarkable chiefly for how little time he's had to spend in bottles. He's a shrewd cookie, Philly Nine, always was. Mad as a hatter, too, of course.'

'I see.' Jane sat down on a desperately fragile Tang-dynasty vase, the molecular structure of which Kiss was able to beef up just in the nick of time. 'So he's dangerous.'

'You might say that,' Kiss responded, spitting out apple pips, 'if you were prone to ludicrous understatements. If midwinter at the South Pole is a bit nippy and the Third Reich was, on balance, not a terribly good idea, then yes, Philly Nine is dangerous. Apart from that, a more charming fellow you couldn't hope to meet. Plays the harpsichord.'

Jane blinked twice in rapid succession. 'Oh God,' she said.

'Ah yes,' Kiss replied, 'I was just coming on to that. If we posit the existence of an omnipotent supreme being—'

'Will you shut up!' Jane looked around for something solid and reassuring in which she could put her trust. Unfortunately, everything she could see had the disadvantage, as far as she was concerned, of having been materialised or otherwise supplied by a genie. Eventually she found her left shoe, which she had brought with her from the life she'd been leading before all this started to happen. She hugged it to her.

'Sorry, I'm sure. Do you want me to make a start on the conservatory?'

'All this,' Jane mumbled. 'It is real, isn't it? I mean …'

Kiss clicked his tongue. 'Try banging your head on it if you're in any doubt. I have to say, I find all this ever so slightly wounding. I mean, I do my level best to make things nice for you, and the first thing I know you're questioning its very existence. Gift horses' teeth, in other words.'

'I thought I told you to be quiet.'

'You asked me a question.'

'Did I? Sorry.' Jane closed her eyes and tried to clarify her mind. 'Will you help me with this?' she asked.

'Depends,' Kiss replied huffily, 'on whether I'm allowed to talk.'

'Oh, stop being aggravating.' Jane took a deep breath. 'There I was,' she said, 'an ordinary person—'

Kiss cleared his throat. 'Jane Wellesley,' he recited. 'Age, twenty-eight. Height, five feet one inch. Weight—'

'Thank you, yes. Following a distressing scene with someone I had thought really cared about me—'

'Vince. Vincent Martin Pockle. Age, thirty-one. Height, six feet two inches. Eyes a sort of—'

'Either help,' Jane snapped, 'or go and empty the dustbins. Following a distressing scene, I resolved – stupidly, I admit – to kill myself. When I opened the aspirin bottle, out jumped a genie.'

'At your service.'

'Or so it seemed. At any rate, at the time I accepted you at face value, and I've been doing so ever since.'

'So I should damned well—'

'Ever since,' Jane went on, 'I've been ordering you to do seemingly impossible things, and you've apparently been doing them. The things you bring appear to be real.'

'You and I are going to fall out in a minute if you carry on with all this seems-to-be stuff,' Kiss growled. 'The last person to call me a liar to my face, namely the erstwhile Grand Vizier of Trebizond, spends most of his time these days sitting on a lily-pad going rivet-rivet-rivet and wondering why people don't bring him things to sign any more. I invite you to think on.'

'And now you tell me,' Jane continued, 'that another genie – was he one of the ones we met at that peculiar night club?'

'No.'

'Another genie is planning to destroy the human race, using overgrown carnivorous plants. And it's not,' Jane added, after glancing at her watch, 'April the first. Now then, what the hell am I meant to make of all that?'

Kiss shrugged. 'The best you can,' he replied. 'It's called coping. Like I said, some people find it helps to posit the existence of an omnipotent supreme being. I know for a fact He does. Other people,' Kiss added, materialising a decanter and a soda syphon, 'get drunk a lot. It all comes down to individual preferences in the long run.'

'Look—'

'As a matter of fact, He's all right, and so's the second one, Junior. It's the Holy Ghost you've got to watch out for. Forever walking through walls with its head under its arm, which for someone in its position is taking light-hearted frivolity a bit too far, in my opinion. Still, there it is …'

'Kiss …'

'Not to mention,' the genie continued, 'jumping out during séances and banging things on tables. And, of course, trying to exorcise it is an absolute hiding to nothing. Sorry, you were saying?'

'What *is* going on?'

The genie shrugged. 'Can't rightly say,' he replied. 'By the looks of it, some raving nutcase or other's decided to annihilate his own species. When you've been around as long as I have, you get used to it. You get used to pretty well everything eventually.'

'I see.' Jane started to pick at the stitching on her shoe. 'Happen a lot, does it?'

'Once every forty years, on average. Usually, though, it's just a war. When We get involved, it tends to get a bit heavy. Still, like I told you the other day, for every genie commissioned to destroy the world there's another told off to save it, so things even out in the long run. Last time I looked, the planet was still here.'

Jane opened her eyes. 'I think I'm beginning to see,' she said. 'Sort of. Just when this other genie – Pennsylvania something?'

'Philadelphia Machine and Tool. Actually there is a genie called Pennsylvania Farmers' Bank III – Penny Three – but he's no bother to anyone.'

'This Philadelphia person,' Jane continued coldly, 'is going to wipe out the human race, you suddenly pop up and stop him doing it. That's why all this is happening. And I'm ...'

She stopped. She felt cold. In her anxiety, she broke the heel off her shoe.

'Look.' Kiss frowned, summoning up soft, heavenly music in the far distance. 'Nice try, but it doesn't quite work like that. Things aren't all neatly ordained and settled the way you seem to think – unless, of course, you posit the existence of a ...'

'But it makes sense,' Jane protested. 'Someone wants the world destroyed. I want it saved.'

Kiss clapped his hands. 'Ah,' he said, 'now we seem to be getting somewhere. That sounded remarkably like a Wish to me.'

'Did it?'

Kiss nodded. 'I reckon so. You Wish the world to be saved. I take it,' he added, 'that you do?'

'I suppose so.'

'Give me strength!' Kiss took a deep breath. 'Either you do or you don't, it's not exactly a grey area. Toss a coin if you think it'll help you decide.'

Jane shook her head. 'Of course I want the world saved,' she said. 'Or at least, I suppose I do. The last thing I can remember before all this was wishing it would all go away.'

'That's just typical sloppy mortal thinking,' Kiss replied crossly. 'This is what comes of giving your lot free will without making you send in the ten coupons from the special offer box-lids first. You mortals,' Kiss went on, with a slight nuance of self-righteousness in his voice, 'think that just because you come to an end, the world comes to an end too. Well, I'm an immortal and I'm here to tell you it doesn't. If you ask me, they should print *Please Leave The World As You Would Wish To Find It* in big letters on the inside of wombs and coffins, and then there'd be no excuse for all this messing about. I'm sorry,' he said, calming down, 'but there are some things I feel strongly about. Well, stronglyish, anyway.'

'Sorry,' Jane said meekly. 'I'm not really used to all this yet.'

'That's all right,' the genie replied, turning the music up a very little. 'Look, take it from me, you want the world saved.'

'Right.'

'Save the world,' Kiss continued, 'and you get merit in Heaven.'

'If we posit its existence, of course.'

Kiss sighed. 'Everyone's a comedian,' he grumbled. 'Look—'

'Save ten worlds and you get a free alarm clock radio—'

'That,' snapped the genie, 'will do. It's quite simple, as far as I'm concerned. The human race is the measure of everything that's prosaic and mundane. If there weren't any humans, there'd be no point being a genie, because there wouldn't be anyone to be bigger and stronger and cleverer than. So, as a favour to me, I suggest you Wish the human race saved. OK?'

Jane squinted into the middle distance, trying to see what the world would look like if she wasn't there. She couldn't.

'Put like that,' she said, 'how can I refuse? But hang on,' she added. 'I thought you said all the nasty plant seeds had got burned up. Doesn't that mean …?'

Kiss grinned unpleasantly. 'It means,' he said, 'that my old mate Philly Nine has failed. If he'd succeeded, the human race would have been annihilated. Since he's failed, with all the loss of face that entails ...' The genie laughed without humour. 'That means,' he went on, 'he's honour bound to get even. Which means,' he concluded, materialising a paint roller and a five-gallon tin of pink emulsion, 'you lot really are in trouble. Are you absolutely dead set on having pink, by the way? It'll make the whole room look as if it's been whitewashed with taramasalata.'

Jane considered for a moment and then nodded. 'Yes,' she said firmly. 'Definitely pink.'

According to the ancient proverb, the worst words a general can ever utter are, 'I never expected *that*.'

In consequence, the military pride themselves on having anticipated every possible contingency. There are huge underground bunkers beneath the floor of the Arizona Desert staffed by teams of dedicated men and women whose sole purpose in life is to dream up the Weirdest Possible scenario, and make plans to meet it.

Some of these scenarii are very weird indeed.

Witness, to name but a few, the elite Special Boot Squadron (the task-force poised to counter an attempt by a hostile power to subvert democracy by glueing the soles of everybody's shoes to the floor while they sleep); the Royal Cleanjackets (the crack special force permanently on yellow alert for the day when alien commandos infiltrate all the major dry-cleaning chains across the Free World); not to mention Operation Dessert Storm (the fast response unit designed to deal out instantaneous retribution in the event of low-level bombing of non-military targets with custard).

The heavy burden of co-ordinating these various forces lay, at the time in question, on the broad shoulders of Major-General Vivian Kowalski: officer commanding,

Camp Nemo. When the day arrived that was to be remembered ever after as the Pearl Harbor of weirdness, Kowalski had just returned from a tour of inspection of the Heliotrope Berets (the hair-trigger-trained haute couture force whose centre of operations is a tastefully decorated concrete bunker directly under the Givenchy salon, Paris). As a result he was feeling rather jaded.

It was good, he decided, to be back.

Returning to his spartan quarters, he removed the HB uniform he had worn for the tour (sage cotton jacquard battledress by Saint Laurent, worn over Dior raspberry silk chemise with matching culottes), lay down on his bunk and covered his face with his hands. It had been a long, hard day.

The telephone rang. The red telephone.

In an instant Kowalski was on his feet, dragging on his discarded uniform and gunbelt. Twenty minutes later, his helicopter landed on the White House lawn.

'Hi there, Kowalski,' the President greeted him, yelling to make himself heard over the roar of the chopper engines. 'Excuse my asking, but why are you wearing a dress?'

In clipped, concise military language Kowalski explained, and they went inside. In the relative peace of the Oval Office, the President explained. He didn't mince his words.

When he'd finished, Kowalski read back his notes and chewed his lip.

'Gee, Mr President,' he said. 'We never expected anything like *that*. Who do you think's responsible?'

The President shrugged. 'No idea,' he replied. 'Does it matter? The important thing is, what do we do? I assume you guys have something up your sleeves out there in the desert that'll zap these mothers into the middle of ...'

He tailed off. Kowalski was shaking his head.

'Sorry,' he said. 'I guess we overlooked that possibility.

You gotta admit,' he went on, countering the implied criticism in the Chief's eyes, 'giant self-propelled carnivorous wildflowers terrorising Florida has got to be one of the longest shots of all. Besides,' he went on, 'since you saw fit to trim the budget …'

'OK.' The President made a small gesture with his hands, guillotining the recriminations stage of the conference. 'So tell me, Viv. What have we got?'

Kowalski scowled and scratched his head. 'Assuming,' he said, 'that saturation bombing with all known weedkillers – you've tried that, yes, of course.' He grinned. 'I'm afraid you're going to have to let us work on that one for a while,' he said.

'But you do have a solution?'

'No,' Kowalski admitted, 'but I know somebody who might.'

The main reason why the world is still here is that genies have little or no initiative.

Command them to do something and they obey. It's not unknown for them sometimes to interpret their instructions with a degree of latitude – for example, if their instructions can be interpreted, however loosely, as a mandate to destroy the human race, and they happen to be psychotic Force Twelves with a personal grudge against mankind in general. Under such circumstances, they spring into action with all the vigour and energy of a supercharged volcano.

But without some tiny speck of mortal authority around which to build their pearls of malevolence, even the nastiest genies can do nothing. And, fortunately enough, mortals unhinged enough to give them that authority are few and far between.

In the most secret bunker of all, half a mile under the bleakest spot in all New Mexico, there is a door.

A big, thick steel door with a combination lock. For the unimaginative there is also a notice, in huge red letters, saying 'DO NOT ENTER'.

Open the door and you find a flight of steps, going down. Just when exhaustion and the disorienting effect of the darkness and the smell of must and stagnant water is about to get too much for you, the steps end and there is another door. It, too, is big, thick and made of steel. There is a notice, in big red letters, saying 'AUTHORISED PERSONNEL ONLY'.

Open that door and you find yourself in a small room, the size of the average hotel fitted wardrobe. The room is empty, apart from a chunky steel safe.

Inside the safe is a bottle.

WHOOSH!

Kowalski reared back, banged his head on the door and sat down hard. Suddenly the room was full of genie.

'Hello,' said Philadelphia Machine and Tool Corporation IX, grinning unpleasantly. 'Your wish is my command. What's it to be?'

Slowly, his eyes not leaving the apparition that surrounded him, Kowalski levered himself up off the floor with all the agility of a dropped fried egg climbing back into a frying pan. 'Hi,' he replied. 'Are you the genie?'

Philly Nine gave him a look.

'Yeah,' Kowalski said, 'I guess you must be. I'm—'

'I know who you are,' Philly Nine replied. 'What can I do for you? To hear,' he added, with a chuckle that belonged to some private joke Kowalski didn't even want even to understand, 'is to obey. Shoot.'

The soldier explained; and as he did so the genie nodded sympathetically. The expression in his fiery red eyes didn't for one instant betray the savage triumph pumping through his heart.

Had it ever occurred to Kowalski to wonder, he asked

himself, why a genie should have *volunteered* to be indentured to a bottle? Why, when all other genies in the history of Creation would do anything – anything at all – to avoid it, Philly Nine (a Force Twelve, no less) had deliberately and at his own request allowed himself to be bound to serve whoever removed the lid of this nasty, smelly glass container? Did the words *ulterior motive* have no place at all in this man's vocabulary?

'I see,' he said, when Kowalski had finished speaking. 'Nasty business. I take it,' he went on, choosing his words with the skill of a lawyer on a fraud charge, 'you want me to do something about it?'

Kowalski nodded. 'Positive,' he said.

'And may I take it,' the genie purred, 'that I have a certain degree of discretion in how I go about this? So long as I get the job done, of course?'

'Naturally,' the soldier said. 'This thing has sure got us licked. Anything you can do—'

'Oh, I can think of a few ideas,' the genie said. Being a Force Twelve, one of the seven most powerful non-divine beings ever to pass through the Earth's atmosphere, he was just about able to keep a straight face. 'A few tricks up my sleeve, that sort of thing. When would you like me to start?'

'Immediately,' Kowalski replied. 'If that's OK with you.'

A wide, slow smile crept like the first spill of lava from the cracks of Vesuvius across Philly Nine's large, handsome face. 'No problem,' he said. 'You just leave everything to me, and we'll see what can be done.'

Kowalski permitted himself a sigh of relief. Just for a moment back there, he'd been worried. 'That's fine,' he said, 'If there's anything you need …'

Philly hesitated. A few atomic bombs might, he felt, come in handy, particularly when it came to apportioning the blame afterwards. On the other hand, he had just been given carte blanche by a mortal – not just any mortal, he

added with infinite smugness, but a duly accredited repre-
sentative of the government of the United States of America
– and asking for a fistful of nukes might just lead to awkward
questions being asked and tiresome restrictions placed on
his mandate. After his carelessness in wiping out the
mortals who had given him his original opportunity, which
he had then squandered (to his infinite shame), he had
managed against all probability to get a chance at getting his
own back. Best not to risk blowing it just for a handful of
fireworks.

'Thanks for the offer,' he said therefore, 'but I should be
able to manage. Have a nice day, now.'

He vanished.

Tinkerbell, Grand Khan of the Hammerhead Pansies, lifted
its flower and roared.

The echoes died away. Then, from every corner of the
Everglades, came answering roars, howls, shrieks and
trumpetings. To the east it could make out the long, shrill
howl of the primroses, under the command of Feldkom-
mandant Trixie. From the north came the dull thunder of
the forget-me-nots, and the laboured snorting of their High
Admiral, Zog.

Where the bloody hell, Zog was asking, *are we?*

Tinkerbell twiddled its stamens in contempt. The forget-
me-nots were, after all, an inferior species; and as soon as
the job in hand was over, there was a place reserved for
them somewhere near the bottom of the compost-heap of
Creation. In the meantime, they might still conceivably be
useful, if only as green mulch.

High overhead the F-111s continued their futile buzzing
like so many demented mayflies; and, for those of them ill-
advised enough to fly too low, with approximately the same
life expectancy.

With a high wave of its right leaf, Tinkerbell motioned its

column to proceed, and the mud churned around their thrashing roots. In the far distance, a reverberating *splat!* indicated that Zog had just tripped over its own tendrils.

Of all the seeds in Philly Nine's bag, only thirty-one primroses, twenty-six forget-me-nots and nineteen pansies had made it through the hole in the atmosphere safely to the ground; and at first Tinkerbell had wondered whether the forces at its disposal were going to be sufficient. As time passed, however, and each individual flower had started to grow and put forth flowers, it realised that its fears were unfounded. The three varieties had been designed to take root in the dry, barren dust of the cities. The rich, wet mud of the swamps was a thousand times more nutritious, and the plants had grown accordingly. Mud, however, is all very well, but for high-intensity carnivores it lacks a certain something. They were feeling, to put it mildly, decidedly peckish.

It was, therefore, fortuitous that the United States Third Armored Division should have chosen that moment to attack.

Ah! Seventy-six telepathic vegetable intelligences simultaneously registered a giant surge of relief. *Lunch!*

The army's battle plan was simple. Lay down an artillery barrage guaranteed to extinguish every trace of life in a thirty-square-mile area. Then another one. Then one more for luck. Then send in the tanks.

For the next ten hours it was noisy in that part of Florida, and visibility was poor because of the smoke. When the noise had subsided into a deadly silence, and the breeze had cleared away most of the smoke and fumes, there was nothing to be seen except desolation –

– and seventy-six enormous flowers towering over a nightmare scrapyard of twisted metal.

Better? asked the primroses.

A bit, replied the forget-me-nots, spreading well-fed

roots among the debris that had once been a complete armoured division and burping. *But you know how it is. You quickly get tired of all this tinned food.*

With a sonic boom that shattered windows and played merry hell with television reception all over the state, Philly Nine flew over Miami, heading for the pall of smoke.

Swooping low, he turned a jaunty victory roll over the straggling column of refugees that clogged the interstate highway in both directions for as far as the eye could see. A ragged cheer broke out at ground level. The poor fools! If only they knew.

The wildflowers weren't hard to find; they were, by now, the tallest things in Florida. Spread out in a loose column, they were lurching at an alarming speed along the deserted tarmac of a ten-lane expressway. Huge lumps of asphalt came away each time their roots moved. Behind them the earth was a glistening muddy brown.

Philly Nine skirted round them in a wide circle, easily evading the outstretched tendrils of the forget-me-nots. As he flew, he hugged himself with joy. This was going to be fun!

He was, however, still in two minds. His original plan had been an unquenchable wave of fire that would shrivel up the flowers and then sweep irresistibly onwards, north-east, until the entire continent was reduced to ash. On mature reflection, however, he couldn't help feeling that that was a waste of the opportunity of an eternal lifetime. America is, after all, only one continent, surrounded on all sides by oceans. As he studied the column of marauding flora weaving its grim course, he couldn't help reflecting that this lot would probably be more than capable of having the same net effect if left to their own devices. What he wanted was something a bit more universal in its application; something that wouldn't grind to a jarring halt as soon as it hit the beaches …

Philly Nine stopped dead in mid-air and slapped his forehead melodramatically with the heel of his hand. Of course! He'd been looking at this entirely the wrong way round.

He accelerated, heading due north. In a quarter of an hour he was over Alaska; at which point he slowed down, rubbed his hands together to get the circulation going and looked around for something to work with.

At the North Pole he alighted, materialised a roll of extra-strong mints, popped the whole tube into his mouth and chewed hard. Then he took a deep breath, and exhaled.

The ice began to melt.

A word, at this stage, about Insurance.

There are your big insurance companies: the ones who own pretty well everything, who take your money and then make you run round in small, frantic circles whenever you want to claim for burst pipes or a small dent in your offside front wing. Small fry.

There is Lloyds of London: the truly professional outfit who will insure pretty well any risk you choose to name so long as you're prepared to spend three times the value of whatever it is you're insuring on premiums. As is well known, Lloyd's is merely a syndicate of rich individuals who underwrite the risks with their own massive private fortunes. Slightly larger fry, but still pretty microscopic.

What about the real risks; the ones that have to be insured (because the consequences of something going wrong would be so drastic), but which are so colossal that no individual or corporation could possibly provide anything like the resources needed to underwrite them?

(Such risks as the sun failing to rise, summer being cancelled at short notice, gravity going on the blink again, the earth falling off its axis; or, indeed, severe melting of the ice-caps, leading to global flooding?)

To cover these risks there exists a syndicate of individuals who possess not mere wealth, but wealth beyond the dreams of avarice.

Wealth beyond the dreams of avarice? Sounds familiar? Suffice it to say that the registered office of this syndicate is a small, verdigrised copper lamp, presently located at the bottom of a locked trunk in an attic somewhere in the suburbs of Aleppo.

For the record, nobody has yet been able to work out exactly what Avarice dreams about, on the rare occasions when it sleeps. It all depends, the experts say, on how late it stayed up the night before, how comfortable the mattress is, and whether it ate a substantial amount of cheese immediately before going to bed.

One of the many advantages that genies have over mere mortals is that they need no sleep. This is one of the few things that makes it possible for a genie to wait on a human being hand, foot and finger without something inside its head snapping. Eventually the mortal will go to sleep, giving the genie eight or so clear hours in which to recuperate and catch up on its social life.

Kiss had got into the habit of spending these few precious hours each day down at the gym, working out. When genies work out, by the way, they don't bother with weights, rowing machines and permanently stationary bicycles. What they exercise is their true potential.

When his bleeper went, therefore, Kiss was in the middle of a simulated battle with thirty thousand blood-crazed snow-dragons. To make it interesting, and spin the exercise out for more than six minutes, he had both arms and one leg tied behind his back, and he was blindfolded and chained to the wall. This made it difficult for him to reach the telephone.

'Yes,' he snapped into the receiver, deflecting a ravening

hologram with his toes as he did so. 'What is it now?'

'I think you should get back here as quick as you can,' said Jane's voice at the end of the line. 'Something rather serious has cropped up.'

'Really?' Kiss tried to keep the weary scorn out of his voice, but not very hard. 'Let me guess. Your eyebrow pencil's broken and you want me to sharpen it. There's a very small spider in the bath. You can't find the top of the ketchup bottle ...'

'The ice-caps have melted and nine-tenths of the Earth's surface is under water. Can you spare a few minutes, or shall I try to find an emergency plumber?'

'I'm on – get off me, you stupid bird – no, not you. I'm on my way.'

Grunting something under his breath about one damn thing after another, he shook himself free of his adamantine chains, swatted the remaining six thousand dragons with the back of his hand and pulled on his trousers over his leotards.

'Don't switch anything off,' he called out to the attendant. 'This won't take a minute.'

I don't know, he muttered as he raced across the night sky.

Never a moment's peace, he complained, as he grabbed a mop and a bucket out of the empty air.

It's not much to ask, an hour or so at the end of the day just to unwind a bit and relax, he said to himself, as he stopped off at the South Pole to fill the bucket with ice. *But no, apparently not. A genie's work is never done.*

He sighed, shrugged his shoulders and pulled out a handful of small hairs from the back of his neck.

Kiss, save the world. Kiss, thwart the diabolical plans of that crazed megalomaniac wizard over there. Kiss, empty the ashtrays and do the washing-up. I dunno. Women!

He rolled the hairs between his palms, spat on them and threw them up into the air. For a moment they hung between the earth and the stars; then they fell and, as they did so, changed into so many full-sized replicas of himself, each with a mop and a bucket of ice. Each replica pulled out a handful of its own hair and repeated the process.

'Ready?' asked the original Kiss. The replicas nodded.

'What did your last servant die of?' they chorused.

'That's enough out of you lot. Get to it!'

In the Oval Office, Kowalski and the President faced each other over the big desk.

'To begin with, Viv,' said the President, 'I was worried. For a moment there, I was beginning to think you'd maybe overreacted.'

Kowalski squirmed slightly, but not enough for the President to notice. 'You did say—' he began.

'Sure.' The President smiled. 'I should have had more faith in you and your guys. But next time—'

'I surely hope there won't be a next time,' Kowalski said, with conviction.

'Me too,' agreed the President. 'Still, it won't have done the polls any harm. Nothing the voters like more, when the chips are down, than a little display of All-American true grit. And the way your guys handled the evacuations was first class.'

Kowalski nodded. What the President didn't know, and with luck would never find out, was that the really big emergencies were the easy ones. For a really big emergency, like evacuating America, all he had to do was phone the insurance people and let them handle it. Which they had done.

'And the, uh, mopping-up operations afterwards,' the President continued. 'I guess I take my hat off to you there, Viv.'

Kowalski's eyes narrowed. 'You aren't wearing a hat, Mr President.'

'I was speaking figuratively, Viv.'

'Ah.' Kowalski left the semi-smug expression on his face, but inside he was still confused. The insurance people hadn't said anything about mopping up the floods. Leave it, they'd said, it'll go down of its own accord in a year or two. If it's still bad in eighteen months, send out a dove.

So who had done the business with the mops and the dry ice? He wished he knew.

Of course! How could he have been so stupid? The genie, of course, Philly whatever-his-name-was. Who else could it have been?

'No problem,' he said. 'We've got guys on the payroll for every contingency, Mr President, like I keep saying.'

'That's good to know, Viv.' The President smiled. 'Just like magic, huh?'

'There you go again,' replied Kowalski uncomfortably. 'You and your figurative speaking.'

Philly Nine sat on the peak of Everest and counted up to ten.

Don't get mad, he told himself, get even.

You bastards are going to pay for this.

As for the details – well, they'd look after themselves. They always did. Sooner or later some other idiot of a human being would give him an opening, and he'd be back. What was forty years or so to an immortal?

Provided, of course, that no interfering little toerag of a Force Twelve saw fit to stick his oar in, saving the planet with a twitch of his little finger before zooming away into the sunset. Some people, he reflected bitterly, don't know the meaning of the word solidarity.

Yes, indeed. He broke off the summit of the mountain, brushed it clear of flags and ate it. Kiss would have to go, or he might as well stay in bed.

But how? Force Twelves can't just be brushed lightly aside. Or even heavily aside, or aside with overwhelming force. It would be like trying to knock down a pterodactyl with a fly-swatter.

There are, however, ways and means. And of all the ways of killing a cat, Philly Nine reflected, drowning it in cream sure takes some beating.

There is a child.

His father was a brutal, sadistic bully; his mother a nymphomaniac married to a man (not the child's father) many years older than herself, and crippled into the bargain.

Left to his own devices for most of his formative years, the child developed serious personality disorders at a very early age. By the time he turned thirteen, he was effectively past hope of cure.

Partly it was heredity, partly it was environment; partly, it was the child's own basically vicious and perverted nature, which nobody ever took the slightest trouble to correct.

By the time he turned thirteen, the boy had developed a morbid fixation with shooting people. Because of his unusually privileged position, he's able to indulge this ghastly obsession with total impunity.

Look at him. Fourteen years old, dressed from head to toe in camouflage gear, with a Stallonesque headband and pimples. He's lying on his bed reading *Soldier of Fortune* magazine, and beside him on the duvet lies a state-of-the-art Macmillan sniper's rifle, with a Bausch & Lomb 21X scope and integral flash suppressor. When he gets bored with doing nothing, he'll go out into the street and start using it.

There's nothing anyone can do about it. Nothing at all.

Despite the fact that this murderous infant ruins the lives of countless innocent people every day of the week, the authorities are powerless to act. They simply accept the situation and look the other way.

Because the child is a Force Thirteen genie – the only one – and his name is Cupid.

FIVE

High up in the Himalaya mountains, the very roof of the world, Kiss crouched low on a ledge a mere inch or so wide, held his breath, and waited.

'It's vitally important to us genies,' he could hear himself saying to Jane in an unguarded moment, 'that we retain our unique cultural heritage and ancient folkloric traditions and way of life.'

Jane had nodded sympathetically, gone away and read up the subject of what genies traditionally did. Accordingly, he had nobody to blame but himself.

'Come on, you goddamn treacherous sonofabitch,' he muttered under his breath. The mutterings froze in the sub-zero air and fell away, tinkling, down the sheer side of the rock-face. Fortunately, the wind drowned the noise.

On the blind side of the jagged outcrop of rock to which Kiss was clinging perched a bird. Not just any bird; the rarest, most fabulous, most acutely perceptive, biggest and worst-tempered bird in existence. Its plumage was a scintillating shower of jewelled colour, sparkling and shimmering in the clear, sharp light. It had a wing-span of fifty feet and claws that could disembowel an elephant as easily as undoing a zip.

'Cone on, my son,' Kiss whispered. Although he couldn't see the bird, he could hear the soft click as its heavily bejewelled, scalpel-sharp beak pecked at the trail of peanuts he had carefully laid the previous afternoon. Fortunately the phoenix, although rare, magical and incredibly dangerous, is not particularly intelligent. When it suddenly finds a trail of dry roasted peanuts extending along a ledge towards the mouth of a cave thirty thousand feet above sea level, it doesn't stop to ask how on earth they got there. Yum, it thinks, lunch.

This, together with the incalculable value of their tail-feathers, is probably the real reason why phoenices are so rare.

There are easier ways of obtaining phoenix feathers, however, than snaring them with peanuts and pitfall traps. The inhabitants of the Himalayas hit on a much more efficient method not long after the discovery of gunpowder. Genies, however, have obtained phoenix plumage the hard way since time immemorial, and so, regretfully, Kiss had left behind the Mannlicher-Schoenauer .600 Nitro Express rifle that common sense suggested was the best way of going about the job, and had instead packed peanuts, string and a folding shovel.

Peck, peck, peck. Aaaaargh! Crunch. About time too, Kiss sighed, and shuffled quickly along the ledge and round the corner, to peer down into the pit he had spent six hours digging the previous evening.

A baleful red eye glared up at him out of the darkness.

'All right,' croaked a hoarse voice. 'It's a fair cop, guv, I'll come quietly. I don't think,' it added.

Kiss frowned. 'Be reasonable,' he said. 'A couple of feathers and you can be on your way. There's no way you can get out of there otherwise.'

From the pit, the sound of unfriendly cackling. 'You want feathers, chum, you come down here and get them. It's quite cosy in here out of the wind, I'm in no hurry.'

The genie rubbed his chin, nonplussed, and drew his collar tighter around his numb ears. His plan, although

admirably simple and flawlessly executed, had only extended as far as getting the phoenix into the trap. Once he'd
reached that stage, he had assumed, the rest of it would
somehow take care of itself.

'Don't be stupid,' he growled. 'You're just being a bad
loser. You make with the feathers, I'll make with the plank
of wood. Agreed?'

'Up yours.'

'I can starve you out.'

'I carry six months supply of nutritional material around
with me in the form of subcutaneous fat,' replied the bird
smugly. 'If that's your game, you'd better have brought
plenty of sandwiches.'

Kiss pursed his lips. The full extent of his preparations
consisted of a thermos flask of, by now, lukewarm tea and
the remainder of the peanuts. True, he could fly back to
Katmandu, stock up on chocolate and be back in thirty
seconds, but he had an idea that by the time he returned the
phoenix would be out of there and circling overhead with its
bowels puckered ready for pinpoint-accuracy bombing.
Phoenix guano is the third most corrosive substance in the
entire cosmos.

'I'll roll a rock on top of you,' he ventured. 'See how you
like that.'

'You'd crush the feathers,' the bird replied. 'A right prat
you'd look going back to the princess or whoever it is you're
doing this for holding something looking like a second-hand
pipe cleaner.'

'All right,' Kiss conceded. 'So it's a stalemate. Let's
negotiate.'

'Bugger off.'

Tiny silver bells started ringing in Kiss's brain. 'Fair
enough,' he said, 'if that's the way you want to play it, don't
say I didn't give you every chance.'

The red eye blinked. 'Bluff,' it snarled. 'Look, you sling

your hook and we'll say no more about it. Can't say fairer than—'

Kiss began to sing.

When they choose to do so, genies can sing well; heart-breakingly, soul-meltingly well. A genie can, if he sets his mind to it, sing solo duets; even barbershop.

Alternatively, they can sing badly. Very badly indeed.

By dint of stuffing its pinion feathers into its ears and banging its head sharply against the side of the pit, the phoenix managed to hold out for an amazing seventeen minutes, during the course of which Kiss sang *Sweet Adeline*, *Way Down Upon The Swanee River*, *Mammy*, *Alexander's Ragtime Band* and three complete renditions of *Seventy-Six Trombones Followed The Big Parade*. Indeed, it was only when he took a deep breath and announced that there were fifty-seven thousand green bottles hanging on a wall that the phoenix screeched like a Mack truck braking on black ice and started throwing feathers.

'Thank you very much,' Kiss called out, stuffing feathers into a sack. 'Do you want a receipt?'

'Shut up and go away, please.'

'And no sneakily crawling out and coming after me, you hear?'

'I wouldn't dream of it. Not unless I saw an affidavit certifying you'd had your larynx removed first.'

Kiss slid the plank down into the pit, waved cheerfully, said goodbye and stepped off the ledge.

As he floated to the ground he entirely failed to notice the small figure huddled in the lee of the rocks, snapping furiously at him through a telephoto lens.

'That's him,' said Philly Nine. 'You think you can do it?'

'I dunno.' Cupid frowned. 'Let's see her again.'

Philly Nine shrugged and produced the other photo-graph. In it Jane was clearly visible, third from the left, second row down, holding a hockey stick.

'Couldn't you get something a bit more up to date?' Cupid demanded.

Philly shrugged again. 'If necessary,' he replied. 'I didn't think it mattered. Anyway, I thought you were supposed to be blind.'

Cupid smiled wearily. 'Man, there's all sorts of dumb things I'm supposed to be,' he replied. 'And this photo is fifteen years out of date. Get me something better and then we can talk business.'

'Wait there,' the genie said. Forty-five seconds later he was back.

'That's more like it,' said Cupid, appraising the picture with a professional eye. 'It's not going to be easy,' he added, after a few moments of close scrutiny.

'Come off it,' Philly said. 'To you, a piece of cake. Five minutes of your time, that's all I'm asking for.'

'Rather longer than that,' Cupid replied. He tried holding the picture sideways, but it didn't seem to help.

'Look.' Philly frowned. 'You owe me, remember?'

About a thousandth of a second later, he wished he'd kept his mouth shut. The child was looking at him in a way that made his blood run cold.

'Mister,' Cupid said, 'I'm a Force Thirteen, I don't owe nobody *nothing*. You'd do well to remember that, unless you want to spend the rest of your life sending boxes of chocolates to a red-arsed monkey. Understood?'

'Sorry.'

Cupid made a small gesture with his hands, signifying that the apology was accepted. 'All I'm saying is,' he went on, 'it's a tough assignment. The ballistics alone are gonna need a lot of careful planning. This ain't gonna be cheap, I can tell you that for nothing.'

Philly Nine smiled. 'That,' he said confidently, 'isn't a problem. Just so long as you can do it.'

'Yeah.' Cupid nodded. 'I can do it.' He laughed without

humour. 'It'll be one for the trade press, I'm telling you. For a start,' he went on, 'there's the problem of the actual projectile. For her, it's got to be a frangible spire-point, or the chances are I'll just blow her away. For him, though, we're talking tungsten-core, full satin jacket stuff, the full treatment. Means there's no chance of a second shot if I miss the first time.'

'You won't miss, Coops. You never do.'

The boy shrugged. 'Always a first time. And supposing I do manage to do the job on them; I still gotta get myself outa there. Once your buddy here realises what I've done to him, he ain't gonna be pleased.'

Philly Nine stood up. 'You'll find a way,' he said confidently. 'That's why you're the best. It'll be worth your while.'

Cupid glanced back at the photographs and grinned wryly. 'It'd better be,' he said, did a thumbnail impersonation of a lovestruck marmoset, and vanished.

Jane hesitated, feather duster in hand, and looked around her.

'What the hell,' she said aloud, 'has come over me?'

It was, looked at objectively, an awe-inspiring sight. Suffice it to say, her mother would have approved. She had ambivalent feelings about that.

Yes, it was tidy. Yes, it was clean. Spotlessly so, in fact. Any passing visitor could have eaten his dinner off the floor without any health risk at all, although he might have found it more convenient to use a plate. Furthermore, the curtains matched the carpets, the carpets matched the loose covers and the loose covers matched the lampshades. It was exactly the sort of interior that furniture polish advertisements are filmed in, and a Swiss mother-in-law couldn't have found a microbe or a granule of dust anywhere.

'Yetch,' thought Jane.

Eight years' living on her own had accustomed Jane to a rather more bohemian environment: second-hand furniture, the floor hidden under discarded clothes and newspapers, a sink full of crockery and a kitchen floor that went crunch! when you stepped on it. She liked it that way. It was a statement, she'd always told herself, about her spiritual enfranchisement as a woman of the last decade of the twentieth century, the logical extension of the glorious principle to which Emmeline Pankhurst devoted her life.

And now look at it. 'Why?' she demanded. No reply.

Perhaps, she mused, catching herself in the act of plumping up a cushion, it's simply a case of reverting to type. That in itself was a disquieting thought, for the women in her family were the sort that ironed socks and regarded any meal that didn't contain at least two boiled vegetables as a badge of heresy. No, it couldn't be that. It had to be something else.

It had to be something to do with the genie. Looking at the scene before her, she realised that what it lacked was a man, entering stage left and being told to take off his muddy shoes and not to sit on the chairs in those trousers. The genie, however, didn't by the wildest stretch of the imagination fall into that category. The only thing he – it – would be likely to tread into the carpets would be stardust or blood, and quite often it didn't even wear legs, let alone trousers. Nor could it possibly be a case of the genie's taste subconsciously subverting her own. Left to himself, Kiss would have done the place out like a cross between the palace of Versailles and Sinbad's cabin. Perhaps …

Perhaps, Jane reasoned as she automatically straightened a picture, it's an instinctive reaction; an urge to counter the intrusion of bizarre supernatural forces into her life by making her environment as brain-numbingly mundane as possible. Well, she was made of sterner stuff than that. She fished a magazine out of the paper rack, opened it and laid it face down in the centre of the floor. Then she straightened it, folded it neatly and put it away again. It was all she could do to stop herself ironing it first.

'This must stop,' she said firmly. The words seemed to soak away into the soft furnishings like water in a desert. Bad vibes.

That nest of tables hadn't been there this morning, had it? If anyone had told Jane a month ago that she'd ever deliberately own a nest of tables, she'd have laughed in his face. Yet there they were; with little coasters on them, to stop cups leaving rings on their sparkling glass tops. In her natural environment, cups grew on every available flat surface like mushrooms, and you had to give them a little tweak to break the gasket of solidified coffee that glued them down before you could remove them. And that, Jane knew in her heart, was the way it was meant to be. Not like this. She felt like a daughter in her own home. It was intolerable.

As soon as Kiss got back from whatever errand she'd sent him on, she resolved, she'd tell him to clear it all away and put it back exactly how it had been, down to the last smeared glass and overstuffed dustbin bag. Until then, she would go out.

Where, though? She didn't know. The last four weeks, she realised, had been spent in an orgy of home-making, with occasional breaks for picnics in exotic places. She hadn't yet come to terms with the fact that she no longer had to work for a living, or go out shopping, or do anything at all. Which left her with nothing whatever to do.

There had been, she recalled, some talk of saving the world, and as hobbies go, she supposed it would do to be going on with; more socially useful than needlework, and cheaper than collecting Georgian silver snuffboxes. It wasn't, however, the sort of thing you could do every day of the week. She needed something else, and she was damned if she was going to spend the rest of her life buying clothes or going to cocktail parties. She wanted …

Adventure? God forbid! Travel, to see strange sights and brave new worlds? She could go anywhere with a wish; but without the hanging about in departure lounges and lugging suitcases off carousels that gave travel its true meaning. All genuine wanderers know that it is better to travel uncomfortably than to arrive. Simply closing your eyes and finding yourself in Madagascar was as pointless as staying at home and arranging plastic flowers. What the hell did she want out of life?

But the idea of telling the genie, thank you very much, the rest of eternity's your own, was somehow repellant; it would be such a waste, like telling God you'd had a better offer. All the wish-fulfilment dreams you've ever had, there for the asking; no, there was no way she could say goodbye to all that. It would be cowardice, she'd never forgive herself, and she'd have to go back to doing her own washing-up.

There must, she reassured herself, be some purpose to all this. Although she'd never taken much interest in fairy stories when she was a girl, she could at least remember that genies didn't just happen to people out of a clear blue sky; there was always a plot of some sort, a sequence of events leading up to the genie, and a series of adventures following its arrival, concluding in the overthrow of evil, the righting of wrongs and the happiness ever after. To jump straight from the middle of the story to the end would violate the first law of narrative, and the laws of narrative make the laws of thermodynamics look weedy in comparison. Break the laws of narrative and you don't get let off with thirty hours' community service; they lock you up in a story and throw away the bookmark. No, something was going to happen, whether she liked it or not, and it was probably going to involve a life-and-death struggle with the forces of darkness. Gosh, Jane said to herself, what a cheerful prospect to look forward to. And aren't I the lucky one?

Why me, though? Well, why not? Presumably everybody else was busy. That was the sort of question she would have to leave to whoever was telling the story.

She glanced at the clock. Even if she was going to have to save the world, she reckoned, she'd probably still have enough time to wash her hair first.

In an upstairs window of the house opposite, Cupid adjusted his headband, chambered a round in his rifle and drew a skin-tight leather glove on to his right hand with his teeth. Through his telescopic sight (with the special rose-tinted filter) he could see Kiss trudging wearily back across the sky, his arms full of feathers. The girl was still under the hair-dryer, reading a book. The timing was going to have to be absolutely right.

No worries. Back in the old bow-and-arrow days, it was true, he had occasionally made a mistake. Now, however, he had technology as well as destiny on his side, not to mention the steadiest trigger finger in the Universe. At anything less than six hundred yards, provided the visibility was even half-way adequate, the course of true love was guaranteed to run smooth. He breathed in and felt his heartbeat slow down.

Now the genie was floating in through the window. The girl was looking up from her book. Here, the genie was saying, where do you want me to put all these feathers? Cupid half-closed his left eye and took up the slack on the trigger.

The first shot brayed out in the still air – only Cupid could hear it, of course – followed by the rattle of the bolt as he worked the second round into the chamber. No need to ask whether the first bullet had found its mark; the genie's mouth had already flopped open in that uniquely gormless way that can only mean one thing. With a half-smile, Cupid brought the crosswires to bear on Jane's heart and let his finger tighten round the trigger …

A spider, which had been spinning its web directly overhead, fell on the back of his neck. At the last moment, just as the sear slipped its bent, he twitched sharply, jerking the rifle sideways –

– and a potted fern, which had accompanied Jane from one flat to another for the last six years without really being aware of her existence, suddenly noticed with heart-stopping intensity how entrancingly her hair curled round the nape of her neck –

– swore, worked the action and steadied the butt in the pocket of his shoulder. Ignoring the spider, which was trying to tunnel down under the collar of his combat jacket, Cupid half-emptied his lungs and eased off the trigger. For a split second the image before his eyes blurred, as the rifle jumped in a fierce spasm of unleashed energy. Then the picture cleared …

Gotcha! The room opposite was suddenly full of pink hearts, floating in the air like big, fat balloons. The whole street was heavy with the stench of roses.

Quickly and carefully, making no more noise than a stalking leopard, Cupid gathered up his equipment and got the hell out.

Fire crackled in the withered stems of the mistletoe, casting an eerie red glow on the lichen-covered stones of the circle. It illuminated seven faces.

'Ready?'

'Yup.'

The Chief Druid winced slightly. Although he was aware of how vitally important it was to attract keen new blood to the Circle, so that the ancient secrets could be passed down to generations yet unborn, he still hadn't come to terms with young Kevin's attitude. The sceptical part of him still harboured a suspicion that Kevin, who was an insurance broker, had only joined in the hope of picking up new clients.

However.

'We shall now,' he said gravely, 'link hands and invoke the Goddess.'

'Ready when you are, Humph.'

Ready when you are, Humph. It was at time like this that he wondered whether there was any point in passing down the ancient secrets. There was a sporting chance, he reflected gloomily, that if the Goddess did materialise Kevin would immediately leap forward and try to sell her a unit-linked endowment policy.

'Everybody join hands,' he went on, 'and keep holy silence in the presence of ... Are you all right back there, Mr Prenderby?'

'Yes, thank you, Chief Druid.'

'It isn't time for your pills yet, is it?'

'Not for another half-hour, thank you, Chief Druid.'

'That's all right, then.' The Chief Druid glanced round. His flock were waiting, with all the silent embarrassment of grown men asked to hold hands with other grown men who they'd probably see again the next day, but wearing suits and ties rather than long grey woollen gowns. He cast another sprig of mistletoe on to the fire and took a deep breath.

WHOOSH!

'Stone the flaming crows!' The Chief Druid recognised the voice of Shane, who was on an exchange visit arranged with the Order's New South Wales congregation. He cringed. Just his rotten luck, he said to himself. The one time the Goddess actually manifests herself in my Circle, and the first person to greet her is this antipodean lout.

'Hello, boys,' said the Goddess.

She stood in the centre of the fire, which had leapt up to meet her like a large, friendly dog. Red tongues of flame licked round her, and her head was surrounded by a chaplet of pale blue light.

'G'day, Miss.' The Australian shook his hand free from the clammy paw of Mr Prenderby (who looked like he was going to need his pills sooner than usual) and extended it gingerly. A long, yellow, spotted snake materialised out of the fire and curled round his forearm as far as the elbow.

'And what,' drawled the Goddess, 'can I do for *you*?'

'Excuse me.' Kevin's voice. The Chief Druid couldn't bear to watch. It shouldn't be like this, he told himself; it wasn't like this in the books.

The Goddess turned her head and smiled politely, like the Queen being introduced to the teams at half-time during the Cup Final. Kevin smiled back, instinctively using the wide grin he used for Putting Clients At Their Ease.

'Excuse me,' he said, 'but I take it you are the, um, Goddess? No offence, but I think we ought to just . . . rivet-rivet-rivet.'

The Circle froze, and the only sound was the sobbing of the wind and the frantic croaking of the small yellow frog that had once been Kevin.

'Satisfied?' asked the Goddess. 'Or would you like me to do something really convincing?'

The six druids fell simultaneously to their knees.

'Now then,' said the Goddess briskly, 'to business. Any requests, anybody?'

No reply. The Goddess clicked her tongue.

'Oh come *on*, people,' she said, 'I'm sure you didn't drag me all the way down here just to chat about the weather. Anybody for a bumper harvest? Rain for the crops? The winner of the 3.15 at Chepstow?'

The Chief Druid ran a desperate scan through the jumbled mess between his ears, but nothing occurred to him. He briefly considered saying, 'All hail!', but decided that She'd take that as a reference to the weather, a subject she apparently wasn't inclined to discuss.

'Well,' said the Goddess, 'if nobody wants anything at all, we'd better just fast forward to the wicker-cage bit, and then call it a day.'

For crying out loud, somebody say something. The Chief Priest swung a hasty glance round the Circle, but nobody was moving. They were all frozen like snakes watching a mongoose; except for Mr Prenderby, who had nodded off again.

'I see.' The Goddess sighed. 'Well then, the wicker-cage it is, then. And whose turn is it to be burnt alive this evening? I do hope somebody's remembered to bring some matches.'

'I have a request, Majesty.'

The Chief Druid's relief was short-lived, because the words were still hanging in the crisp night air when he realised that the voice that had spoken them was his own.

'Splendid,' the Goddess said. 'Right, what'll it be?'

'Um.' The Chief Druid felt his tongue dragging like sandpaper across the roof of his mouth. 'Do you know,' he went on, 'it's just slipped my mind for a moment.'

'Has it really?'

'Yes, Majesty.'

'Would it help,' the Goddess went on, 'if I just quickly read your mind? It won't take me two seconds.'

'Please don't trouble yourself, Majesty.'

'It's no trouble.' Suddenly the Chief Druid was horribly aware of the Goddess's eyes; he could feel them poking into his brain like knitting needles. No question at all that she could see exactly what he was thinking.

'I see,' said the Goddess. 'Yes, I can see your request in there, plain as day.'

'You can?'

'Of course I can, silly.' The Goddess smiled at him. 'You

want me to afflict the world with seven plagues, don't you?'

'I do? I mean, yes, of course. How clever of you to—'

'You want me to trample the Unbeliever like a worm under the claw of the gryphon. You want me to unleash the fury of the Nine Terrible Winds, and visit the wrath of Belenos upon the heads of the ungodly.'

The Chief Druid nodded. As he did so, he was aware that he was on the receiving end of some pretty old-fashioned looks from the rest of the Circle (particularly Mr Cruick-shank, who taught Drama at the local junior school and had a Greenpeace sticker in the back window of his Citroën) but he ignored them. 'Quite right,' he stuttered. 'My sentiments exactly, er, Majesty.'

The Goddess nodded. 'Fine,' she said. 'Ordinarily, that'd be a pretty tall order, but since it's you—'

'Excuse me.'

The Chief Druid's head whirled round like a weath-ervane in a hurricane. Mr Cruickshank had raised his hand. 'Yes?'

'Excuse me, Goddess,' said Mr Cruickshank, his eyes nearly popping out of his head, 'but, if you don't mind me asking—'

'Yes?'

'These seven plagues …'

'Ah yes.' The Goddess dipped her head placidly. 'Mr Owen will correct me if I'm wrong,' she said, dropping a smile in the Chief Druid's direction, 'but what I think he had in mind was plagues of hail, brimstone, frogs, sulphur, locusts, giant ants and burning pitch. That's right, isn't it?'

The Chief Druid felt his head nod.

'In any particular order, or just as it comes?'

'Oh, as it comes. Whatever's the most convenient for you.'

'Thank you.' The Goddess considered for a moment. 'In that case,' she said, 'I think we'll set the ball rolling with locusts. Is that all right with everyone?'

A flash of blue lightning rent the night sky, and six heads rapidly nodded their agreement.

'You're sure? It's your request, after all.'

'No, really,' gabbled the Chief Druid. 'Locusts, by all means.'

'Locusts it shall be, then,' the Goddess replied. 'Will Tuesday be soon enough, do you think?'

The Chief Druid shuddered. He had spent that afternoon planting out his spring cabbages. He assured the Goddess that there was no hurry.

'Oh, I think I should be able to manage Tuesday. Now then, any more for any more?'

Apparently not. A few seconds later, the Goddess was gone. As she sped through the fog and filthy air, she gave herself a little shake and turned back into the genie Philadelphia Machine and Tool Corporation IX.

A genie with a mandate.

The small yellow frog that had once been Kevin hopped slowly across the blasted heath.

Right now, he might be a small yellow frog; but not so long ago he had been an insurance broker, and we have already seen how insurance is like a pyramid –

(Huge, incomprehensible, hideously expensive, completely unnecessary and specifically designed only to be of any benefit to you once you're dead? Well, quite; but also …)

– a pyramid, with tens of thousands of little people like Kevin at the bottom, and a small number of very big people indeed at the top.

If one of the little people at the bottom shouts loud enough, one of the big people at the top will hear him.

Exhausted, the little yellow frog crawled the last few agonising inches and flopped into a stagnant pond. For two minutes he lay bobbing in the brackish water, gathering his strength.

They will hear him, because there is money at stake; and money is the ultimate hearing aid.

The little yellow frog stretched his legs and kicked feebly. A small string of bubbles broke the surface of the water. Deep down, among the pondweed and the mosquito larvae, Kevin rested, took stock of his position, and reflected on what he had to do next.

First, he had to file a claim. Without the policy document to hand, he couldn't be sure that there wasn't something in the fine print that excluded being turned into a frog from the All Risks cover; Act of Goddess, probably. But there was no harm in trying.

Second, he had to report to his superiors.

The loss adjusters at the top of the pyramid have a refreshingly dynamic approach to their art. Instead of simply coming on the scene when the dust has settled and trying to make the best of a bad job, they prefer to think positive. The best way to adjust a loss, they feel, is *retrospectively*.

Not long afterwards, a small yellow head appeared above the surface of the pond, blinked, and turned its snout towards the waning moon.

'Rivet,' it said. 'Rivet-rivet-rivet.'

SIX

'Would you like,' Jane asked, 'a cup of tea?'

Kiss nodded, unable to speak. Genies, of course, can't stomach tea. The tannin does something drastic to the inexplicable tangle of chemical reactions that makes up their digestion. He grinned awkwardly.

'I brought you some feathers,' he mumbled, and thrust the bundle at her. She simpered.

'Gosh,' she said. 'Aren't they pretty? Let me put them in some water.'

She grabbed the feathers and fled into the kitchen, leaving Kiss to speculate as to what in hell's name was going on.

Heatstroke? He hadn't been anywhere hot. Malaria? Genies don't get malaria. A recent sharp bang on the head? No. Then what …?

Eliminate the impossible –

'Impossible!' he said aloud.

– and whatever remains, however improbable –

'No way,' he muttered. 'Biological impossibility.'

– must be the truth …

'*Shit!*' he said.

And yet. Weirder things have been known. It's a fact that human beings (and genies count as human for this purpose) can get attached to almost anything, with the possible exception of Death and lawyers. And there was something indescribably charming about the way the corners of her mouth puckered up when she smiled …

'Oh, for crying out loud!' the genie exclaimed. And then the truth hit him. He peered down at his chest and saw, on the left side, a small round hole in his shirt. A few minutes later and it wouldn't have been there; the holes Cupid makes in cloth heal themselves in about a quarter of an hour, on average.

The bastard, Kiss said to himself. The absolute bastard.

But what could he do about it? Well, he could try changing himself into a woman – a piece of cake for a Force Twelve – but he had the feeling that that wouldn't make things better in the slightest degree; in fact, it would complicate matters horrendously. The same was true of turning into a cat, an ant or a three-legged stool.

He could get hold of that bloody aggravating child and twist his head off. That would make him feel better, for a while; but he knew perfectly well that even Cupid was incapable of undoing the damage. All he could realistically hope for was that with the passage of time the wound would heal of its own accord. But how long? With mortals, he knew, the process usually took somewhere between three and sixty years, and he didn't have that much time. Marriage, of course, was a recognised form of accelerating the process, but even so …

And why? The question flared in his mind like an explosion in a fuel dump. What possible reason could Cupid have for a stunt like this?

He could think of a reason. Cold sweat began to seep through his pores.

The door opened and Jane sidled through, holding a teacup and a large cut-glass vase full of soggy-looking phoenix feathers.

'There,' she said, 'don't they look nice?'

Kiss nodded dumbly. He had been an observer of human behaviour long enough to know perfectly well what came next; that excruciatingly embarrassing hour or so that you always get when two people realise that they're in love, but both of them would rather be buried alive in a pit full of quicklime than raise the topic in conversation. There would also be much staring at shoelaces, averting of eyes, feelings of nausea and meaningless small talk marinaded in sublimated soppiness.

'It was really kind of you to get them for me,' Jane was saying. 'It's something I've always wanted, a vase full of feathers. I think I'll put it here, where I can look at it when I'm sitting on the sofa.'

Jesus wept, Kiss thought, if only you could hear yourself! 'I'm glad you like them,' he heard himself reply. 'It was no bother, really.'

'I'm sure it was.'

'No, it wasn't.'

First, Kiss's subconscious was saying, we'll take the little bastard's rifle and wrap it round his neck and then shove it right up his …

'You sure?'

'Sure.'

There are rules, very strict rules, about when a genie may or may not read the mind of a mortal to whom he is indentured. Kiss broke them all. It was some small comfort to him to find that Jane's innermost thoughts were along more or less the same lines as his. *What on earth is going on?* he noticed with approval. *It can't really be, surely,* he was pleased to see. *What, him?* he read, with somewhat mixed feelings. *Pull the other one, it's got bells on it* was, he couldn't help feeling, just a trifle too emphatic. Without realising he was doing it, he made a few subliminal alterations to his bone structure and general physique.

Look, screamed his soul, this is ludicrous. Why don't you just tell her what's really happened, and find some way of sorting it out?

His consciousness turned to his soul and told it to get lost.

Yes, but …

Don't you understand plain Arabic? Bugger off. Can't you see the lady and I don't want to be interrupted?

'More tea?'

'Yes, please.' *You idiot, can't you see what's happening? Are you just going to stand there and let them …? Hey, there's no need to get violent, I was just going anyway …*

'Would you like a biscuit?'

'No, no, I'm fine, thanks.'

'You're sure?'

'Sure, thanks all the same.'

'It'd be no trouble at all.'

'No, really, I'm fine.'

As he spoke, Kiss marvelled at the moral fibre of the human race. A lesser species, faced with all this mucking about as an integral part of the procreative process, would have died out thousands of years ago. Salmon battling their way up waterfalls were quitters in comparison.

'Was it cold out?'

'Sorry?'

'I said, was it cold out? The weather.'

'No, it was fine. A bit nippy actually up the Himalayas themselves, but otherwise very, um, clement. For the time of year.'

'They must be very interesting,' Jane croaked. 'The Himalayas, I mean.'

'Yes, very.'

'And you had no trouble finding the phoenix?' Jane went on. It was painfully obvious that she was suffering too, but there was nothing at all he could do about it. He was having to call upon hidden resources of superhuman power just to stop himself from standing there with his mouth open like the rear doors of a cross-Channel ferry.

'No, it was easy enough. I just looked for some rocks with lots of white splashes and bits eaten out of them.'

'Ah. Right.'

Inside his heart, the bullet began to decompose. Cupid's bullets do that; the outer jacket, which is pressure-formed out of 99 per cent pure embarrassment, is soluble in sentiment and dissolves, leaving the bullet's core: 185 grains of cold-swaged slush. Any minute now, Kiss knew, he'd be staring at the carpet and muttering that there was something he'd been meaning to say to her for some time.

'Jane.'

'Yes?'

'There's something I've been meaning to say to you for some time.'

'Me too.'

'Sorry. Fire away.'

'No, no, you first.'

Thanks a heap. 'It's like, well—'

'Yes?'

He took a deep breath and said it. While he was saying it, the small part of him that was still functioning normally, albeit on emergency back-up systems and with a chair wedged behind the door in case the build-up of pink slop outside tried to force its way in, was working feverishly on the original very-good-question, *Why?*

Why should Philly Nine go to all the trouble and expense of hiring the ultimate hit-man, breaking all the rules in the Genies' Code of Conduct (it was cold comfort, but as soon as the Committee got to hear of this, Philly Nine was going to be spending a very long time in a confined space looking at green, curved, opaque walls) just to get his own back? Genies don't …

('… *Feelings that are, well, stronger than just ordinary friendship and, well, I guess that what I'm trying to say is…*')

Genies don't conduct their feuds like that; they hit each

other with solid objects, sometimes even mountains and small asteroids, and pelt each other with lightning and divert major rivers down the backs of each others' necks, but at least they're open about it. And, once the air had been cleared and the damage to the Earth's surface has been made good and the mountains put back in their proper place, they forget all about it and carry on, as if nothing had happened. This sort of thing …

('… *and I was sort of hoping that if you somehow might find you feel sort of the same way about me then we might sort of …*')

And then the penny dropped. The shock was so great that for a few moments Kiss was suddenly taken stone-cold sober, and he stopped in mid-sentence and stared.

'The *bastard!*' he said. 'The complete and utter bastard!'

Jane looked up sharply. 'I beg your pardon?'

'Sorry.' The tide of slush, temporarily checked, started to flow again. 'I was miles away. As I was saying …'

Let's do everyone a favour and fade out on Kiss for the moment …

('… *Make me the happiest man, well, genie, in the whole wide world …*')

… And just consider the situation, calmly and without getting carried away. Ready? Good.

What do you get if you cross a genie with a human being? Answer, you don't, because you can't. It's a simple matter of chemistry; or physics; or, when you come right down to it, mythology.

Genies do not, of course, exist. This doesn't mean that there aren't any. There are, as should be now be only too obvious, rather more of them than the universe can comfortably accommodate. Any cosmos that contains fragile, breakable things, such as planets, is better off with a ratio of as near to zero genies per cubic kilometre as possible.

Genies exist at a tangent to reality. They intrude into the continuum we inhabit, in much the same way as an iceberg intrudes into a major shipping lane. Only a tiny proportion of the huge complex of forces that go to make up a genie is ever present on this side of the thin blue line at any given time. Of the genie known as Kiss, for example, 87 per cent is sprawled across the Past and the Future like a cat sitting on the Sunday paper.

Let your imagination do its worst, and then you will agree that any sort of lasting relationship between a genie and a human being is out of the question. And if that wasn't bad enough, please also bear in mind that regardless of the physical shape it chooses to adopt, a genie always weighs a minimum of 72 tons and has a normal skin temperature of 700 degrees Celsius. It takes as much effort for a genie just to shake hands with a human without crushing him to pulp or shrivelling him up into ash as it would have to expend on juggling with the Pyrenees while standing on one leg on the head of a pin. And relationships are hard enough as it is without any added complications.

There is, however, an escape clause. It's totally irreversible and unbearably romantic, and its consequences to the genie are so horrendous that it has never been used; but it does exist.

A genie can become a human.

Think about it. Never to be able to fly again; never to uproot mountains or conjure up storms, change shape, travel through time, work magic. To forswear eternal life, and accept the inevitably of old age and death. To throw away divinity and embrace mortality, and all for love.

A hiding to nothing, in fact.

But the option exists; and it's a basic rule of life in an infinite universe that if something is possible, no matter how dangerous, unpleasant or downright idiotic it might be, sooner or later some fool will do it. Because it's there.

Or because they have no choice.

While we're on the subject of genies, consider this. Given that genies are by temperament cruel, arbitrary, uncaring, destructive and deeply interested in wealth beyond the dreams of avarice, isn't it inevitable that at least some of them should end up in the legal profession?

The offices of Messrs Fretten and Swindall are on the fifth floor of a large Chianti bottle with a hole drilled in the side and a bulb stuck in the neck, somewhere in the fashionable suburbs of Baghdad. This is no dog-and-stick operation over a chemist's shop in the High Street; even the receptionist is a Force Nine genie, with the power to harness the winds, raise the dead from their graves and convince callers that Mr Fretten really is on the other line and will call them back as soon as he's free.

(A staggering achievement, considering that Mr Fretten has been imprisoned in an empty gin bottle on a back shelf of the golf-club bar ever since Jesus Christ was a teenager; but there it is. There are at least two callers who have been holding for six hundred years.)

Hoping very much that wealthy beyond the dreams of avarice meant just that, Kiss made an appointment and took a strong easterly trade wind to Baghdad. Having given his coat to the receptionist, handed over a bottomless purse by way of a payment on account and read the March 1453 edition of the *National Geographic* from cover to cover, he was ushered into Mr Swindall's office and permitted to sit down.

'It's like this,' he said. He explained.

'You're stuffed,' said Mr Swindall, a big, fat bald Force Twelve with six chins. 'Completely shafted. He's got you on the sharp end of a very long pointy stick and there's bog all you can do about it. Forty thousand years in a Tizer bottle will seem like paradise compared to what you're about to go through.'

'Oh.'

Mr Swindall grinned. 'As neat a piece of buggeration as I've ever been privileged to hear about,' he went on. 'You've got to hand it to this friend of yours, he really knows how to insert the red-hot poker. If he came in here tomorrow I'd offer him a job like a shot.'

'I see.' Kiss frowned. 'I thought you're supposed to be on my side,' he said.

Mr Swindall nodded. 'Oh, I am,' he said. 'One hundred and twelve per cent. But face facts, you're dead in the water this time. Won't do yourself any favours by burying your head in the sand.' Mr Swindall rubbed his hands together. 'Now then, first things first. You'd better make a will.'

'Had I?'

'Absolutely.' The lawyer nodded, setting his chins swinging. 'After all, now that you're going to snuff it – pretty damn soon by our standards – it's imperative that you set your affairs in order. In fact, you're going to need some pretty high-level tax planning advice while you're at it, because there'll be none of this beyond-the-dreams-of-avarice stuff once you're one of Them.' A slight cloud of worry crossed Mr Swindall's shiny face. 'You did pay in advance, didn't you?'

'Yes.'

'That's all right, then. Next you'll be needing somewhere to live, so I'll just give you a copy of our housebuyer's special offer package; and it'll be some time before you get used to not being invulnerable any more, so we'll put your name down for a couple of personal injury actions in advance. It's a good scheme, this one; it means you can start paying for the lawyers' fees before you have the accident. Ah, yes,' said Mr Swindall, rubbing his hands together and grinning like a hyena, 'we'll be able to provide you with a *full* range of legal services before you're very much older, you mark my words.'

'I see. Thank you very much.'

'Don't mention it. Oh yes, and of course there'll be the divorce as well …'

'The div …'

Mr Swindall smiled sadly. 'You don't think it'll last, do you? Be realistic, please. Ninety-nine-point-seven per cent of marriages between supernaturals and mortals don't last out the year, so if I were you I'd put a deposit down now while you've still got a few bob in your pocket. Much easier that way.'

Kiss raised his hand. 'Just a minute,' he said. 'Before we get completely carried away …'

'We are also,' Mr Swindall interrupted quickly, 'authorised by the Divine Law Society to conduct investment business, so if you'll just fill in this simple questionnaire …'

'Before,' Kiss insisted, 'we get completely carried away, what's the procedure for doing this …?'

'The renunciation of eternal life?' Mr Swindall opened a drawer and pulled out a thick sheaf of forms. 'Piece of cake. You just fill these out, in quadruplicate, and take them with the prescribed fee to the offices of the Supreme Court between 9.15 and 9.25 on the first Wednesday in any month, and six months later you'll have to attend a short hearing in front of the District Seraph …'

It took Mr Swindall twenty-seven minutes to describe the procedure.

'It's as simple as that,' he concluded. 'And if you run into any problems along the way, just give me a shout and I'll put you back on the right lines. Now, where were we? Oh, yes. For a mere thirty per cent commission, I can put you on to some very nice unit trusts which ought …'

'The forms, please.'

'You don't want to hear about the breathtaking new equities portfolio we're putting together for a select few specially favoured clients?'

'No.'

'Oh.' Mr Swindall frowned. 'Oh well, sod you, then. The receptionist will give you the final bill on your way out.'

Organising a plague of locusts, even if you're a Force Twelve genie, is several light years away from a doddle, as anyone who's ever organised anything will readily appreciate.

First, catch your locusts. Actually producing nine hundred million locusts wasn't a problem. Let there be locusts! And there were locusts.

A plague of locusts. The phrase trips easily off the tongue. But consider this. The average locust needs a certain amount of food each day, or it dies. Nine hundred million locusts, gathered together in one spot awaiting distribution in plague form, need nine hundred million times that amount. Neglect to provide nine hundred million packed lunches, and before very long you'll have a plague of nine hundred million dead locusts; untidy, but no real long-term threat to humanity.

Another point to bear in mind is that locusts are in practice nothing more than the sports model of the basic production grasshopper; and grasshoppers hop. Up to six feet, when the mood takes them. Trying to keep nine hundred million of the little tinkers together long enough to organise properly structured devastation parties is, in consequence, not a job for the faint-hearted.

Furthermore, they chirp. They stridulate. The sound they produce is extremely similar in pitch, frequency and tone to the sound of fingernails on a blackboard. Nine hundred million locusts stridulating simultaneously takes noise pollution into a whole new dimension.

Half an hour into the plague, Philly Nine was beginning to wish he'd gone with the flow and specified a plague of frogs instead.

The final straw was the huge flock of ibises which suddenly appeared, hovering in the air just out of genie stone-throwing range and darting in whenever Philly's back was turned to gorge themselves on the biggest free lunch in ibis history. The few who overdid it to such an extent that they were unable to get off the ground again met with appropriate retribution; but there were plenty more where they came from.

Three hours into the plague, with nothing achieved except a massive feed bill, a net loss from starvation, desertion and enemy action of about seventeen million locusts and a lot of very happy ibises, Philly Nine sat down, put his head in his hands and began to whimper.

The locusts, who had finished off the latest consignment of rice (sacks included) and were beginning to feel peckish again, ate his shoes.

'Excuse me.'

Philly Nine looked up. Hovering above his head was a helicopter, out of whose window hung a man with a clipboard and a megaphone.

'Excuse me,' the man yelled above the roar of the engine and the chirping of the locusts, 'but are these insects yours?'

Philly nodded. By now they'd finished off his socks and were working their way up his trousers.

'Then I'm very sorry,' the man went on, 'but I'm going to have to ask you to move them. They're causing an environmental hazard, you see, and we can't have that. There's regulations about this sort of thing.'

Philly Nine laughed bitterly. 'Move them,' he said. 'Right. Where would you suggest I move them to?'

'Not my problem,' the man replied. 'But while we're on the subject, I take it you do have a permit for livestock transportation?'

'What?'

'A permit,' the man said. 'Transportation of livestock without a permit is a very serious offence.'

'No, I haven't,' Philly growled. 'What precisely are you going to do about it?'

The man shook his head. 'I'm sorry,' he said, 'but if you haven't got a permit, then I can't allow you to move these insects. They aren't going anywhere until I see a Form 95, properly endorsed by the Department of Transport ...'

'But you told me yourself to get them shifted.'

'Agreed,' the man said, nodding. 'But not without a permit.'

'All right,' Philly snarled, just managing to stay calm. 'So what do you suggest I do?'

'Not my problem. You could try getting a permit.'

'How do I do that?'

The man sighed. 'You can't,' he said. 'Sorry. In order to apply for a permit, you have to give twenty-eight days' notice in writing to the Inspector of Livestock Transportation, and like I just said, you haven't got twenty-eight days because you've got to remove them immediately on environmental grounds. Bit of a grey area in the regulations, I'm afraid. Oh, and by the way ...'

'Yes?'

The man pointed with his clipboard towards the ibises, which had settled down en bloc in the middle of the swarm and were munching a broad swathe through it with impressive speed. 'You're not allowed to do that, I'm afraid.'

'Do what?'

'Do or permit to be done anything which tends to prejudice the well-being of an endangered or protected species. If any of those ibises dies from over-feeding, I'm afraid it'll be your head on the block.'

'I see.'

'So I suggest you move them on. Although,' the man

continued, 'disturbing the habitat of an endangered or protected species is also forbidden, and the expression habitat does include any well-established feeding-ground—'

Philly slowly got to his feet. 'All right,' he said, 'it's a fair cop. Looks like you're going to have to impound my locusts.' He grinned. 'No hard feelings,' he added. 'I know you guys have a job to do. OK, they're all yours.'

The man in the helicopter shook his head. 'Sorry,' he said, 'but we can't do that. Regulations state that we can't accept surrender of property from members of the public without an authorisation from the Secretary of State, and to get an authorisation we'd need to give twenty-eight days' notice …'

'Fine.' Philly's mental computer fixed on the helicopter, estimating its airspeed and mass, and calculating the necessary trajectory a good gob and spit would need to follow in order to hit the man square in the eye. 'So what are you going to do?'

The man frowned. 'I hate to have to do this,' he said, 'but if you won't co-operate you leave us no choice. All right, Wayne, over to you.'

Wayne? Who's Wayne? Philly Nine looked sharply round, just in time to see a tall figure in overalls standing over him with an empty milk-bottle in his hand. He tried to dodge, but he slipped on a wedge of squashed locusts, lost his footing and staggered backwards into the bottle. A cork appeared, blotting out the light from what had suddenly become a very small, cramped universe.

'Twenty-eight days,' said a small voice, very far away. 'For contempt. When you get out, we'll also be filing a civil suit for public nuisance and forty-six breaches of the planning regulations. Sorry.'

Nine hours later, the locusts ceased to be a problem. Starvation, ibises and a freak virus which spread like wildfire had accounted for them all; all except the one which had hopped into the milk bottle just before the cork was inserted.

Twenty-eight days turned out to be a very long time.

Genies can do, and have done, pretty well everything; but one field of endeavour in which they have little experience, for obvious reasons, is organising stag nights.

Call to mind the old adage about not being able to organise a highly convivial party in a brewery. Focus on that thought.

'We ought,' insisted Acme Waste Disposal Services III, a small Force Two, 'to have a stripagram.' He scratched his head. 'It's traditional,' he added, 'I think.'

The other members of the Committee shrugged and waved to the bartender for more goat's milk. These were uncharted waters.

'What's that?' asked Nordic Oil IX.

Awds Three frowned. 'What I've heard is,' he said, 'you hire this female mortal to come along and take her clothes off.'

'Why?'

'And then she sings a song or recites a poem or something.'

'No wealth-beyond-the-dreams or anything?'

Awds Three shook his head. 'Nope,' he replied. 'Off with the undies, do the song, say the poem, and that's it.'

'How very peculiar.'

'And sometimes,' Awds added, wishing he hadn't raised the subject, 'they jump out of cakes.'

'Get away!'

'So I've heard,' the genie mumbled. 'Never seen it myself, but …'

There was a puzzled silence.

'Let's just go over this one more time,' said a thoughtful genie by the name of Standard Conglomerates the First.

'There's this female mortal imprisoned in a cake, and ...'

'Not imprisoned, exactly ...'

'... and she jumps out and *doesn't* grant three wishes ...'

'As I understand it. Like I said, this is all strictly hearsay ...'

'... festoons the floor with her dirty laundry ...'

'Hey, we don't have to do her laundry for her, do we, because I've got sensitive skin ...'

'... sings a song and goes away again. For which,' he added, 'she expects to be paid money. And this,' he concluded, 'is fun.'

'Male bonding,' suggested Nordic Oil.

'I think that's extra.'

Stan One drew a deep breath. 'I think we'll pigeonhole that one for the time being, people. Which leaves us with excessive drinking ...'

'Well, that oughtn't to be a problem, provided they skim the cream off first ...'

'Excessive drinking,' Stan One continued, 'singing raucous songs and being sick in people's window-boxes in the early hours of the morning.' He paused. 'It's all a bit jejune, isn't it?'

'What sort of cake, exactly?'

'That's what mortals do,' Awds replied defensively. 'Don't blame me, I'm only repeating what I've heard.'

Stan One shrugged. 'If he's dead set on becoming a mortal, I suppose that's what he's got to learn to expect.' He took a long pull at his goat's milk and spat out a tiny knob of rennet. 'The sooner he starts, I guess, the sooner he'll get used to it.' He grimaced; not entirely because of the rennet.

'Because if it's one of those creamy ones with jam in the middle, she won't half be sticky and yeeuk by the time she's jumped up through the middle of it. Bits of glacé cherry in the hair, all that sort of—'

'I think,' said Imperial Unit Fund Managers IV, a big,

slow genie, 'that at some stage we have to tie shoes to a car.'

Awds shook his head. 'You're wrong there,' he said. 'It's horses you tie shoes to. Cars have tyres.'

'Oh. Sorry.'

'Damned odd, the whole thing,' mused Stan One. 'Anyone know why he's doing it?'

There was a general shaking of heads. 'For charity?' suggested the Dragon King of the South-East. 'One of these sponsored things?'

Impy Four shook his head. 'Can't see how it'd work,' he replied.

'Well,' replied the Dragon King, 'he's becoming a mortal, right? So he gets people to sponsor him, so much a year, to see how long he'll live. So suppose we sponsor him, oh, five gold dirhams a year, and he lives say twenty years …'

'That's a bit extreme, isn't it?'

The Dragon King shrugged. 'People do weird things for charity,' he said. 'I heard once where this bloke allowed himself to be chained in the stocks and have wet sponges thrown at him.'

Awds shook his head. 'I don't think it's that,' he said. 'I think it's more *cherchez la femme*.'

'Find the lady? You mean like a card game?'

'And anyway,' interrupted a slender Force Six, 'from what you say, all you have to do to find mortal females is look in the nearest Victoria sponge. There's got to be more to it than that.'

'I think,' said Awds, 'he's in love.'

A long, difficult silence.

'Just say that again, will you?' asked Stan One, slowly.

'I think he's in love,' Awds repeated, red to the tips of his ears. 'Just a rumour, of course. No idea where I heard it.'

'With a mortal?'

Awds nodded.

'A *female* mortal?'

'It's only what I've heard.'

Another long silence.

'Well,' said the Dragon King briskly, 'if he's doing it for charity, then I reckon I'm good for ten dirhams a year. Any takers?'

Jane frowned.

'The first one again,' she commanded, 'but without the sequins.'

There was a voiceless sigh, and out of nothingness appeared a dress. It was long, white and shimmering. Twenty thousand tiny white flowers sparkled on the sleeves. So light and insubstantial was the material that a gnat sneezing in the jungles of Ecuador set the hems dancing. It hung in the air, full of some sort of nothing that accentuated its breathtakingly graceful lines. Jane thought.

'All right,' she said. 'Let me see number three just one more time.'

'Sign here.'

Philly Nine took the clipboard, squiggled with the pen, and handed them back.

Sulphur, he thought. Nice, inanimate, noiseless sulphur. Ninety-nine-point-eight-nine per cent pure. Easiest thing in the world, a plague of sulphur.

'Just stack it neatly over there,' he said. 'Thanks a lot.'

The delivery man nodded, and started shouting directions to his colleagues. The long queue of lorries started to move.

''Scuse my asking,' went on the delivery man, 'but that's a lot of sulphur you got there.'

Philly Nine looked up from the bill of lading. 'Sorry?' he said.

'That's an awful lot of sulphur you got there, mate,' the delivery man went on. 'You want to watch yourself.'

Philly Nine favoured him with an icy grin. 'I know what I'm doing,' he said. 'Believe me.'

'OK,' replied the delivery man, as the genie stalked away and broke open a crate. 'So long as you realise that this stuff's highly …'

Philly Nine wasn't listening. To distribute sulphur in plague form: first, grind it up into a fine powder. Use this to salt rain-clouds all over the Earth's atmosphere. The sulphur will dissolve in the rain-water, forming (with the help of a little elementary chemistry) H_2SO_4, otherwise known as sulphuric acid. He chuckled, took a long drag on the butt of his cigar and threw it aside.

There was a flash –

'. . . inflammable.'

SEVEN

Kiss lay on his back, stared at the ceiling, and screamed.
And woke up.

Genies rarely have nightmares, for the same reason that elephants don't usually worry about being trampled underfoot. With the possible exception of bottles, there's nothing in the cosmos large enough or malicious enough to frighten them, or stupid enough to try.

There are, however, exceptions. Kiss reached out for something to wipe his forehead with, and breathed in deeply.

He'd dreamed that he could no longer fly; that all his strength and power had deserted him and that one day, not too far in the future, he was going to die. As if that wasn't bad enough, he was going to have to spend what little time he had doing something futile, degrading and incredibly boring – the term his dream had used was *a full-time job* – just to earn a little money, money well within the dreams of avarice, simply to keep himself alive. And on top of that, what little time he had left over wasn't going to be spent in the back bar of Saheed's, playing pool, because his wife got upset if he kept going out in the evenings.

Weird dream. Talk about morbid …

His eyes shot wide open, and then closed again.

There must be some way out of this.

★

There were times, even now, when Vince felt just a little bit wistful about splitting up with Jane. Sure, she was difficult, querulous and, not to put too fine a point on it, on the chubby side of plump. And she had moods. And she didn't like Indian food or the right music. And her voice, when you got to know it well, had that tiny edge to it that eventually had roughly the same effect as a dentist's drill on an unanaesthetised tooth; on the other hand …

Lucky escape, Vince congratulated himself. Lucky escape.

Not, he realised as he switched out his bedside light and set his mind adrift for the night, like Sharon. True, Sharon had just enough brain to make up a smear on a microscope slide, but there were compensations. Sharon was what one might have expected to result if Pygmalion had been a photographer working on Pirelli calendars rather than a sculptor. He grinned at the darkness, and slipped away into sleep.

And dreamed a very peculiar dream.

He dreamed that he was asleep; and over his bed stood a huge, monstrous shape, towering above him like Nelson's Column, all gleaming muscles, fiery red eyes and big canine teeth. And it seemed as if the vision spoke to him, saying …

Listen, sunshine. Jane loves you and you love her. If you know what's good for you, that is. Get my drift?

And in his dream he had cried out and tried to wriggle away; but the monstrous vision had grabbed him round the throat with a huge, clawed hand, and had said –

Now you may be thinking, all that's over, I don't want to risk another broken heart. Well, there's other bits that can get broken too, take my word for it, not to mention tied in knots and yanked out by the roots. So you can either listen to the promptings of your secret heart, or you can spend the rest of your life drinking all your meals through a straw. Think on.

And then he'd woken up.

'AAAAAA!' he'd started to say; but before he could develop this line of argument the dream had stuffed a pair of socks into his mouth, lifted him up by the lapels of his pyjama jacket and held him about an inch from the tip of its huge, flaring nose.

'Not,' the dream went on, 'that I'm trying to influence you in any way. Heaven forbid. Just ask yourself one question. Is this Sharon the sort of girl who'd stick by you, come what may? Would she always be there to plump up the pillows, change the bedpans, maybe wheel you down the street as far as the library once a week? You reckon she is? Well, very soon you may well be ideally placed to find out. Sleep tight, punk.'

Then he fell, landing in an awkward heap on the mattress, and the dream turned out just to have been a dream after all. After three-quarters of an hour, he'd stopped shaking enough to switch out the light and …

In case I forgot to mention it before, looks aren't everything. And even if they were, it'd be a bit academic anyway if you couldn't see, on account of both your eyes having been pulled out and rammed up your ears. Hypothetically speaking, of course.

With a fantastic effort, Vince managed to ungum his mouth. 'Hey,' he said.

In case you've lost it, I'll just write Jane's phone number on your chest with this red-hot – oh, you can remember it? That's fine, then. Just remember, all the world loves a lover.

Vince gurgled and closed his eyes; then opened them again. Made no difference.

Last point, before I go. If I were you, I'd lay off the cheese last thing at night. Gives you bad dreams. Cheerio.

There was an old fisherman and he had three sons. They were called Malik, Ibrahim and Asaf.

Malik was very brave. Often when the wind was blowing in from the Gulf and the waves were so high that they seemed to splash against the clouds, Malik would take the boat and come back with his nets bursting with big, fat fish. Eventually Malik passed all his exams and became a chartered surveyor.

Ibrahim was very wise. Many a time, when the fish refused to leave the bottom and everybody else's nets were empty, Ibrahim would bring his boat to shore and his nets would be so heavy with fish that it took five men to lift them out. In due course, Ibrahim won a scholarship and qualified as an accountant.

But Asaf was always lazy and good-for-nothing, and while his father and brothers were out with the nets he would stay at home lying on his bed and dreaming of far-off lands and beautiful princesses. As a result, when his two brothers had both left home and his father came up lucky in a spot-the-infidel competition in the *New Islamic Herald* and retired, Asaf was left with nothing but a leaky old boat, a lot of split old nets and the prospect of a lifetime in the wholesale fish trade. Which served him, of course, bloody well right.

On one particular day, Asaf had been out since first light, and when evening came he still hadn't caught a single fish. Sadly he looked out over the Gulf, towards the burnt-out oil rigs that stood out from the leeward shore, and sighed. As he did so, a little voice inside him seemed to say, 'Throw out your net just once more, Asaf, and see what Providence may bring you!'

And why not? Asaf asked himself, and he flung the net out as far as he could throw it, and started to draw it in. As it came, he could feel how light it was; no fish again this time, he reflected sadly, isn't that just my bloody luck?

He was just about to stow the net away and head for home when he saw, hidden in the corner of the net, a tiny jewelled fish no bigger than a roulette chip. He picked it up in his cupped hands and was on the point of throwing it back when something caught this attention. He checked himself, and looked down at the little tiny body squirming in his hands.

'Just a cotton-picking minute,' he said.

The fish kicked frantically, opening and shutting its round little mouth. Asaf peered down at it and frowned. Then, quick as a flash, he grabbed his thermos flash with his other hand, shook out the dregs of tea, filled it with seawater and dropped the fish into it.

'Hello,' he said.

The fish released a stream of bubbles, flicked its tail and darted down into the bottom of the flask. Asaf considered for a moment, then covered the neck of the flask with the flat of his hand and shook it up and down for a few seconds.

'You're not a fish, are you?' he said.

The fish flopped round through 180 degrees and burped drunkenly. 'Fair crack of the whip, sport,' it gurgled. 'What d'you take me for, a flamin' King Charles spaniel?' It froze, mouth open in a perfect O. 'Ah, shit,' it added.

'Quite.'

'Let the cat out of the old tucker-bag there, I reckon,' the fish went on, hiding its face behind a fin. 'All right, fair dos, I'm not a fish.'

'Sure?'

'Fair dinkum,' the fish replied. 'Since you ask, I'm the Dragon King of the South-East, and if you've quite finished ...'

Asaf stroked his chin. 'A Dragon King,' he mused. 'I read about your lot once. You grant wishes.'

The fish thrashed its fins irritably. 'Look, mate,' it spluttered 'get real, will you? If I could grant flamin' wishes, my first wish'd be *I wish I wasn't stuck in this bastard jar.* My second wish—'

'Other people's wishes, I mean,' Asaf corrected. 'The

poor fisherman catches you, he takes pity on the poor little
fish trapped in his net and throws it back, and next thing he
knows he's knee-deep in junk mail from the financial
services boys. It's a standard wish-fulfilment motif in Near
Eastern oral tradition,' he added. 'Usually three.'

'Three what?'

'Wishes,' Asaf replied, 'for fulfilment. Now we'll start off
with a nicely balanced eight-figure portfolio made up of say
fifty per cent gilt-edged government stocks, twenty-five per
cent offshore convertible …'

The fish squirmed. 'Sorry,' it said.

'I beg your pardon?'

'No can do.' Fish can't sweat, but the Dragon King was,
by definition, not a fish. 'Look, mate, if it was up to me it'd
be no worries, straight up, Bob's your uncle. But …'

'*But?*'

'Yeah,' replied the fish. 'Dragon King of the *South-East*,
remember? With responsibility for the Indian Ocean,
southern sector.'

'You mean,' said the fisherman, 'Australia?'

The fish nodded. That is to say, it moved up and down
in the water, using its small rear fins as stabilisers. 'And New
Zealand,' it added, 'not forgetting Tasmania. But excluding
the Philippines. And where I come from, blokes don't wish
for the sort of thing you do.'

'They don't?'

The fish shook its head; the same manoeuvre, but in
reverse. 'One, all the beer you can drink. Two, sitting in
front of the TV watching the footie with a big bag of salt and
vinegar crisps. Three, more beer. Interested?'

'Not particularly.' Asaf frowned. 'In case you didn't
know, this is a Moslem country.'

'Is it? Jeez, mate, get me outa here quick. Talk about a fish
out of water …'

'Quite.' Asaf lifted the flask and began to tilt it sideways towards the deck of the boat. 'Are you sure that's all you can do?' he said encouragingly. 'I'll bet you anything you like that if you really set your mind to it—'

'Watch what you're flamin' well doing with that …'

Asaf nodded, and restored the flask to the vertical. 'What you need,' he said, 'is more self-confidence. And I intend to give it to you. Inexhaustible wealth, now.' He started to count to ten.

'Just a minute.' The fish was cowering in the bottom of the flask, frantically feathering its tail-fin for maximum reverse thrust. 'Um, will you take a cheque?'

'No.'

'Plastic?'

'No.'

'Then,' said the fish, 'it looks like we got a problem here.'

'We have?' The flask inclined.

'Yes.'

Asaf shrugged. 'Fair enough, then. What can you offer?'

The fish oscillated for a moment. 'How about,' it suggested, 'a really deep bronze tan? You know, the outdoors look?'

'Don't be stupid, I'm a fisherman.'

'Right, good point. I guess that also rules out a magic, self-righting surfboard.'

'Correct.'

'All right, all right.' The fish twisted itself at right angles and gnawed its fins. 'What about stone-cold guaranteed success with the sheilas? Now I can't say fairer than that.'

'Yes, you can. To take just one example, inexhaustible wealth.'

The fish wriggled. 'Stone-cold guaranteed success with *rich* sheilas?'

Asaf nodded. 'I think we're getting warmer,' he said.

'Rich, good-looking sheilas?'

'Marginally warmer. Still some way to go, though.'

'Rich, good-looking sheilas who don't talk all the flamin' time?'

'Better,' Asaf conceded, 'but I still think you're missing the point somewhat. I think if you zeroed in on the rich part, rather than the sheilas aspect …'

'I got you, yes.' The fish turned over and floated on its back for a second or two. 'What about,' it suggested, 'rich old boilers who'll pop off and leave you all their money?'

Asaf shook his head. 'Too much like hard work,' he said. 'And besides, you're displaying a very cynical attitude towards human relationships, which I find rather distasteful. Let's stick to rich, shall we, and leave the sheilas element to look after itself.'

'Could be a problem with that,' the fish mumbled. 'The sheilas are, like, compulsory. Chicks with everything.'

'How depressingly chauvinistic.'

'Yeah, well.' The fish waggled its tail-fin. 'Sort of goes with the territory, mate. You don't have to treat 'em like dirt if you don't want to,' it added hopefully. 'I mean, if you want to, you can buy 'em flowers.'

Asaf sighed. 'Gosh,' he said, 'how heavy this flask is. If I have to stand here negotiating for very much longer, my arm might get all weak and …'

'All *right*, you flamin' mortal bastard!' the fish screeched. 'Just watch what you're doing with that thing.'

'Well?'

'I'm thinking.' The fish swam in slow circles, occasionally nibbling at the sides of the flask. 'OK,' it said. 'But this is the best I can do.'

'I'm listening.'

'Just the one sheila,' said the fish persuasively. 'And she's stinking rich—'

'Beyond the dreams of avarice?'

'Too right, mate, too right. Richest chick this side of the black stump. And all you've got to do is rescue her, right?'

Asaf scowled. 'You haven't been listening,' he said. 'All I'm interested in is the money. Climbing up rope ladders and sword-fights with guards simply aren't my style. I get vertigo.'

'No worries,' the fish reassured him. 'I'll handle all that side of things, just you see.'

'Sure,' Asaf growled. 'In case you hadn't noticed, you're a two-inch-long fish. Don't you think that'd prove rather a handicap when it comes to rescuing wealthy females?'

'Huh!' The fish sneered. 'Now who's the bigot?'

'But …'

'Just 'cos I'm small and I've got fins …'

'Be reasonable,' Asaf said. 'You can't escape your way out of a thermos flask. How are you going to cope with heavily guarded castles?'

'I'll have no worries swimming the moat,' the fish replied. 'Anyway, I'm only a fish right *now*. As soon as I can get home and out of this flamin' fish outfit, I can go back to being a dragon. Dragons can rescue anybody, right?'

'I suppose so.' Asaf rubbed his chin. On the one hand, the Dragon King hardly inspired confidence. On the other hand … He looked down at the boat, the empty nets, the threadbare sail. 'Very well, then. So long as it's guaranteed success.'

'Trust me.'

'I was afraid you'd say that.'

'Look …'

'All right,' Asaf said. 'So what do I do now?'

The fish darted up the meniscus of the flask. 'Just chuck me back in,' he said, 'and then row to the shore. I'll be there waiting.'

'Straight up?'

'On me honour as an Australian,' the fish replied solemnly. 'No bludging, honest.'

'Oh, all right then.' Asaf jerked the flask sharply sideways, emptying its contents into the sea. There was a soft splash.

'Waste of bloody time,' he muttered to himself. Then he rowed to the shore.

He was just pulling his boat up on to the beach when there was a sharp WHOOSH! immediately behind his back, and sand everywhere. He turned slowly around and saw a very old, very battered Volkswagen dormobile, with lots of stickers inside the windscreen. He frowned; and suddenly realised that instead of his comfortable old fishing smock, he was wearing strange new clothes: a denim jacket with the sleeves cut off, shorts, trainers and no socks. There was also some sort of sticky white stuff all over his nose and lips.

'Hey!' he said angrily.

WHAM!

Hovering over his head was a huge, green scaly lizard.

'G'day,' it said. 'Jeez, mate, you don't know how good it feels to get me proper duds back on again after being squashed inside that poxy little fish skin. Ready to go?'

Asaf stepped back. He had to retreat quite some way before he could see the whole of the dragon. He began to wish he hadn't started this.

'Hey,' he said, 'what's going on? Who are you, anyway, the local area franchisee for the Klingon Empire?'

The dragon chuckled. 'I'm a dragon, mate,' he replied. 'What did you expect, a little skinny bloke with glasses? Now, are you ready for off?'

'Off where?'

'Off to see this incredibly rich sheila,' the dragon replied. 'Now I'd better warn you, she's not exactly a real hot looker, but so what? Like we say in Oz, you don't care what's on the mantelpiece when you're poking the fire.'

'All right,' Asaf muttered. 'But what's with the broken-down old van? Why the stupid clothes?'

The dragon looked offended. 'We're going on our travels, right?'

'I suppose so, yes.'

The dragon's lips parted in a huge smile. 'Well,' he said, 'if we're going walkabout, we might as well do it properly.'

Asaf was on the point of objecting vehemently when it occurred to him that the Dragon King was perfectly right. Wherever you go, he remembered his brothers telling him, whichever inhospitable corner of the globe you wind up in, you can always be sure of finding three tall, bronzed Aussies in beach clothes and a beat-up old camper. And you can bet your life that when the chips are down, they're not the ones whose fan-belt breaks three hundred miles from the nearest garage.

The Dragon King waves a giant forepaw and vanished. A moment or so later, when he'd recovered, Asaf noticed that the dormobile now had a chrome dragon mascot on the bonnet where the VW insignia ought to have been.

'This is silly,' he told himself. Then he climbed into the van and turned the key.

Love, according to all the best poets, works wonders. Under the influence of love, men and women scale impossible mountains, brave tempestuous seas, face down dangers that any rational human being would run a mile from; love does for the heart and the soul what a five-year course of anabolic steroids does for the muscles. Mankind will do virtually anything for love.

Blind terror, however, knocks love into a cocked hat.

It wasn't love, for example, that brought Vince, white as a sheet and jumping like a kitten at loud noises, round to Jane's front door at nine o'clock sharp, clutching a huge bunch of flowers and wearing the tie she'd given him at the office Christmas party (hastily unwound from a dripping tap and ironed).

The door opened.

'Hello, Vince,' Jane said. 'What lovely flowers! Goodbye, Vince.'

The door started to close. Love at this point would have given it up as a bad job and gone home.

'Jane,' Vince said. 'Hi there. It's been a long time.'

'Not nearly long enough. Get lost.'

Through the quarter-open door, Vince could see strange things: miles of plush carpet, acres of richly patterned wallpaper, stacks and rows of colour-supplement furniture. Somewhere in his subconscious, the change in Jane's environment registered. He smiled, trying as he did so to keep his teeth from chattering.

'I think we ought to talk,' he said.

'Do you? Why?'

'Um.' Vince dredged his mind for something to say and, in the silt at the bottom of his memory, came across a phrase. It had lodged there, muddy and forgotten, ever since he'd idled away a day's flu watching one of the afternoon soaps.

'We've got to sit down and talk this thing through,' he said solemnly. 'Otherwise we might regret it for the rest of our lives.'

Jane considered. 'You might,' she said. 'Depends on how thick-skinned you are. If being called a heartless, two-timing little scumbag is likely to scar you for life, I'd suggest you leave now. Mind you,' she added, 'I expect you're well used to it by now. Must happen to you all the time.'

'Does that mean I can come in?'

Jane sighed. 'I suppose so. It'd make shouting at you easier.'

Weak-kneed, Vince crept into the living-room …

AAAAGH!

There, sitting on the sofa, apparently putting a plug on an electric hair-dryer, was the Monster. For a fraction of a second it raised its eyes and looked straight at him; during which time he did his level best to swallow his own Adam's apple.

'Vince,' Jane said in a bored voice, 'this is Kiss. Kiss, this is Vince. I didn't ask him to come here,' she added.

The Monster was on his feet. 'That's all right,' he said, 'I was just going. I expect,' he added, 'you two have a lot to talk about.'

'No, we don't,' Jane said. 'It doesn't take long to call somebody a bastard.'

'See you later,' said Kiss, and walked out through the wall.

Vince sat down heavily in an armchair. 'Your friend—' he said.

'Fiancé,' Jane interrupted.

'Ah.'

'Bastard.'

'Yes.'

'What do you mean, yes?'

Vince tried to think what he did mean, but his brain wasn't working too well. 'Um,' he said.

What you mean is, yes, I admit I behaved like a bastard, but I promise I'll make it up to you. Got that?

It isn't actually possible to jump out of one's skin, but Vince did his best. The voice seemed to be coming from two inches inside his left ear.

'Do you mind not squirming about?' Jane asked wearily. 'You'll damage the furniture.'

'Sorry.'

I'll say it one more time. I admit I behaved like a bastard. Go on, say it.

'I admit,' Vince said, staring straight ahead, 'I behaved like a bastard …'

'Good.'

But I promise that I'll make it up to you. Come on, say it.

And try and put some feeling into it, for God's sake.

'But I promise,' Vince gasped, 'that I'll make it up to you. Somehow,' he added.

Don't ad lib.

'Sorry.'

'What?'

Sorry for all the pain my heartless and misguided behaviour must have caused you. Now, however …

'Hang on,' Vince said. 'Sorry for all the pain my heartless and misguided behaviour …'

'Oh, for crying out loud!' Jane exploded. 'Look, buster, whoever writes your scripts for you, tell him not to pack in the day job.'

The part of Vince's subconscious currently under enemy occupation smirked.

Stupid cow. No! Don't say that. Listen, Jane, I can explain everything. Go on, you fool, cat got your tongue?

'Listen, Jane, I can explain everything.'

'So can I. You're a bastard. Explanation complete.'

Any suggestions?

Shut up. Jane, when two people feel the way about each other that we do, it's never too late to start again.

'Jane,' Vince enunciated, 'when two people feel the way about each other that we do, it's never too late to start again.'

'Would you like,' Jane asked, 'a cup of tea?'

A whoop of triumph rocked Vince's inner brain, playing havoc with his centre of balance. Yo, buddy, we're in! Go for it!

'Yes, please,' Vince said.

'Won't be a tick.'

Jane retreated into the kitchen. As soon as the door had closed, Vince felt a tremendous rushing in his ears, and—

WHOOSH!

'Hi,' he mumbled. 'How'm I doing?'

The genie gave him a cold, hard look. 'If I couldn't read your mind,' he growled, 'I'd swear you were deliberately trying to bugger this up. Fortunately for you, I can see you're shit-scared and you wouldn't dare. So just do exactly what I say and everything'll be just fine.'

'Sure,' Vince muttered. 'Er, excuse me saying this, but what exactly do you want me to *do* to her?'

The genie raised an eyebrow. 'Marry her, of course. What do you think?'

'Ah.' Vince cowered slightly. 'In that case,' he said, 'I'd rather have the violent and painful death, if it's all the same to you.'

For a moment, there was sympathy in the genie's eyes. 'Look, chum,' he said, 'it's you or me, right? And I'm bigger than you, which means it's you. Sorry, but that's the way it goes. At the moment,' he went on, deleting the sympathy and replacing it with a glare of heart-stopping ferocity, 'we're doing this the easy way.'

'But she's so damn *sloppy*.'

Kiss winced. 'Do you mean sloppy as in over-sentimental, or sloppy as in extremely untidy?'

'Both.'

'Agreed. Believe me,' he added, 'I'm really grateful to you for doing this. It's not just the fact that I can't stand the woman, I assure you. It's just that unless I can get her to let me off the hook, I'm going to have to become a mortal in fourteen days' time. Hence,' he added meaningfully, 'the sense of urgency. I'll make it up to you one day, genie's honour. Unlimited wealth, all that sort of thing. In the meantime, however …'

The door started to open. With a stifled *Oh shit!* the genie vanished, and Vince once again became aware of a dull presence against his inner ear, as if he'd just been under water.

'Tea,' said Jane.

'Thanks.'

'Drink it while it's hot.'

You heard the lady.

Vince smiled broadly and drank. A fraction of a second later most of the tea had turned into a fine mist, sprayed all over the room.

'Oh dear,' said Jane. 'Something go down the wrong way?'

By way of response Vince choked, gasped and made a peculiar gurgling noise in the back of his throat. He was still smiling, but only because some paranormal force had grabbed control of his jaw muscles and frozen them.

'Perhaps,' Jane continued sweetly, 'it's because I put five teaspoonfuls of salt in it instead of sugar. When you've finished retching, you can leave.'

Strewth, whispered the voice in the back of Vince's brain with horrified admiration, *she really is a tough cookie, your girlfriend.*

Vince stood up slowly, wiped tea off his face, closed his mouth tightly and pinched his nose hard between thumb and forefinger. Then he blew.

PLOP!

Kiss hit the floor like a sack of potatoes, rolled and came to rest against the opposite wall. He was dripping-wet and shaking.

'Well,' Vince said, scrambling for the door, 'been nice seeing you again, Jane. All the best to you and your . . . All the best. Bye.'

The door closed behind him.

EIGHT

Philly Nine sighed. He was having a hard time.

The brimstone had been a complete washout. Literally – it had started raining just as he was lugging the crates of the stuff off the lorry, and industrial spec brimstone is water-soluble.

The frogs had been an absolute nightmare. They'd just sat there. No sooner had he shooed one consignment of, say, five thousand out of the delivery pond than the previous batch had hopped back in and sat down, resolutely croaking and wobbling their chins at him. Magically generated flash floods dispersed them for a while, but their homing instinct was such that at least ninety-five per cent of them were back home within the hour. They way they got through pondweed was nobody's business.

'Sign here,' the Frenchman said. 'And here. And here. Thanks, monsieur. It's a pleasure doing business with you.'

Philly nodded sombrely, and waved as the convoy of trucks rattled away into the distance. If you stretched the definition to breaking point, a worldwide chain of Provençal Fried Frogs' Legs bars might be taken to constitute a plague, but it probably wasn't going to bring the world to its knees; not, at least, in the short term.

What, he asked himself wretchedly, next? His own fault, he reflected, for letting himself be carried away by the gothic splendour of the language. If he'd been content to settle for a nice straightforward plague of, say, plague, the entire human race would by now be coming out in suppurating boils, and he'd be home and dry. As it was ... He took out the crumpled envelope on which he'd jotted down his notes.

X   Locusts
X   Sulphur
X   Brimstone
X   Frogs
   Hail
   Giant ants
   Burning pitch

Never usually a quitter, Philly sighed, folded the envelope and put it away. Was there, he asked himself, really any point in going on?

And then he remembered.

The brochure. The smiling face. The slogan, 'We're here to help you.'

'Of course!' he said aloud, and his face broke into a silly grin. Virtually the only useful thing they teach you at Genie School: don't bother learning the Knowledge itself, so long as you know where to go to look it up. He took out his diary and thumbed through the business cards wedged in the inside flap until he found the right one.

THE GENIE ADVISORY SERVICE
Central office: the Djinn Palace, Street of the Lamp-Makers,
Samarkand 9
Have you got a problem? Bring it to us!
Your wish is our command!

GAS headquarters had only recently relocated to an imposing suite of purpose-blown bottles in a crate round the back of Number 56, Street of the Lamp-Makers, and there were the inevitable settling-in problems associated with the migration of any large enterprise. For example, the phones weren't working yet, only twenty per cent of the staff knew where the toilets were, and all the files had been sent to a hurricane lamp in the Orkneys by mistake, along with most of the typewriters and the coffee machine. Apart from that, it was business as usual.

After five minutes in the waiting room reading a back number of the *National Demonological*, Philly was greeted by a small, round genie who extended a tiny, moist paw and introduced himself as 'GAS 364, your Personal Business Adviser'. GAS 364 chivvied him into a small cell with two deep armchairs, a vase of flowers and a large framed print of Picasso's *Guernica*, offered him coffee, and asked what the problem was.

Philly explained.

'Right,' said GAS 364, 'got you. The old, old story.'

'It is?'

GAS 364 nodded. 'Bitten off more than we can chew,' he said, smiling. 'Trying to swoop before we can glide. It's basically a time management/resources allocation problem.'

'Ah. Is that serious?'

'Depends.' GAS 364 waggled his hands. 'There's a lot of variables. How your operation is structured, for example, lateral as against vertical command groups, properly demarcated zones of responsibility, incentive-related leadership packages, that sort of thing.'

'Gosh,' Philly said. 'Actually, there's only me.'

GAS 364 rubbed his various chins. 'Sole practitioner, huh?' he said. 'Now that means a whole different subgroup of potential dysfunction hotspots. The left hand not knowing whether the right hand's been left holding the baby. And, of course, carrying the can.' He shook his head. 'You know,' he said, 'if only you'd come to see us earlier, a lot of this could well have been avoided. But there we are.'

'Are we?'

GAS 364 spread his hands in an eloquent gesture. 'Are we indeed?' he said. 'Like we always say, you can't destroy the world without breaking eggs.'

Philly's brow clouded for a moment. 'Eggs,' he said. 'You're thinking of the giant ants?'

'Let's stay off the specifics for the time being,' GAS 364 replied, glancing at his watch, 'and zoom in on the generals. Which means, first things first, software.'

'Software?'

'Mortals,' GAS 364 translated. 'As opposed to hardware, meaning us. It's basically a question of approach, you see. You sole practitioners, you simply have no idea of how to delegate.'

'Delegate? Delegate the annihilation of the human race?'

GAS 364 nodded. 'The only way,' he said. 'Think about it. Sure, you're a Force Twelve, rippling muscles, big turban, the works. But at the end of the day, when pitch comes to shove, there's just you. Just you,' the genie repeated, 'to open the mail, answer the telephones *and* wipe out all sentient life-forms on the Planet Earth. Result: you're overstretched. Which means,' he went on, leaning back and folding his hands behind his head, 'when the van arrives with the crates of frogs, you can't cope. As we've seen.'

Philly nodded. 'So?'

'So,' GAS 364 replied, 'let somebody else do the donkey work for you. Get the software to do the actual extermination stuff, while you maintain a general supervisory and administrative role, which is what you're supremely qualified for. It's as simple as that.'

Philly, who had just begun to feel he was dimly glimpsing what the small genie was driving at, scowled. 'Please explain,' he said.

GAS 364 beamed at him. 'Easy,' he said. 'Start a war.'

★

'Hello,' Jane said.

Kiss got up slowly and started wringing out his wet clothes. 'Hello,' he replied.

'He's gone.'

'Has he?'

'Yes. You're all wet.'

'Yes.'

'Just as well,' Jane said, 'that you can't catch colds.'

'Isn't it.'

They stood for a while, looking at each other. Between them, so nearly solid that it was almost visible, the question *What were you doing in Vince's ear?* hovered in the air.

Somebody once defined Love as never having to explain what you were doing in somebody's ear. It's not a particularly accurate definition.

'Fancy a picnic?' asked Jane.

'Don't mind.'

'Or we could stay in and I'll cook something.'

Kiss smiled feebly. 'Let's have a picnic,' he said.

For want of anywhere better to go, they went to Martinique. It wasn't the most joyous picnic in history –

(For the record, the most joyous picnic in history was the time seven Force Fives decided to have a barbecue in the back garden of a house in Pudding Lane, London, in the year 1666. The genies had a great time and London got St Pauls, various Wren churches and a nursery rhyme or two by way of belated compensation.)

– and after they'd eaten the sandwiches and drunk the champagne they sat in silence for a full seven minutes, looking at the dark blue sea.

'Jane,' Kiss said eventually.

'Yes?'

How to put it, exactly? How to explain that the ferociously passionate feelings they both harboured were nothing but a device contrived by a supernatural fiend as part of his plan to annihilate humanity? How to explain all that, *tactfully*?

'Nothing.'

Jane poured the last dribble of the champagne into her glass. It was lukewarm and as flat as a bowling green. 'I thought that was very romantic,' she said.

Kiss suppressed a shudder. 'What was?'

'You hanging around like that when Vince was there. I think you were jealous.'

Well of course, you would. 'Ah.'

'Were you?'

'Sorry? Oh, yes. Yes, I was.'

'You needn't be.'

'That's good to know.'

Jane picked at the strap of her sandal. 'The moment I saw him,' she went on, 'I knew it was all over between us. In fact, I can't imagine what I ever saw in him, really.'

'Can't you?'

'No.'

Kiss breathed in. For some reason, he found it harder than usual. 'I quite took to him, actually,' he said. 'Not a bad bloke, when you get to know him. I expect.'

'Oh Kiss, you *are* sweet.'

That particular phrase, *Oh Kiss, you are sweet*, stayed with him the rest of the day and deep into the night, with the result that he couldn't sleep. By two-thirty in the morning, it had got to him so much that he put on his coat and went to Saheed's.

In the back bar he met two old friends, Nordic Industrial Components IV and Consolidated Tin IX. They were sitting in a corner sharing a big jug of pasteurised and playing djinn rummy.

'Hi,' he said, joining them. 'Would you guys say I was sweet?'

Nick and Con stared at him. 'Sweet?'

'You heard me.'

Nick shook his head. 'To be frank with you, Kiss, no.'

'I'm very relieved to hear it. Same again?'

Three or four jugs and a game of racing genie later, Nick asked why he had wanted to know.

'Oh, no reason. Somebody accused me of sweetness earlier on today, and it's been preying on my mind.'

'Ah.' Nick dealt the cards. 'Well, my old mate, you need have no worries on that score. Who's to open?'

'Me,' said Con. 'Three earthquakes.'

'See your three earthquakes,' Nick replied, 'and raise you one famine.'

'Twist,' said Kiss. 'I think it's a horrible thing to say about anybody.'

'Agreed,' said Con. 'Who said it, and what had you in mind by way of reprisals?'

'My fiancée,' Kiss said. 'Your go, Nick.'

'Your *fiancée?*'

'That's right.'

'See your famine and raise you a pestilence. Since when?'

'Recently,' Kiss answered. 'Can we change the subject, guys? I'm trying to enjoy myself.'

'Your pestilence,' said Con, 'and raise you one. This is pretty heavy stuff, Kiss. She must be some doll if you're thinking of packing in the genieing on her account.'

'Repique,' Kiss said (he was banker), 'and doubled in Clubs. My clutch, I think.'

'Buggery.'

'That's forty-six above the line to me,' Kiss went on, jotting down figures on a milk-mat, 'and one for his spikes, makes seventy-seven to me and three to play. My deal.'

'I've had enough of this game,' said Con. 'Let's play Miserable Families instead.'

So they played Miserable Families; and two hands and a jug of pasteurised later, Kiss was ninety-six ahead and held mortgages on seventy-five per cent of Antarctica, which was where Con lived.

'No thanks,' Con said, when Kiss suggested another hand. 'I get the impression your luck's in tonight.'

'Tell me about it,' replied Kiss gloomily.

'This girlfriend of yours.'

'Fiancée.'

'Quite.' Con paused. Generally speaking, genies don't kick a fellow when he's down, just in case he grabs hold of their foot. There are, however, exceptions. 'Lucky in cards, unlucky in love, they say.'

'They're absolutely right.'

Nick grinned. 'I take it,' he said, 'you're not overjoyed?'

'It's that bastard,' Kiss blurted out. No need to say who the bastard was. 'He hired Cupid to shoot me. It's not,' he added dangerously, 'funny.'

There was a difference of opinion on that score. When he had regained control of himself, Nick asked why.

'He's going to destroy the world …'

'Not *again.*'

'… and he wants me out of the way first. I call it diabolical,' Kiss concluded, draining his glass. 'He shouldn't be allowed to get away with it.'

'Oh, I dunno,' Con replied mildly. 'All's fair in—'

'Don't say it. Not the L word.'

'War,' Con continued. 'You've got to hand it to Philly, he has brains. And vision. And that indispensable streak of sheer bloody-minded viciousness that you need to get on in this business.'

Kiss frowned. 'Well, so have I,' he said. 'Trouble is, *she* won't let me use it.'

'Bossy cow!'

'Or at least,' Kiss amended lamely, 'she wouldn't like it.

And as things are at the moment …'

Nick winked. 'Say no more,' he said. 'What you need, I think, is a little help from your friends.'

Kiss looked up. 'Really?'

'We might consider it,' Con replied. 'Get a mate out of a hole. Can't watch a good genie go down, and all that.'

Kiss's frown deepened. 'But what can you do?' he asked. 'Philly's a Twelve and you're both Fives. He'd have you for breakfast.'

Con cleared his throat. 'We weren't thinking of that,' he said. 'No, what we had in mind …' He looked at Nick, who nodded. 'What we were thinking of was more by way of getting your beloved off your back. Weren't we?'

'Could be fun,' Nick agreed. 'How long have you got?'

Kiss shuddered. 'Thirteen days,' he said, 'before the papers go through. Any ideas?'

Nick poured the last of the pasteurised into his glass and chuckled. 'I expect we'll think of something,' he said.

Battered Volkswagen camper van speeding across the desert.

The Dragon King was beginning to get on Asaf's nerves. After a long struggle, he had managed to jury-rig the primitive radio so that it could receive Radio Bazra's easy listening music channel; but he needn't have bothered, because he couldn't hear a thing over the Dragon King's Mobius-loop renditions of *The Wild Colonial Boy*. It would have been slightly more bearable if the King had known more than 40 per cent of the words. As if that wasn't enough, the King had taken his shoes and socks off, and his feet smelt.

''Twas in eighteen hundred and sixty-two,' the King informed him for the seventeenth time that day, 'that he started his wild career/Tum tumpty tumpty tumpty tum tee tumpty tumpty fear/ He robbed the wealthy squatters and …'

'Do you mind?'

The King looked up. 'Yer what, mate?' he enquired.

'Do you mind,' Asaf said, 'not singing?'

The King looked hurt. 'Sorry, chum,' he said. 'Thought a good old sing-song'd help pass the time.'

'You did, did you?'

'No offence, mate.'

'Quite.'

The King turned his head and looked out of the window. 'I spy,' he said, 'with my little eye, something beginning with . . . S.'

'Sand.'

'Too right, sport, good on yer. Your go.'

'No, thank you.'

'Fair enough.' The King sighed and opened a can of beer, which hissed like a bad-tempered snake and sprayed suds all over the place. Asaf wiped his eye.

'That's another thing,' he growled. 'This car smells like a brewery.'

'Glad you like it.'

'As a matter of fact, I don't. Can't you wait till we stop?'

'Anything you say, boss.' He drained the can and chucked it out of the window. No point, Asaf reflected, in raising the subject of pollution of the environment and the recycling of scrap aluminium. Deaf ears.

'Not much further now, anyway,' the King said, 'till we reach the first Adventure.'

Asaf applied the brakes, bringing the van to a sudden halt. 'What do you mean,' he asked dangerously, 'adventure?'

The King looked at him. 'Gee, mate, this is a quest, right? You gotta have a few adventures in a quest. Don't you worry, though, she'll be right.'

'Who will?'

'It'll all go beaut,' the King translated. 'No worries on that score. Trust me.'

'I was afraid you'd say that.'

The next half-hour was relatively painless. True, the King hummed *Do You Ever Dream, My Sweetheart* in a Dalek-like drone under his breath, but with the radio and the groaning of the suspension over the rocky, potholed road, he was scarcely audible. It could have been worse, Asaf rationalised. It could have been *My Way*.

'Here we are,' the King said, pointing with his right forefinger into the middle of the trackless waste of their left. 'Anywhere here'll do.'

Asaf sighed and pulled over, leaving the engine running. 'Now what?' he said.

The King chuckled. 'You'll like this,' he said. 'Right up your alley, this is. Watch.'

A flicker of movement in the far distance caught Asaf's eye. The King handed him a pair of binoculars, through which he could see a girl on a donkey being hotly pursued by three men on camels. The girl had a good lead on her pursuers, but they were gaining fast.

'The low-down is,' said the King, 'the chick is the daughter of some Sultan or other, and the three blokes on the camels are wicked magicians. All clear so far?'

Asaf nodded.

'Well,' the King continued, 'she's running away from them because she's just stolen the Pearl of Solomon, which gives them sort of magic powers. You go to meet her, she gives you a magic bow and three arrows. You fire the first arrow at the first magician—'

'Excuse me …'

'And,' the King continued, 'he turns back into a beetle – that's what he really is, you see, a beetle – and you tread on him and that's that. You fire the second arrow—'

'Excuse me …'

'The second arrow at the second magician, and *he* turns back into a scorpion, which is his true shape, and you drop a rock on him. You shoot the third …'

'Excuse me,' Asaf shouted. The King looked up.

'Sorry, mate, am I going too fast? The first …'

'I won't do it.'

The King stared at him with a wild surmise. The surmise couldn't have been wilder if he'd just said that Dennis Lillee was a slow bowler.

'I don't want anything to do with it,' the fisherman reiterated. 'You're asking me to aid and abet a theft, commit murder …'

Jeez, mate, they're *insects.*'

'Insecticide, robbery with violence, obstruction of the highway and heaven knows what else, for no readily apparent reason—'

The King was almost in tears. 'For crying out loud,' he said, 'it's a flamin' *adventure.* What sort of a bloke are you?'

'Basically law-abiding,' Asaf replied coldly. 'Has it also occurred to you that I might miss? With only a very scanty knowledge of archery and just three arrows—'

'It's a magic bow, you dozy bastard!' the King yelled. 'You can't miss. Believe me.'

'It's still wrong,' Asaf replied. 'If there's a dispute between these people, they ought to take it to the proper authorities.'

The donkey was quite close now, and slowing to a gentle trot. The camels, however, were accelerating.

'*Look,*' shouted the King. 'Unless you rescue the chick, she won't be able to give you the three white stones, which—'

'What three white stones?'

'The three *magic* white stones which have strange and supernatural powers, you stupid drongo!' the King snapped. 'Of all the …'

Asaf sighed, and opened the door. 'Oh, all right,' he said.

'But I'm not shooting anybody, and that's final. You wait here and don't interfere.'

He climbed out of the camper. His legs were stiff with cramp after the long drive, and his left foot had gone to sleep. He hobbled over to where the donkey had come to an expectant halt.

'Allah be praised!' the girl exclaimed. She was radiantly beautiful, and around her neck hung a single white pearl which shone with a strange inner light. 'Quick, my prince, take this bow and—'

'Be quiet!' Asaf snapped. 'I'll deal with you in a minute.'

He trudged past her and stood between her and the camels, which slewed to a halt. The lead camel-rider drew a curved blue sword and brandished it ferociously.

'Out of the way, infidel,' he snarled, 'or I shall cut off your head!'

Asaf shook his head. 'Don't be silly,' he said briskly. 'And for your information, I'm not an infidel.'

The camel-rider reined in his steed and frowned. 'Yes, you are,' he said. 'By definition,' he added.

'Rubbish.'

The other two camel-riders drew their scimitars and waved them, but with rather less enthusiasm.

Asaf didn't move. 'Well?' he said.

'Well what?'

'Ask me a question about Islamic belief and culture. That'll show whether I'm an infidel or not.'

'It's just an expression,' the second camel-rider started to say, but his superior shushed him.

'All right, Mister Clever,' said the first camel-rider. 'What's the first verse of the fortieth chapter of the Koran? You don't know, do you? I thought you …'

Asaf cleared his throat. 'This book is revealed by Allah,' Asaf recited in a loud, clear voice, 'the mighty one, the all-knowing, who forgives sin and accepts repentance, the bountiful one, whose punishment is stern. Want me to go on?'

The camel-riders looked at each other.

'OK,' said the first camel-rider. 'So you're not an infidel. Now will you please shove off and let us get on with our work?'

Asaf stayed where he was. 'Bet you don't know the next bit,' he said.

The camel-rider glowered at him. ''Course I do,' he said.

'Go on, then. Prove it.'

'Huh.' The first camel-rider sniffed. 'There is no god but Him, all shall return to him, none but the unbelievers dispute the teachings of Allah—'

'Excuse me,' the second camel-rider interrupted.

The first camel-rider whirled round in his saddle. 'What?' he said.

'It's not teachings, it's revelations. The revelations of Allah.'

The first camel-rider scowled. 'It says teachings, son of a dog!' he growled. 'Do you dare—?'

'Actually,' muttered the third camel-rider, 'he's quite right, it is revelations. Here, have a look. At the bottom of the second page, three lines up.'

'What!' roared the first rider. 'You dare to contradict me, spawn of filth! I shall cut off—'

'Here, look for yourself, it's there in black and . . .'

'He's right, you know, Trev. It does say . . .'

There was the sharp, brittle sound of steel clashing on steel. Asaf sighed, shook his head sadly, and sauntered back to where the girl was waiting.

'Idiots,' he muttered softly. 'All right, give me the stones and sling your hook.'

'Allah be praised, oh my prince,' said the girl nervously, rather as if she'd been expecting a rather different cue. 'Thanks to you—'

'Yes,' Asaf said. 'We'll take all that as read, shall we? The stones, please.'

Behind him there was a roar of triumph. The third rider lay slumped on the sand, and the first rider was brandishing his sword again.

'If I were you,' Asaf said, 'I'd hand them over and get the hell out of here before those two sort out their differences. Keep straight on down this road about ten miles and you'll find a telephone box. Phone the police. OK?'

The girl nodded, confused, and handed him a white cloth bag which held something heavy. Before she could say anything else, Asaf turned on his heel, hobbled back to the van and slammed the door.

'I trust,' he said, putting the van into gear and driving off, 'that there's not going to be much more of this sort of thing, because a man can only take so much pratting around before his patience starts to wear thin. I'm telling you this,' he added, 'just so's you'll know. OK?'

'OK, mate. Actually . . .'

Asaf turned his head and gave the King a long, cold look. 'Don't tell me,' he said. 'There's more.'

'Fair crack of the whip, chum, it *is* a quest.'

Asaf glanced quickly in the mirror, slowed down and started to turn the van around.

'Hey,' the King protested, 'what are you . . .?'

'Going home,' Asaf replied. 'Look, I may just be a simple fisherman, but I have my self-respect. So let's just call it quits. You get out of my life and stay out, and everything will be fine.'

'But the sheila,' the King said. 'It's all fixed up!'

'Then unfix it.'

'I can't!'

Asaf stopped the van. 'What,' he asked quietly, 'does that mean?'

The King bit his lips. 'Like I said,' he replied mournfully.

'Everything's set up. You *wished*, remember?'

'Wealth without limit was what I wished for,' Asaf replied. 'There wasn't anything in the original specifications about running amok killing and stealing half-way across the blasted continent.'

'For pity's sake, mate, this is my job on the line here. I've made arrangements . . .'

Asaf leaned back in his seat and closed his eyes. 'All right,' he sighed. 'On three conditions.'

'Anything.'

'One, you don't sing.'

'No worries, mate, not another note.'

'Two,' said Asaf, 'we keep these stupid adventures to the basic minimum. No magic spells, no more beautiful maidens than absolutely necessary, and positively no gratuitous folklore. Agreed?'

'You got it.'

'Three.' He leaned forward and turned the key in the ignition. 'Keep your bloody shoes on.'

Two genies, rather the worse for six pints apiece of semi-skimmed with double-cream chasers, lurched out of Saheed's and hailed a taxi.

'Where to?'

'Isson this bitta paper,' mumbled Nick. 'Fastasyoulike.'

'You're the boss,' replied the taxi. It hovered for a moment, straightening out its corners, and lowered itself to ground level. The genies climbed aboard.

'Home, James,' Con declaimed, 'an' don't spare the Axminster.'

The carpet rose like a very flat Harrier, made itself stiff in every fibre of its being, and shimmered away into the night sky.

The cold air, rushing past their ears, served to cut the milk fug, and by the time they arrived at the destination scribbled on the milk-mat both genies were – not sober, exactly, but at least 90 per cent in charge of their principal motor functions. The ideal state, in other words, for attempting something very silly indeed.

'Right,' said Nick. 'You ready?'

'As I'll ever be,' Con replied. 'Here, I'm not so sure this is a very brilliant idea . . .'

'Shuttup.' Nick rubbed his eyes and said the shape-changing spell aloud. It worked. 'Your turn,' he said.

'I still think—'

'Get on with it.'

'All right.' Con mumbled the magic words; and he too changed shape. The carpet braked smoothly and began its descent.

'Here, Con,' Nick whispered. 'Remind me. Which one am I supposed to be?'

Con shrugged. 'I've forgotten,' he admitted. 'Let's have a look at you.'

'Well?'

Con rubbed his chin. 'I think,' he said after a while, 'you're the tall one. Wossisname.'

'I see. So you're . . .?'

'The other one.'

'Fine. I'm glad we've got that sorted out.'

The carpet came to rest. The two genies climbed off and paid the fare, and then looked round. Nobody about. Probably just as well. What they were doing was, of course, unethical and probably highly illegal by genie standards. On the other hand, virtually everything genies do is.

'Here goes.'

'Break a leg.' Con extended a slightly unsteady arm and rang Jane's doorbell.

'What do you mean,' Nick asked, 'break a leg?'

'It's something mortals say,' Con replied as the porch light came on. 'Something to do with good luck.'

'It's not good luck breaking a leg,' Nick said doubtfully. 'Not if you're a mortal, that is. Takes weeks to mend, a mortal leg does.'

'It's just an expression.'

'Bloody silly one, if you ask me.'

The door opened and Jane stood in the doorway. She was wearing a pink winceyette dressing-gown and fluffy slippers.

'Ah,' said Nick, as smoothly as he could (but another half of pasteurised would, he realised, have been a wise precaution), 'good evening, um, miss. My name's Robert Redford and this is my friend Tom Cruise. Our car's broken down and we were wondering if we could borrow your phone.'

Jane frowned. 'It's two o'clock in the morning,' she said.

If Nick was fazed for a moment, he didn't show it. 'Exactly what I was saying to Mr Cruise,' he replied. 'Face it, Tom, I told him, chances of there being a garage open at this time of night are practically nil, so we'd better phone the breakdown service. And then, would you believe it, neither of us had any change. So we thought . . .'

In the background, the carpet lifted smoothly into the air, waggled its seams and glided away. 'You'd better come in,' Jane said.

'Thanks.'

Jane shut the door. 'You're genies, aren't you?' she said.

'Ah.'

'It's the carpet,' Jane said over her shoulder, leading the way through into the living-room. 'It's a dead giveaway, that. Also,' she added wearily, 'you obviously haven't seen Mr Redford for quite some time. Not that he hasn't worn quite well, but . . .'

Con took a deep breath. 'Hey,' he said, 'is this guy really a genie? Gosh, isn't that . . .?'

'And so are you,' Jane sighed. 'You're still wearing your slippers.'

The soi-disant Tom Cruise glanced down at his feet,

which were encased in curly-toed gold slippers with jewels stuck to the uppers. 'Damn,' he said.

'Sit down,' said Jane.

Nick smiled feebly. 'Listen, Miss,' he said, 'this has all been a big mistake, and . . .'

'Sit *down*.'

They sat down.

'And take those silly faces off, for heaven's sake.'

They changed back into their proper shapes.

'Sorry,' Nick said.

'And so you should be.' Jane folded her arms and gave them each a look that would have made a woolly mammoth feel at home. 'Men!' she added.

'I'm sorry?'

'Typical male idea of a joke,' Jane went on. 'Oh gosh, Kiss is getting married, let's go and play a joke on him. Puerile.'

'Ah.'

'Posing as extremely handsome film actors, you said to yourselves, let's make some excuse to get in to her flat, so that when he comes round the next morning he'll jump to the wrong conclusion, get madly jealous and they'll have a row. How utterly childish!'

Nick swallowed hard. 'Yes,' he said, 'I see that now. How silly of me.'

'Me too,' Con mumbled. 'Won't be doing anything like this again in a hurry, you can bet your life.'

Jane glowered at them. 'Actually,' she said, 'you're closer to the truth there than you think. Stay there.'

She swept out, and came back a few seconds later with two tomato ketchup bottles and a saucepan. 'It's just as well,' she said, 'that I was planning on making a bolognese anyway.'

She emptied the bottles into the saucepan, put them down on a coffee table, and snapped her fingers. 'Right,' she commanded. 'In you get.'

The two genies stared at each other.

'You can't be . . .'

'You heard me. Come on, jump to it.'

Quickly, the two genies assessed their position. On the one hand, Jane had invoked no magic spell or charm sufficient to force them into the bottles. They didn't have to go. They would be perfectly within their rights to stay exactly where they were and simply explain, calmly and rationally, exactly what they thought they were playing at.

WHOOSH!

Jane nodded and screwed down the lids. Then she put the bottles away in the kitchen cupboard and went back to bed.

NINE

Start a war.
   Using hail, giant ants and burning pitch.
Piece of cake.

The atmosphere was electric.

Around the packed arena, a hundred thousand spectators watched dry-mouthed as the synthesized fanfare sounded, the gates opened and –

– the teams appeared!

They had said it couldn't happen, not in our lifetimes. The political, cultural and ideological gulf was too great, they said. They'd been wrong.

As the teams ran on to the field, one man sat back in his seat in the President's box and swelled with pride like an overfed bullfrog. Rightly so; he had devoted the last three years of his life to making this moment possible. He had dreamed the impossible dream, and it had become a reality.

The first ever international sporting event between the pathologically hostile Latin American states of San Miguel and Las Monedas. The symbolic resolution of a feud that threatened the peace of the whole world. Here, in the Stadio Ricardo Nixon, San Miguel City, the differences of these two bitter rivals would be fought out, not with tanks and bombs but the click of heels, the swirl of petticoats, the snap of castanets. The great Tango Showdown between the San

Miguel Tigers and the Las Monedas Centurions was about to begin.

Secretary General Kropatchek sighed with pure pleasure. One small two-step for a man, he reflected, a giant entrechat for Mankind.

The contestants lined up, magnificent in their gaudy splendour. Nervously, the orchestra tuned their instruments for the last time. One false note, they knew, could even now lead directly to Armageddon. The Master of Ceremonies took the field – just for today, he had dispensed with the curule chair and his customary robes, and was dressed in a simple purple tuxedo – and read a brief prayer before shouting, '*Ariba!*' and standing well back. The contest began.

In the clear blue sky, a small black speck appeared, too small to notice …

Accounts of what happened next vary, naturally. If you believe the San Miguel version, a Starfighter of the Las Monedas air force swooped down low over the arena, discharged a drop-tank of napalm on to the dead centre of the specially installed dance-floor, and roared away. The Las Monedians, of course, say that it was a San Miguel MiG that dropped the incendiary device. The truth will probably never be known. The truth, in circumstances like these, is generally irrelevant anyway.

What did matter was the sudden explosion of activity in the President's box. As the flames roared up to the sky from the middle of the stadium, the delegates from the two countries flew at each others' throats and started throwing punches, plates of vol-au-vents and souvenir programmes. Their aides, meanwhile, were yelling into their radio handsets, demanding punitive air strikes and massive retribution. Secretary General Kropatchek managed to escape to safety, but only by stunning a passing waiter, snatching his tray and edging out backwards handing out canapés.

Three hours later, just before hostilities could begin in earnest, a hasty cease-fire was lashed together: involving a three-mile neutral zone along the common frontier, a UN peacekeeping force and a unilateral ban on all forms of ballroom and flamenco dancing throughout the front line states. It held. Just.

Which pleased the human race no end but irritated Philly Nine, who had put a lot of thought and effort into the attack, and had quite reasonably expected a result. Back to the drawing board.

High in his solitary eyrie, he watched the tanks withdraw, clicked his tongue, and took out his crumpled envelope.

He ran his pen down the margin and drew a cross.

X Burning pitch

Ah well, he muttered to himself. Better luck next time.

One small random particle, working its way steadily towards the centre ...

'That signpost,' said Asaf, with deadly patience, 'says *Ankara, 15km.*'

The Dragon King lifted his sunglasses and squinted. 'Too right, mate,' he said. 'Well, stuff me for a kookaburra's uncle.'

Asaf breathed out slowly through his nose. 'I may yet,' he replied. 'Admit it,' he went on. 'We're on the wrong road.'

The King looked out of the window. 'Hell,' he said, 'it all looks different from down here. I'm used to the aerial view.'

Asaf snarled, put the camper into reverse and started to back up. The King put a hand on his arm.

'Just a second there, mate,' he said. 'While we're here, we might just as well ...'

He tailed off. Asaf scowled.

'We aren't lost, are we?' he said accusingly. 'You've lured

me out here for another of your goddamn poxy adventures.
Admit it.'

'Fair dinkum, mate, you'll like this one. Stand on me.'

Asaf stamped on the accelerator, sending the camper
hurtling backwards. 'Oh no, you bloody well don't,' he
snapped. 'Not after the last time.'

'Yes, but—'

'And the time before that.'

'Hang on just a—'

'*And* the time before that, with the talking shrub. I nearly
died of embarrassment.'

The King shut his eyes, took a deep breath and stalled the
engine. Or rather, he caused the engine to stall. Then he
tried his best at an ingratiating smile.

'Adventure,' he said weakly, 'is the spice of life.'

'Get out.'

'Pardon me?'

'Get out of my van,' Asaf growled. 'And you can bloody
well walk home.'

'You haven't seen the adventure yet.'

Just then, at precisely the moment when Asaf was leaning
across to work the passenger-door handle, a beautiful white
gazelle sprang out in front of the camper, stopped dead in
its tracks, raised its head for an instant and then ran on. Asaf
stared.

'Is that the adventure?' he said.

The King drew breath to explain, thought better of it and
nodded. 'You see?' he said. 'Told you you'd like it.'

Asaf frowned. 'I must be mad,' he muttered. 'Stark
staring—'

'She'll be right, mate. Trust me.'

Still muttering, Asaf climbed slowly out of the camper, shut the door and walked slowly towards the
gazelle, which had stopped about seventy-five yards away
and was feeding peacefully on a discarded cheese roll. He

had covered half the distance when –

WHOOSH!

It seemed as if the ground split open at his feet, as a huge apparition reared up and loomed over him. Generally humanoid in form, it had three heads, five arms and the legs of a wild goat. Out of the corners of its mouths projected weird curling tusks, and in its hands it held a variety of archaic but imagination-curdling weapons. It crouched in a fighting pose and said, 'Ha!'

'Oh, for pity's sake,' said Asaf, disgustedly. 'Not you again.'

And justifiably; because all three of the monster's heads were the same, and the face on each of them was identical to the one Asaf had so far encountered on one camel-riding magician, one magic-carpet-riding Grand Vizier, one man-eating Centaur, one seven-headed magic bird and, improbable as it may seem, one evil but enchanting houri. It was a face that was starting to get on Asaf's nerves.

'Tremble!' the monster commanded, a mite self-consciously. It was the tone of voice a policeman might use when arresting someone who, on closer inspection, turned out to be his elder brother.

'Bog off,' Asaf replied. He turned on his heel and started to walk back to the van.

'Wretched mortal, I shall devour . . .' the monster started to say; then it realised that its audience was fifteen yards away and walking briskly. It scampered after him; a manoeuvre that wasn't helped by the goat's feet.

'Wretched . . . mortal . . . I . . .' it puffed. 'Here, wait for me!'

Asaf turned and scowled, hands on hips. 'Look,' he said, 'I told you the last time. I'm not interested. Go away.' He turned and quickened his pace, and the monster had to sprint to keep up with him.

'But I shall devour . . . oof!'

Before the monster could halt its teetering run (imagine Godzilla in a pair of two-inch-heel court shoes, each shoe on the wrong foot) Asaf had whirled round and prodded it hard just below the navel. It wobbled for a fraction of a second and then sat down hard on a sharp boulder.

'Ouch!' it said. 'That hurt.'

'Good.' Asaf grabbed a pointed ear and twisted it. 'Look, chum, so far I've killed you twice, imprisoned your soul in a bottle, thrown you off a cliff and nailed your ears to a tree. What exactly do I have to do to you before you get the message?'

'I'm only doing my job,' the monster replied.

'Find another job, then,' Asaf snapped. 'Carpentry, for instance. Plumbing. Chartered surveying. Anything which doesn't involve meeting me ever again. Otherwise,' he added, 'I shall get seriously annoyed. Got it?'

'Finished?'

'Yes.'

'Thank you.' The monster clicked its tongues. 'Now then, where was I? Oh magnanimous one, spare my life and I shall . . .'

'Hold on,' Asaf interrupted, turning the ear in his hand a few degrees clockwise. 'This doesn't involve three wishes, does it, because I've had all that and as far as I'm concerned you can take your three wishes and you can—'

'No, it doesn't,' replied the monster irritably. 'And my ear is not a starting handle. Thank you very much.'

'Get on with it, then.'

'Spare my life,' growled the monster, 'and I shall show thee the most wondrous treasure.' It glanced up with its unencumbered heads. 'Interested?'

'Not very,' Asaf replied. 'But it's an improvement. Go on.'

'Not three leagues from here,' said the monster, 'there lies an enchanted castle, under whose walls—'

'Hold it.'

'Well?'

'Three leagues,' said Asaf. 'What's that in kilometres?'

'Fourteen and a half,' snapped the monster. 'Not four-teen and a half kilometres from here there lies an enchanted castle, under whose—'

Asaf shook his head. 'No way,' he said. 'A fifteen-kilometre detour on these roads, there and back, that's best part of an hour. We wouldn't reach Istanbul till gone nine.'

'Hoy!' the monster broke in angrily. 'We're talking about a wondrous treasure here.'

'Sorry,' Asaf replied. 'Not even with free wine-glasses.' He gave the ear a final twist, for luck, and let go. 'So long,' he said. 'I have this strange feeling we'll meet again soon. Till then, mind how you go.'

'Gold!' the monster yelled after him. 'Silver! Precious stones!'

'Balls,' Asaf replied.

'You can't do this,' screamed the monster. 'I've signed for it now, they'll have my guts for—'

'I expect you're used to that by now,' Asaf said. 'Ciao.'

'Bastard!' The monster shook its many fists, spat into the dust and started to sink into the ground. Asaf walked a few more yards, and then stopped.

'Hey!' he said.

The monster paused, waist-deep in the earth. 'Well?'

'Did you say gold?'

'Yes.'

'And silver? And precious stones?'

'Yes.'

'Stay there, I'll be right with you.'

Asaf turned and hurried back. The monster was leaning on its elbows, drumming its fingers on a rock.

'You really like causing problems, don't you?' it said.

'You do realise I'm stuck here till they can get a maintenance crew out?'

'Gosh,' said Asaf. 'Sorry about that.'

'Either you can materialise,' grumbled the monster, 'or you can vanish. One or the other. You try mixing the two, you get stuck.'

'That was thoughtless of me,' Asaf admitted. 'By the way, I don't think I caught your name – your actual name, that is. Like, when you're off-duty.'

'Neville.'

'I'm Asaf.'

'Hello.'

'Hello. Now, about this gold.'

'And silver.'

'Quite. How exactly do I set about—?'

'*And* precious stones.'

'Great.' Asaf broadened his smile a little. 'Can you give me specific directions, because then I won't have to trouble you to come with me, I can just . . .'

The monster shook his heads. 'Oh, no, you don't,' it said. 'This time we do it by the book.'

Asaf sagged a little. 'Do we really have to?' he asked.

'Yes.'

'Sure? I mean, wouldn't it be far simpler if you just drew me a map or something?'

'Out of the question,' Neville replied. 'First, you've got to fight the hundred-headed guardian of the pit, and then—'

'Hang on,' said Asaf. 'This hundred-headed guardian. That'll be you, right?'

Neville bit his lips, then nodded. 'That's right,' he mumbled.

'And I win, right?'

'Yes.'

'And you get killed.'

'Yup.'

'Again.'

Neville furrowed all his brows simultaneously. 'Yeah,' he said. 'A bit pointless, really, isn't it?'

'Futile, if you ask me.'

'Anyway,' Neville went on, 'after you've killed the hundred-headed guardian, then you've got to guess the secret riddle of the Mad Witch of the North—'

'You again, right?'

Neville nodded. 'In a frock,' he added. 'Three sizes too small, too. Stops your circulation.'

'Must be awful.'

'It is. After that,' he went on, counting off on his fingers, 'there's the monstrous cloud-stepping ogre—'

'Guess who.'

'Followed by the wicked Grand Vizier who tries to have you thrown in the snake-pit . . .'

'You again?'

'No,' Neville replied, 'that's my cousin Wilf.'

'Ah. Let me guess, you're the snakes.'

'You got it.'

'I escape, naturally?'

'Naturally.'

'The snakes, I anticipate, aren't quite so fortunate?'

Neville shuddered. 'I do so hate death by drowning,' he added. 'Makes your ears go pop. I always get this headache, stays with me the whole of the rest of the day.'

'In fact,' Asaf said, 'the way I see it, I'm going to have to spend the rest of today, and probably most of tomorrow as well, kicking shit out of you, and it's all a foregone conclusion anyway.'

'Wretched, isn't it?'

'Childish,' Asaf agreed. 'Look, couldn't I just beat you to a jelly now and get it all over with in one go?'

There was a long pause. 'Put like that,' said Neville slowly, 'it does sort of make sense.'

'In fact,' Asaf went on, 'a token clip round the ear would probably do just as well.'

Neville frowned. 'I'm not sure about that,' he said. 'Standing orders specifically require—'

'Yes,' Asaf interrupted, 'but who'll ever know? I won't tell anybody.'

'You won't?'

'Scout's honour.'

The monster thought about it for a while. 'Can I get you to sign a receipt?' he asked. 'Just for the books, you understand.'

'Sure,' said Asaf.

'Deal!' The monster cried, and it reached down into the bowels of the earth. A moment later its hand reappeared holding a parchment, a quill pen and a bottle of ink. 'So much more sensible this way,' it said.

'Quite.'

'So if you'll just sign here . . .'

'Where your finger is?' asked Asaf, unscrewing the ink bottle.

'That's it. Goodbye, idiot!' he added. 'See you in Hell!'

And, so saying, it grabbed Asaf by the scruff of the neck, squashed him head-first into the ink bottle and screwed down the cap.

And vanished.

Meanwhile, the small frog that was Kevin, the insurance broker, had filed his report. It made interesting reading.

Only a genie of Force Seven or above could have deciphered the pattern of nibble-marks on the lily-pad, and known that they read:

rivet-rivet-rivet-rivet-
RIVET-RIVET-RIVET-RIVET!!!!!!-RIVET!!!!!!

Only a genie of Force Eight or above, fluent in frog, could have translated the message and grasped its terrible significance.

Only a genie of Force Nine or above would have the authority to take the necessary remedial action.

Only a genie of Force Eleven or above (or God, at a pinch) would have the necessary technical knowledge and basic common sense required to put that remedial action into effect.

Fortunately, the report found its way on to the right desks, was understood and taken seriously. The necessary action was proposed, approved and set in hand.

As for the frog that was Kevin, it found itself coming to terms with its new lifestyle rather more quickly than it had originally anticipated. Not only were the hours better and the pressures less; the inhabitants of the pond were remarkably receptive to the idea of insurance and he was doing excellent business when a heron, new to the area, swooped down and ate him.

Regrettable; but that's nature for you, and it's a comfort to reflect that his last conscious thought must have been relief that his loved ones would be adequately provided for by a comprehensive insurance package specially tailored to his needs and circumstances.

Or would have done, if he'd had any loved ones, and if the policy hadn't contained a special no-herons clause. But it's the thought that counts.

A scrumpled ball of paper looped through the air and added itself to the small pyramid on top of the waste-paper basket.

Philly Nine yawned. It was late, he was tired, and he wanted to go to bed. Giant ants . . .

He got up and prowled round the room. Nobody to blame but himself, of course; he'd chosen giant ants of his own free will. He could have had anything he liked, but no, he had to be clever.

Ants, for pity's sake.

He sat down on the arm of a chair, closed his eyes and rallied his thoughts. What, he demanded of himself, do ants *do*?

Well. They build nests. They run around aimlessly. They get into picnic baskets and scamper about over the boiled eggs. This, Philly had to admit, wasn't exactly the stuff of Armageddon.

They chew things up. With their snippy little mandibles, they make mincemeat out of old dry timber. They dig. When you pour boiling water on them, they die.

He looked up at the clock on the wall, and shuddered. Would it be possible, he wondered, to claim a typographical error and instead have a plague of giant *aunts*? More scope there, he felt sure; something you could get your teeth into . . .

Nah. It'd be just his luck to get found out; to annihilate humanity and then have the whole thing set aside on a technicality. Long gone were the old, free-and-easy days of his imphood when near enough made no mind. These days, you had to be precise. No good putting a princess to sleep for ninety-nine years, three hundred and sixty-four days, twenty-three hours and fifty-nine minutes. You could bet your life there'd be some weasel-faced little sod with a clipboard and a stopwatch somewhere, just willing you to foul up.

Ants. Harmless, industrious, ecologically-friendly ants. Bastards.

He snatched another piece of paper out of the packet and started to scribble.

An anthill, he wrote, *so big that it cuts off the light from a major European city. Giant ants undermining Beijing, so that it falls down to the centre of the earth. The New York subway system infested with giant ants . . .*

Scrumple. Whizz. Flop.

He stood up again, and then sat down. *Giant* ants. Yes. Perhaps.

Giant ants, he wrote. *What causes giant ants? And whose fault would it be?*

Pay dirt. Ideas started to flood into his mind like water through a breached sea-wall, and he scribbled furiously. So furiously in fact, that it was half an hour before he realised he was writing on his best white linen tablecloth.

Giant ants. Yes. Yes indeed.

What do you call it when a genie has a really good idea? Genius.

It was late. Even Saheed's, which is never empty, was down to its last hard core of residual customers; a few sad types sitting at tables, two more playing the fruit machine, and one very sad customer with his foot on the brass rail.

'Don't you think you've had enough?' murmured the barman.

Kiss scowled at him. 'Not yet,' he grunted, and pushed his empty glass back across the counter. 'Yogurt. Neat. No fruit.'

The barman shrugged. He was, of course, only doing his job, and it was none of his business; but the idea of a Force Twelve wandering about with an attitude problem and five quarts of natural yogurt under his belt wasn't an attractive one. He filled the glass and shoved it back.

Time, he said to himself, to start a conversation. More goddamn unpaid social work.

'What's up, mac?' he enquired softly. He assessed the symptoms; it wasn't difficult. 'Trouble with your girl?'

Kiss nodded.

'You could say that,' he replied.

The barman nodded sympathetically. 'Found herself another guy, huh?'

'No.'

'I see. Just plain not interested, you mean?'

'Far from it,' Kiss sighed. 'That's the problem.'

Well, thought the barman, it takes all sorts. 'You mean,' he said, 'you can see it's all over between you, but you can't figure out how to tell her? That's tough.'

'No,' Kiss yawned, 'it's not that. We're in love. Head over heels in bloody love.' He snarled. 'Made in heaven, you could say.'

'Ah.' The barman shrugged. 'But there's some reason why you can't get together, is that it?'

Kiss lifted his head and looked at him. 'What is this,' he asked, 'some sort of blasted sociological survey?'

'Just passing the time, mac. Talking of which . . .?'

'Put another one in there,' Kiss said. 'With a cream chaser.'

'You're the boss, mac.'

'And stop calling me mac.'

'You got it, chief.'

There was a frantic chiming from the direction of the fruit machine and suddenly the floor was covered in oranges and lemons, tumbling out of the pay-out slot and rolling around on the floor. One came to rest beside Kiss's heel. He stood on it.

'I mean,' he said suddenly, in the general direction of the barman, 'it's not my fault, is it? I never asked to be the one to save the world.'

'Yeah,' said the barman. 'Have you seen what time it is, by the way?'

'I don't give . . .' Kiss leaned over, picked up an orange and squashed it into pulp between his thumb and middle finger. 'I don't give *that* for the world. None of my damn business.'

'You said it, chief.'

'But it's my damn responsibility!' Kiss scowled horribly, and then looked down at his hand. 'Hey, have you got a towel or something?'

'Just a second.'

'So why,' Kiss continued, wiping his hands, 'does it have to be me? Go on, you tell me, it's your stinking planet. Why me?'

The barman shrugged. 'Somebody's got to do it?' he suggested.

Kiss shook his head. 'Not good enough,' he said. 'I'm a genie, right? We're ...' He closed his eyes, fumbling through a fog of draught yogurt for the right words. 'Free spirits,' he said. 'No. Loose cannons. We do our own thing. That's unless somebody gets us by the balls and makes us do theirs. But that,' he concluded defiantly, 'goes with the territory. We can handle that.'

'Glad to hear it, buddy.'

In the background there was a dull squelch, as the fruit machine tried unsuccessfully to pay out a grapefruit through a four-inch slot. Kiss sighed.

'You don't want to hear all this, do you?' he asked.

The barman looked at him with old, warm eyes. 'I can take it,' he said, 'I've heard worse.'

Kiss nodded. 'You must have heard it all,' he said.

'Maybe.' The barman picked up a glass and polished it. 'But maybe I wasn't listening.'

Somewhere in Kiss's brain, the dinar dropped. 'You're a genie?' he asked softly.

'You bet, squire.'

'What Force?'

The barman shrugged, breathed on the rim of the glass in his hands and eased away a mark. 'Twelve,' he replied.

'Twelve?' Kiss looked at him. 'Then what the blazes are you doing in a dump like this?'

The barman looked back, and his eyes were like the view through the wrong end of the binoculars. 'Hey,' he said. 'You know how it is when you're bound by some curse to a bottle?'

Kiss nodded.

'Well, then.' The barman half-turned and with an eloquent but economical gesture he indicated the shelves behind him. 'Me,' he said, 'I got *lots* of bottles.'

'Gawd!'

'It's not the way I'd have liked things to pan out,' the barman agreed. 'But you find yourself in a situation, what can you do? Me, I serve drinks to people. That's from six pee-em to maybe four-thirty ay-em. The rest of the time . . .'

Kiss leaned forward. 'Yes?'

'The rest of the time's my own,' the barman replied. 'Same again, is it?'

On his way home, Kiss turned out the cupboard under the stairs of his mind and found it to be mainly full of junk. There he found the ironing-board of duty, the broken torch of hope, the unwanted Christmas presents of obscure function that represent the random operations of fate, the dustpan of experience, the stepladder of aspiration, the hoover of despair; there also he found the raffia-covered Chianti-bottle table-lamp of love, which had seemed such a good idea at the time, which promised to cast light where before there was darkness and which now got under his feet whenever he wanted to get out the ironing-board. Its shade was as pink as ever, but its bulb had gone.

Not, Kiss hastened to add, my fault. I'm the goddamn victim; and she is as well, of course, but *she's* not expected to give up being a Force Twelve genie. His thoughts returned to the genie behind the bar at Saheed's; another Force Twelve fallen on hard times. They could form a support group; well, not a group. The best they could do with the manpower available would be a very short, truncated heap.

I've got to get myself out of this. But how?

★

The inside of an ink-bottle turned out to be remarkably spacious, all things considered.

Admittedly, you have to sit with your knees round your ears and your arms behind your back; and it doesn't do to sneeze violently for fear of knocking yourself silly on the walls. The fact remains; getting six foot of retired fisherman inside three inches of bottle without pruning off several indispensable components is some achievement. Try it and see.

'Let me OUT!'

Some people, it seems, are never satisfied. There are successful young executives in the centre of Tokyo who pay good money for not much more *lebensraum*, and are glad to get it.

'Are you deaf or something? Let me OUT!'

Asaf paused to catch his breath. Yelling at the top of one's voice in a confined space is physically demanding and, besides, it didn't seem to be working.

If I were a baby bird, he said to himself, and if this was an eggshell, I could peck my way out.

Ah, but it isn't. And you're not.

It would be overstating the case to say that Asaf stiffened, because after nine hours in the bottle he was pretty conclusively stiff already; but he went through the motions.

There is someone, he said to himself, in here with me.

Hope he's as uncomfortable as I am.

Not really. You get used to it after a while.

This time, Asaf felt a definite twitch in his sphincter.

Don't be like that.

'What?' Asaf said aloud. His voice, he couldn't help noticing, seemed to be coming out through his socks; something to do with the rather unusual acoustics inside an ink-bottle.

Hostile. I can definitely sense hostility. I'm only here because I thought you might be feeling lonely.

'How the hell am I supposed to feel lonely in something this size?'

Fair point. I'll be going, then.

'Wait!'

Silence. But then again, he reflected, there would be, wouldn't there? Since, apparently, whoever it was in here with him was either a disembodied spirit or . . .

A telepath. Bit of both, actually. Go with the flow, that's always been my motto.

'Who are you?'

Name? Or job description?

'Both.'

All-righty. My name's Pivot, and I'm the duty GA.

'GA?'

Guardian angel. Since whatever it was was simply a suggestion of words in his mind, there was no way it could actually sound embarrassed. But it somehow gave the impression.

'Bit late, aren't you?' Asaf grumbled. 'Nine hours ago I could have used you.'

I know, Pivot replied. *But like I said, I'm duty GA for this whole sector. I got held up on a call the other side of Bazrah. I came as quick as I could.*

'I see.' Asaf took a deep breath; or at least, the top slice of one. 'Well, now you're here . . .'

I can keep your morale up and comfort you with homely snippets of folk wisdom and popular philosophy.

'That's it?'

Sorry.

'Like, It's a funny old world, that sort of thing?'

You've got the idea.

'Fine. Well, I expect you've got lots of other calls to attend to, so don't let me . . .'

I know, replied Pivot sadly, *it's not exactly a great help. But that's all I'm able to do for you under the scheme. Lots of people actually do find it remarkably helpful.*

'I see.'

If you were being tortured, of course, or even briskly interrogated, that'd be another matter entirely. I could remind you of your rights and exhort you to display fortitude and moral courage in the face of adversity.

'Gosh. Well, it's just as well I'm not, then, isn't it?'

There was silence in Asaf's mind for a while, and he spent the time thinking all the most uncharitable thoughts he could muster, in the hope of persuading Pivot to leave quickly.

It'd be different if you were a fee-paying client, of course.

'Sorry?'

Morale-raising and verbal comfort are all I'm allowed to offer under the scheme. If you want to go private, of course, I'm sure I could be even more helpful still.

'Such as?'

Such as getting you out of here, for a start.

'Done.'

Plus, there's our fully comprehensive after-care package, of course. We don't just ditch our clients the moment they get out of the bottle; oh dear, no. We can offer advice on a wide spectrum of issues, including financial advice, investment strategy, pensions . . .

'Whatever you like. Just get me out of—'

If you'd just care to sign this client services agreement. There, there and there . . .

Asaf growled ominously. 'I'd just like to point out,' he said, 'that my hands are wedged against the side of this bottle so hard my circulation stopped about seven hours ago. I think signing anything's going to be a bit tricky.'

Oh. Oh, that is a nuisance. Because, you see, the rules say I can't really do anything for you unless you sign the forms. I have my compliance certificate to think of, you know.

Asaf gritted his teeth. 'I promise I'll sign them the

moment I'm free,' he said. 'Word of honour.'

Ah yes, Pivot replied, *but how do I know you're not a FIMBRA agent in disguise? You could be trying to entrap me.*

'Why not take the risk? I'll have you know I'm shortly going to come into wealth beyond the dreams of avarice.' He paused significantly. 'I shall need,' he said, biting his tongue, 'all sorts of financial advice, I feel sure.'

Is that so?

'Definitely.'

Life insurance?

'As much as I can lay my hands on.'

Pensions?

'By the bucketful. I shall want as many pensions as I can possibly get.'

Stone me. It's been months since I sold a pension. Are you sure you're not a FIMBRA agent?

'Absolutely bloody positive. Now, could you please get me out of this fucking bottle?'

At the back of his mind, Asaf could feel Pivot wriggling uncomfortably. *I still have bad feelings about all this. The rules really are terribly strict.*

'Couldn't you ...' Asaf squirmed with agony as a spasm of cramp shot down his spinal column. 'Couldn't you sign them for me? As my agent or whatever?'

Hum. Not really. Not unless you sign a power of attorney. I happen to have one with me, by the way.

'Oh, for crying out loud...'

I'm sorry, sighed Pivot. *I'd really love to help, but you know how it is. Now, are you ready for some homely snippets yet? We could start with, 'It's always darkest before the dawn', or we could ...*

'No!' Asaf jerked violently in protest, and in doing so fetched the back of his head a terrific crack on the wall of the bottle. 'Just you dare, and the moment I'm out of this sodding contraption—'

He stopped in mid-snarl. The walls were creaking. Obviously, the blow from his head had damaged the glass. Now if he could only . . .

I've also got one about not beating your head against a brick wall, continued Pivot helpfully. *And I can customise it to refer to the sides of glass bottles for a very modest . . .*

Crash. The glass gave way and suddenly Asaf was out, sprawled full-length – six feet of cramp and muscle spasms – on a flat field of grass. There were shards of broken bottle sticking into him in all sorts of places.

There, I told you we'd have you out of there in no time, said Pivot, recovering well. *That'll be, let's see, seven minutes at a hundred dirhams an hour, so by my reckoning that's . . .*

Asaf lifted his head, and thought long and hard about what he would like to do to the next supernatural being who crossed his path. By the time he'd finished, something told him he was very much alone.

TEN

Jane looked around her, and clicked her tongue.
She was bored.

Not just bored in the nothing-to-do sense; she was bored to the marrow, half-past-four-on-a-Sunday-afternoon-in-Wales bored. And nothing much, as far as she could see, to be done about it.

Bloody genie! What the hell was the point of being able to have anything you want if all you have to do in order to get it is want it?

Still, she consoled herself while moving a small china ornament two inches to the right, once we're married there won't be any more of *that*. No more of this supernatural nonsense. We can just be ordinary people . . .

Ordinary people . . .

Yes, well. At least ordinary people can go shopping. When you're the proprietress of a Force Twelve genie, one thing you can't do is shop. No sooner have you written down something on your list than it's there, delivered in a fraction of a second, very best quality, from Harrods. But what's the point of having things if you can't shop for them first?

Jane steeled herself. She was a free woman, with an inalienable right to shop. And shop she would.

She glanced down at her feet and noticed that on the patch of floor directly below her, approximately five feet by seven, there was no rug. Everywhere else there were rugs;

the very finest rugs ever, whisked here by arcane forces and precisely, down to the last fibre, what she'd wanted. Well, it would have to stop somewhere, and here was as good a place as any. She would go *out*, and *buy* a rug.

The resolution once made, she softened slightly. All the other rugs in the place – all the furniture and fittings, come to that – were her choice, and she knew for a fact that Kiss didn't really like them much. A bit thin on the barbaric splendour, he considered, while maybe slightly overstressing the cosy and colour-coordinated.

There, now. Two birds with one stone. She would buy a rug, in (she almost hugged herself with pleasure at the thought) a *shop*, and it would be the sort of rug Kiss would like. Persian or something. She could stand a coffee-table on it so that she wouldn't have to see it, but he would still know it was there.

Problem; although all Oriental carpets looked exactly the same to her, she was sure she remembered something about each one being unique, and some sorts being wonderfully marvellous works of art, and others being the sort of thing that's left unsold after a church bazaar. Obviously, it was incumbent upon her to buy one of the approved models.

Why is life so *complicated*?

The thought had scarcely crossed her mind when she caught sight of a book on the arm of the sofa. It was big and fat, and on the cover it had a photograph of a Persian rug. She picked it up.

It was written in Arabic.

That aside, it was promising; it was full of pictures of rugs, all of which looked pretty well identical to her, but it stood to reason that nobody, not even an Arab in the grips of vanity-publishing mania, would go to the trouble of producing a chunky great tome full of pictures of just one rug. Even if he was desperately attached to it, he'd probably just have its portrait painted and let it go at that.

Therefore, she argued, this must be a book, belonging to Kiss, on the subject of rugs; approved rugs, presumably. All she had to do was go to an emporium, find a rug which looked tolerably similar to the pictures in the book, and buy it. Problem solved. She dumped the book in her bag and went out.

Arguably, a more perceptive person might have noticed the wires coming out of the spine, and wondered what business a book had with sockets and electrodes.

The young man (his name was Justin) was tall and thin. L.S. Lowry would have hired him as a model without a moment's hesitation. He was wearing a hairy tweed jacket whose sleeves appeared to have eaten his hands right down to the middle joints of the fingers. He seemed nervous.

But not as nervous as the other man (his name was Max). If Justin resembled a golf club, Max was a dead ringer for the ball.

'Now you've got the number?' Max said.

'Yes, Uncle.'

'And you'll phone me if there's any problems? Any problems at all?'

'Yes, Uncle.'

'And you know where everything is?'

'Yes, Uncle.'

Max chewed his lip. 'The key to the safe is in the coffee tin on the top shelf of the stockroom, just under the—'

'Yes, Uncle.'

'And you're sure you'll be all right?'

'Yes, Uncle.'

There's only so much you can do, thought Max; and I'll only be gone two hours, and there's never any customers on a Thursday afternoon, and all the prices are clearly marked, and I've told him nineteen times not to let anybody haggle . . .

'Justin.'

'Yes, Uncle?'

'Remember, don't let anybody haggle. The prices as marked are non-negotiable. You've got that?'

'Yes, Uncle.'

... Twenty times, so what could possibly go wrong? no, don't even think that. Just keep everything crossed, and hurry back as soon as possible.

'Oh, and Justin.'

'Yes, Uncle?'

'Don't buy anything.'

'No, Uncle.'

It's impossible, Max reassured himself, completely out of the question, that the boy could be as dozy as his mother. For a start, he seems able to remember to breathe regularly without anybody having to remind him. The shop will be in safe hands. Everything's going to be all right.

'Is there anything,' he said, taking a deep breath, 'you want to ask before I go?'

'No, Uncle.'

Max shut his eyes, broadcast a prayer to any passing gods and smiled wretchedly.

'Right,' he said, winding his scarf round his neck, 'it's all yours.'

He took three steps towards the door, stopped and looked round. Of course he would see it all again, and when he came back everything would be all right. But there was no harm in taking one last, long look, just to be on the safe side.

''Bye, Uncle.'

'See you, Justin.'

The bell on the door clanged and Justin was alone with the shop, the till, the books and seventy square miles of the choicest, rarest, most valuable Oriental carpets in the whole of the United Kingdom.

He sneezed.

Carpets attract dust, and dust played hell with Justin's sinuses. The next two hours, he just knew, were going to be very, very long.

He sat down behind the desk and found his place in his book, trying his best to breathe in through his mouth only. He hadn't read more than five or six pages when the bell tinkled. He looked up.

'Can I help?' he asked, and froze.

During the previous night, when he'd been lying awake fretting about having to mind the shop on his own the next day, he had finally managed to reconcile himself to the thought that there might be customers. He had squared up to that one, looked the imposter Fear straight in the eye and stared him down. It hadn't occurred to him, however, that there might be female customers. Young female customers. If the thought had crossed his mind, come to that, he wouldn't be here now.

'I expect so,' Jane replied, looking round. 'I want to buy a rug.'

'Gosh.'

'Looks like I've come to the right place.'

'Crumbs.'

'I mean,' Jane went on, with that awful feeling you get when you know you've got to keep talking because the silence that'll follow when you stop will be too embarrassing to contemplate, 'you look like you've got a very wide selection.'

'Have we? Yes.'

Jane subsided. What she really wanted to do now was leave the shop and never come back; but it looked like there was a sporting chance that the implied rejection would drive the young man behind the desk to slash his wrists, if he didn't break his thumbnail getting the big blade out first. She was stuck.

'Gosh,' she said, selecting a carpet at random, 'what have we here?'

The young man said nothing. His expression seemed to suggest that as far as he was concerned, all carpets were too ghastly for words and he wanted nothing to do with them, ever, not in this world or the next.

'No,' Jane muttered, 'maybe not. Or rather,' she added quickly, in case the negative vibes might just be the final shove that would send him over the edge, 'it's a really nice carpet, but not quite in keeping with . . . Yes, this one's even nicer. Don't you think?'

The young man lifted his head and gazed at the example she'd put her hand on. 'Do you want to, er, *buy* . . .?'

His tone of voice suggested that Jane was trying to seduce him into committing some luridly unnatural act. 'Well,' she mumbled, 'I do quite like . . .'

'I'll look,' said the young man, 'in the book.'

He ducked under the counter, and for on awful moment Jane wondered if he was ever going to reappear. Just when she was steeling herself to go and see what he'd done to himself under there, he bobbed back up again with a shoebox full of tatty notebooks.

'It'll be in here somewhere,' the young man said hopelessly.

Oh Christ, Jane thought, I'm going to be here for the rest of my life. Kiss, where the devil are you when I need you? Beam me up *quick*.

'Look, if it's any trouble . . .'

The young man favoured her with a look that wouldn't have been out of place on the face of a sheep in an abattoir. 'I'm quite capable of looking it up, thank you very much,' he said, with a sort of hideous mangled dignity that made Jane wish very much that her father had never met her mother. 'I'll try not to keep you.'

'I'll buy it anyway,' Jane whimpered, 'if that's all right with you, I mean.'

The young man didn't reply. He was nose-deep in the box. It looked very much as if he was going to be there for some considerable time.

Eventually, just as Jane was wondering whether she could surreptitiously roll herself up in the carpet like Cleopatra, wait till he'd gone and then make good her escape, the young man lifted his head and coughed nervously.

'Excuse me.'

'Yes?'

'Can you see a ticket on it anywhere? It should say 2354/A67/74Y.'

'Ah.' Jane examined the carpet. 'Doesn't seem to be.'

'No?'

'No.'

'Oh.' The young man winced, as if the book in his hand was red-hot. 'I'd better just look, I suppose,' he muttered, and crossed the floor towards her. 'Maybe it's on the back of something. There *should* be one somewhere,' he added poignantly.

They were both standing on the carpet. 'Can I help?' Jane asked.

'It's all right, really, I can manage.'

'What does it say in the book?'

'It's a . . .' The young man squinted. 'Sorry, I can't quite pronounce it. Bokhara something or other.'

'And that's what you think this is?'

'I think so. Mind you, I'm really not an expert. If you wouldn't mind waiting till Uncle gets back, I'm sure he'd be able to . . .'

Oh no, thought Jane, I wasn't born yesterday. This is one of those traps, like the Flying Dutchman or the Lorelei. You promise to wait ten minutes, and five hundred years later you're still there, and everybody you ever knew on the outside has died. 'Here,' Jane said, press-ganging the first words ill-advised enough to come near her, 'I've got a book here, let's see if there's a picture we can identify it from.'

She opened Kiss's book, and as she was rather pre-occupied she failed to notice the slight hum, or the pale blue glow from the endpapers.

God, she thought. I wish I was out of here.

COMPUTING

The voice was inside her, tiny, clear and sharp. She was sure she'd heard it. Oh wonderful, now I'm going potty. If ever I get out of this alive, it's going to be wall-to-wall lino for ever and ever.

I wish, she added in mental parenthesis, Kiss was here.

DOES NOT CORRELATE

'Did you say...'

'Sorry?'

'Nothing.'

Definitely, Jane said to herself, I want to be out of here. Immediately.

WHOOSH!

'Good on yer, mate,' said the Dragon King of the South-East, emerging from behind a pile of coiled-up rope.

'Look...'

'Like a rat,' the Dragon King continued, 'up a drain. No worries. Like they say out Paramatta way: you can take the bloke out of the bottle, but you can't take the bottle out of the bloke.'

This remark was so puzzling that Asaf dismissed his daydream of making the King swallow his own tail, and he sat down on a barrel. 'Where the hell am I?' he asked.

'On the high seas, me old mate,' the King replied. 'On your way to seek fame, fortune, and the sheila with the big—'

'Please be more specific.'

The King smiled; that is to say, the corners of his jaws lifted, and his bright, small blue eyes sparkled even more than usual. 'We're on a ship,' he said.

'I had in fact come to that conclusion already. What bloody ship, and why?'

The King chuckled. 'Because,' he replied, 'you'd get pretty flamin' wet trying to cross the old surf without one. Eh?'

Asaf sighed. It wasn't, he said to himself, fair; not on him, and not on everybody else. Why should the rest of the world be deprived of their ration of idiots just so that he could have an embarrassing profusion?

'Where,' he asked, 'are we going?'

'Pommieland,' the King said. 'The old country. Gee, you'll love it there, mate. It's really beaut, trust me.'

'England?'

'That's the ticket.'

Asaf frowned. 'But that's crazy.'

'That's where she lives, chum. The jam tart with the . . .'

'Fine.' Asaf drew in a deep breath and counted up to ten. 'And this ship . . .'

'Hitched a lift with an old cobber of mine, actually,' said the King. 'A really bonzer old bastard, do anything for you. Knows these seas like the back of his hand.'

Something horrible seemed to slide down the back of Asaf's neck, only on the inside. 'Please,' he said, raising a hand feebly, 'reassure me. Tell me we haven't hitched a lift with Sinbad the Sailor.'

'You know Simbo?'

'Heard of him,' Asaf muttered. 'But—'

'Simbo and me,' the King went on, 'we go way back. Me and old Simbo . . .'

Asaf lay back on the deck and covered his face with the edge of a redundant sail. 'I think I'd like to go to sleep now,' he said. 'And if I don't wake up, never mind.'

'But—'

'Look!' Asaf sat bolt upright, and stabbed the King in the

left pectoral with his forefinger. The scales, he noticed in passing, were harder than his fingernail. 'This time last week,' he said, 'I was content. Not happy, but content. I had a sleazy little hovel with a hole in the roof, my own poxy little business that wasn't going anywhere, fish three times a day, some grubby old clothes, several people I hadn't borrowed money off yet. I was content. And then you turn up, with your bloody three wishes—'

'Steady on, mate . . .'

'I will not steady on!' Asaf shouted. 'Take me home again, now. And that's a wish.'

The King sighed, filling the hold with damp green steam. 'I know what it is,' he said, 'you're hungry. A bit of good honest tucker inside you and you'll be as right as—'

'NOW!'

'Sorry.'

'What?'

'No can do,' replied the King awkwardly. 'It's a bit late for all that now, mate. You should have thought about it before you came.'

'What the hell do you mean?' Asaf growled. 'You got me here, you get me out. And while we're on the subject, what the fuck was all that stuff with that damn bottle?'

'How about,' said the King – he was disappearing, fading into the pale sunlight that streaked down into the hold through an unfastened hatch – 'a nice egg and tomato sarny? Or I can do you pilchards.'

'But . . .'

The King had gone, leaving behind him a few airborne sparkles and a memory of the word 'sarny'. Overhead, the unsecured hatch slammed shut, and Asaf heard the sound of bolts shooting home. He sat for a moment, speechless with rage and confusion. Then he shrugged, folded the corner of sail into a pillow and lay down.

'I hate pilchards!' he shouted, and closed his eyes.

★

And here's the latest, warbled the television, *on the nuclear tests story. And we're taking you live to our man on Pineapple Atoll. Danny, can you hear me?*

Philly Nine grinned, propped his feet on the footstool and used the handset to turn up the volume.

Loud and clear, Bob, chirruped the reporter, who had replaced the studio set on the screen. Behind him there was a view of blue skies and coconut palms. *And the latest seems to be that we now have confirmation of the existence of the giant ants. The giant ants have, in fact, been sighted. By me. I saw them.*

The reporter seized up and stood, gazing into the camera lens. After a gentle prompt from the studio, he continued.

So far, he said, *we've sighted sixteen of the giant ants. They're big, like twenty feet tall at the shoulder, and they're making a real mess of the landscape, I can tell you. Also, attempts to deal with them by way of aerial dusting with ant powder and dive-bomb attacks with kettles of boiling water have proved basically futile. A spokesman for the World Wildlife Fund who chained himself to the leg of one ant in protest against these culling attempts has been eaten, but otherwise there are no reports of casualties.*

It was the studio's turn to say something, but nothing was said. The reporter, by now smiling disconcertingly, continued.

More importantly, the diplomatic exchanges over how these ants came to mutate so drastically is really beginning to hot up. I think all the superpowers are now in agreement that the mutation was caused by clandestine nuclear weapons tests, although I should add that there haven't been any seismic readings to confirm this theory. Where everyone seems to disagree is over who actually did the test. In fact, everybody is accusing everybody else, and the situation really is beginning to get a bit fraught. In fact, we could be looking at the end of the multilateral disarmament initiative here, so for anybody out there with a redundant coal-cellar, the message is, start taking bookings now, because . . .

As the screen hurriedly reverted to the studio set, Philly Nine lay back in his chair, closed his eyes and smiled.

I did that, he told himself smugly, with my little hatchet.

WHOOOOOOSH!

The carpet streaked across the sky like a flat, embroidered meteor, skimming off satellite dishes and the older pattern of weather-vane as it went by sheer force of air displacement. The wonderful aerial view available over its side was wasted on Jane, who was lying flat on her face clinging on to two clenched handfuls of carpet. Justin had blacked out.

'Where to, lady?'

Jane looked up, received an eyeful of fast-moving air and ducked down again. However, she saw enough in the fraction of a second's viewing time she had before the air-blast sandpapered her eyeballs to confirm to herself that there was nobody else on the damn rug but herself and the wimp. The voice was, therefore, entirely her imagination.

'No, I'm not. I'm your automatic pilot for what I hope will prove to be a relaxing and pleasurable flight to the destination of your choice.'

'Bugger off.'

'Pardon me?'

'I said bugger off,' Jane barked over the howling of the turbulence. 'I know you're just a hallucination inside my head, and I'm not standing for it. Go on, hop it, before I set my subconscious on to you.'

There was a pause. If it's possible for a pause to sound hurt, it did.

'You're the boss,' said the voice (and for some reason, it didn't have to shout; it was as clear as a bell over the background noise). 'However, I feel I should point out that I'm not in any way a figment of your imagination. If it helps you to relate better, you can call me George.'

Jane set her jaw firmly. She refused absolutely to be drawn into conversation with her own unbalanced mind sitting on a flying rug doing close on Mach One at just above rooftop level over Croydon. Especially a part of her own unbalanced mind called George. Never lower your standards for anyone, as her mother used to say.

'To explain,' George continued. 'The rectangular object you took to be a book is in fact a state-of-the-art carpet navigation system, compatible with all leading designs of magic floor coverings. Once installed on the carpet of your choice, the system automatically activates the carpet's propulsion and guidance systems, and receives directional input direct from your brainwave patterns by telepathic interfacing, made possible by our revolutionary fifth-generation textile chip technology. You said get me out of here fast, so . . .'

'I did?'

'You thought it,' George corrected itself. 'And that's good enough for me. Your wish is my—'

'NO!' Jane howled. 'Not another one!'

'Pardon me?'

'Look.' In her wrath, Jane knelt upright, oblivious to the enormous volume of nothing directly below. 'I have had it up to here with bloody genies, all right? My wish is *not* your bloody command. To hear is *not* to obey, O mistress. Got that?'

'We copy.'

'Good. Now get me down off this bloody contraption, fast as you like.'

George said nothing. The carpet continued flying straight and level, only appreciably faster. Had Jane been in the mood, she could have glanced down and seen an Alp, real close.

'Are you deaf or something?'

'On the contrary,' replied George affably. 'All our products have new enhanced sensor capability uprated to provide for instantaneous spoken inputting. This feature alone—'

'Then do as you're told and put me *down!*'

'Sorry.'

For a count of maybe three Jane was, literally, speechless; partly because she was so angry she couldn't speak, partly because something small and airborne flew into her open mouth, and the momentum of the collision nearly knocked her over the side. She struggled to her knees again and thumped the carpet with her fist.

'What d'you mean, sorry? I told you—'

'You told me,' George interrupted, 'that your wish was not my command, and that when I heard I shouldn't obey. You got it?'

'But look, I didn't mean . . .'

'Sorry. But you're the sentient being, I'm only a computerised guidance system. Policy formulation's down to you.' George paused, as if for effect. 'You guys are supposed to be *good* at that.'

'But . . .'

'Further clarification,' George continued, as they missed one snow-capped peak by a few thousandths of an inch, 'would, however, be appreciated. For example, when you say something, do you want me to ignore it completely or do the exact opposite?'

Jane blinked twice. 'Do the opposite,' she said quickly. '*Don't* put me down. Fly *faster.*'

'Thanks.'

The carpet flew on: same course, same momentum, Jane screamed and clouted it with the heel of her shoe.

'Just checking,' said George. 'You told me to do the exact opposite, I'm programmed to disobey all orders, therefore I ignore you. That right?'

'No. Yes. Both.'

'Thank you.'

The carpet flew on.

Kiss sat bolt upright. He felt as if a truck had just ploughed into the back of his neck.

Someone was calling him – someone frightened, in danger, in need of protection. No prizes for guessing who.

Bloody woman!

Moon of his delight, entrancing vision of sublime love-liness who gave a purpose to his existence, yes; but bloody woman nevertheless. What, he asked himself bitterly as he searched for his left shoe, has she gone and done now? Locked herself out of her car? Forgotten which level of the multi-storey she'd parked on? Something, he felt sure, like that.

Without dawdling, but without unduly frantic haste either, he dressed and put on his curly-toed shoes. As if, he muttered, he didn't have enough to do. Clean handkerchief. Where in buggery are the clean handkerchieves?

Let there be clean handkerchieves. Problem solved.

Not, he added, that we'll be able to do *that* for much longer. Oh no. And who'll come whizzing along across the tops of the clouds then whenever she's at the station and wondering whether she's left the gas on?

Pausing only to collect the milk off the doorstep, he somersaulted up into the sky, looped the loop and traipsed away through the empyrean.

Jane looked up.

On a scale of one to ten of Sensible Things To Do, that was maybe a Two; above putting your hand in a moving circular saw or enrolling in law school, but definitely below, say, investing in gilt-edged stock or leaving a burning oil refinery. She regretted it almost immediately.

Before the regret set in, however, making her stomach turn over like a well-tossed pancake and tightening her intestines into a small knot, she saw a broad, gently undulating expanse of sand. It might have been a beach somewhere, except that beaches tend to have blue edges, and this lot didn't. In fact, it didn't seem to have any edges whatsoever.

The desert.

Which desert, Jane neither knew nor cared. All that registered with her as relevant information was that she was probably a very long way from Haywards Heath.

'Help,' she said.

Said rather than screamed; she was, at heart, a reasonably practical person, and there was nobody who could help her as far as the eye could see. That was assuming that Justin, who was beginning to come round, wasn't likely to be much use. On the basis of her experience of him so far, that seemed a pretty safe assumption.

Now then, she reassured herself, don't let's go all to pieces. Kiss'll be along in a moment, he'll switch this blasted thing off and we can all go home. My wish is his command, after all. And, she remembered, it was his bloody gadget that got her into this mess in the first place.

Having nothing better to do, she reflected for a while on that. Of all the stupid, careless things to do, she mused, leaving something like that lying about. She looked at the device, which was sitting smugly on the top edge of the carpet. Perfectly reasonable to assume that it was a book. It looked exactly like a book: pages, spine, covers, the works. What sort of an idiot leaves something like that lying around, just begging innocent passers-by to pick it up and leave it on carpets?

Not, she added quickly, that she didn't worship the

ground he stood on (or, to be accurate, more usually hovered about six inches over); but that was either here nor there. Being absolutely adorable and gorgeous is no excuse for rank carelessness. She'd have a word or two to say to him when he finally condescended to show up.

Yes, and where in blazes was he, anyway? Genies, she felt sure, were capable of moving from A to B at the speed of light; and here she had been, for what seemed like hours and hours, stuck on top of a fast-moving flying tapestry over a desert. She'd have expected prompter service from the electricity board.

'Grrng,' said Justin.

It was, as far as she could remember, the most sensible thing he'd said since she'd met him. She turned round, smiled, and said, 'It's all right.'

Justin blinked and lifted his head. 'The shop,' he said. 'Uncle.'

'Everything's under control,' Jane said, as reassuringly as she could. 'One of your carpets took off, with us on it, and I think we're over a desert somewhere, but my genie'll be along in a minute and he'll take us home. So long as you don't look down . . .'

Justin, of course, looked down.

'AAAAAAAAAGH!' he observed.

'Well, quite,' Jane said, 'my sentiments exactly, but there's no need to worry, honestly. You see, it's a magic carpet.'

'A ma—'

'Or at least,' Jane amended, 'it is now. I put a book on it, you see.' She turned up the smile a notch or so. 'I expect we'll all have a jolly good laugh about this as soon as we get back home again.'

'Your *genie*?'

'That's right,' Jane replied. 'No, don't back away, you'll fall off the edge.' The carpet wobbled vertiginously as Justin converted his shuffle backwards into a lunge forward. 'There now, you just lie still and everything will be—'

'Put me down,' Justin said, with a degree of urgency in his voice. 'Put me down put me down put me *down*!'

The carpet juddered slightly.

'Your wish is my command, O Master.'

Suddenly the world was at thirty degrees to itself, and Jane felt herself slide forward. The book, also; it flopped over and was just about to plummet over the side when Jane, stretching full length, managed to catch it. She wasn't sure she understood any of this at all, but it seemed reasonable to assume that if the book fell off the carpet would lose its supernatural capacity and turn back into an ordinary domestic floor covering. And ordinary domestic floor coverings as a rule don't fly.

'Ah,' said Jane. 'You again.'

'Mistress.'

'Look, I know we got off on rather the wrong foot back there in the shop,' said Jane, 'but I think it might be a good idea if we made friends and started again, don't you? Before we fly into a cliff or something.'

'There are no cliffs on our projected route, Mistress.'

'Look ... Look, forget about cliffs. Just don't take any orders from him, all right? He's not quite ...'

'Mistress?'

Justin was staring at her, wondering perhaps why she was talking to the carpet. Could he even hear the bloody thing, she wondered. 'All right,' she whispered, 'you do it your way. Only for pity's sake, do look where you're going.'

'Our fully automated guidance systems,' replied the carpet huffily, 'are computer-aligned to ensure a comfortable, incident-free itinerary. State-of-the-art LCD displays let you know at a glance—'

'LOOK OUT!'

The carpet swerved viciously, just in time to avoid the

ground. Jane opened her eyes again, to see the carpet apparently on top of her. And then, after a heart-stopping roll, underneath her again.

'Sorry. I mean, systems error.'

'Shut up and fly.'

'To hear is to—'

There was an uncomfortable twentieth of a second.

'Don't,' Jane hissed, 'even consider it.'

'But you said—'

'I'm warning you.'

'Your express wish,' said the carpet, flustered, 'was that I ignore anything you tell me to do. Your wish is my command. Oh, *sugar!*'

The carpet hurtled groundwards. Jane shrieked.

'Mistress?'

'Don't worry about it,' Jane said quickly. 'When I said look out, you ignored me. Very sensibly, however, and quite independently of anything I may have coincidentally said, you decided not to crash and took appropriate action. Got that?'

'Yes, Mistress,' said the carpet gratefully. 'Although strictly speaking I should ignore that too.'

'You just try it.'

'Sorry?' said the carpet. 'Did you just say something?'

The carpet levelled, and Jane patted a hem. 'That's the spirit,' she said.

'Excuse me.'

Jane looked round and saw Justin, clinging with both hands, his face buried in the pile. 'Yes?'

'I don't want to be a nuisance,' Justin mumbled through the fabric, 'but do you think we can go home soon? Uncle will be . . .'

Jane wasn't listening. She was looking, unbelievably, down.

'Gosh,' she said.

Underneath the carpet was the sea – a huge, flat blue spread, extending from horizon to horizon. Jane considered for a moment.

'If we jump,' she said aloud, 'we'll land in the sea.'

'I can't swim.'

'I can. And you've got to learn sometime.'

'Why?'

'Because ...' Jane searched her mind for a reason. 'Because it'd be very handy if, for instance, you were sitting on a carpet miles above the surface of the sea and somebody were to push you off.'

'Who'd do a thing like ?'

'That depends,' Jane said firmly, 'on how co-operative you were being at the time.'

You would think, reflected Asaf bitterly, that after escaping from a small glass bottle, escaping from a ship ought to be a piece of cake. Not a bit of it.

Wearily, he lifted the cask of nails above his head and tried once again to use it to smash through the battened hatch. By dint of ferocious effort he managed to deal a featherweight biff to the objective before his arms crumpled and the cask fell heavily onto the deck at his feet, narrowly missing his toes.

For one thing, his thoughts continued, although I didn't know it at the time, I probably had help getting out of the bottle – well, I definitely got help – whereas they want to keep me on the ship. Also, he couldn't help reflecting, the bottle hadn't been surrounded by deep, cold water; and the ship was.

That is, he parenthesised, always supposing I actually *am* on a ship and this isn't all some sort of tiresome meta-physical illusion, the sort of thing Captain Kirk and the crew of the *Enterprise* seem to spend most of their working hours in. The bottle now, that probably was an illusion.

Bloody small illusion; and they might have had the decency to illude the ink out first. Then again, he was beginning to feel that whoever was doing all this to him had a fairly limited imagination.

Sinbad the Sailor, for crying out loud. Whatever next. Puss in Boots?

Now then. Be practical. This is a ship. I am a fisherman, I'm at home on ships. Ships hold no terrors for me . . .

Not strictly accurate. During his fishing career the only ship he'd ever been on was his father's vessel, and that wasn't a ship, it was a boat. Definitely a boat. And as between that boat and this ship, there were many significant differences. There wasn't any water coming up through the floor, for example; likewise, you could scratch your ear on board this thing without the risk of hitting someone in the eye with your elbow.

However, he rationalised, all sea-going craft have certain things in common. Not that he could think of anything offhand that might be of use to him; but he felt sure he was somewhere on the right lines, pursuing this . . .

The ship moved.

More than that; it seemed to jump up in the air. Leaping about is, of course, something that ships as a rule simply don't do (ask any fisherman); but since this was probably an illusion anyway, Asaf wasn't prepared to be dogmatic about anything. Right now, he'd have settled for an illusion that wasn't showering articles of displaced cargo on his head.

He was just struggling out from under a crate of some description which had fallen on him, soliloquising eloquently as he did so, when he noticed the light. A lovely great shaft of sunlight, slanting in through a now open hatch.

Told you, he muttered to himself. Told you it'd be a piece of cake.

★

'Now then,' Jane said, treading water, 'the first thing I'd like you to do is kick with your feet.'

'Aaaaaaagh!'

'It's all right, I've got hold of your neck, you can't – oh, bother.' She kicked hard and managed to get Justin's chin clear of the water. 'Now if you'd have done what I told you—'

'Help!' Justin screamed. 'Help help help heblublublublub . . .'

'You're not trying, are you?' Jane said wearily. 'Look, it's really very simple, any child can do it. You just paddle with your feet, and let your body sort of float . . .'

Jane suddenly realised that she was in shadow, and glanced upwards. There, directly over her head, was the carpet.

'Your wish,' it said politely, 'is my command.'

Jane scowled. 'I thought I'd told you to clear off,' she said.

'I wasn't,' the carpet replied, 'talking to you.'

'What? Oh. Oh you mean him.'

'*Help!*'

'Yes,' said the carpet. 'His wish, my command. So if you'd just shift over a bit, I can—'

'What about me?'

'What about you?'

Jane spluttered as a wave flipped a cupful of salt water into her open mouth. 'You've changed your tune a bit, haven't you?' she observed. 'Not long ago it was all "Our state-of-the-art microcircuitry, designed to make life easy for you".'

'That was different,' the carpet replied severely. 'I was in user-friendly mode then. Now I can please myself.'

'Charming.'

'You're welcome. Now, are you going to shift so that I can rescue my client, or are we going to hang about here all day chatting?'

'You're just going to ignore me, then?'

The carpet shrugged; that is to say, it undulated from its front hem backwards. 'That's what you told me to do, remember? Do you people understand the concept of consistency?'

'Help help *he*glugluglug . . .'

Jane bit her tongue. 'Tell you what I'll do,' she said. 'I'll let you rescue him if you agree to rescue me too. Now you can't say fairer than that, can you?'

The carpet hovered for a moment, thinking.

'I also,' Jane added, as casually as she could, 'happen to know a Force Twelve genie, and I was thinking, if he got hold of one of those carpet-beater things, you know, the ones shaped like a tennis racket . . .'

'All right then, all aboard that's coming aboard. I can take you as far as the ship.'

'Ship? What ship?' Then Jane remembered. 'Oh,' she said. 'That ship.'

That ship. The quaint old-fashioned one with the big square sails which they ought by rights to have crashed straight down on top of, if it hadn't somehow moved a hundred yards sideways at the very last moment. She'd forgotten all about it.

'Well?'

'That,' Jane said, 'will be just fine.'

ELEVEN

The reason why Kiss hadn't shown up yet was that he'd bumped into an old friend.

'Why the hell,' said Philly Nine, picking himself up off a bank of low cloud, 'don't you look where you're damn well . . . oh, it's you.'

'Hello there,' Kiss replied. 'How's you?'

'Oh, mustn't grumble. And you?'

'Persevering. Keeping busy?'

'Mooching about, you know. Nothing terribly exciting, but enough to keep me off the streets.'

'Ah, well. Is that a war I can see starting away down there?'

Philly turned and peered over his shoulder through the thin layer of cumulo-nimbus. 'Where?' he asked.

'Sort of south-east. Look, you see that mountain range to your immediate right? Well, follow that down till you meet the river, and . . .'

'Got it,' Philly said. 'Gosh, yes, it does look a bit like a war, doesn't it? Tanks and planes and things.'

Kiss gave him a long, hard look. 'One of yours, Philly?' he asked quietly.

'Gosh, what is it today, Thursday . . . Oh, *that* war. Yes, well, I may have had something to do with it.'

'You and your obsessive modesty.'

Philly shrugged. Far below, in the vast deserts of Mesopotamia, fleets of armoured personnel carriers speeding across the dunes threw up clouds of dust that blotted out the sun. 'It's only a little war,' Philly said.

'Small but perfectly formed?'

'One likes to keep one's hand in.'

Kiss frowned. 'Like I said, Philly, you're too modest. Why do you do it exactly?'

'Why do I do what?'

'Start wars. I mean, is there some sort of annual award for the best war, like the Oscars or whatever? First of all I'd like to thank my megalomaniac fascist dictator, that sort of thing?'

Philly smiled, a little sadly. 'It's what I do,' he replied.

'You're very good at it. Have they started shooting yet?'

Philly glanced at his watch and shook his head. 'Two abortive peace initiatives to go yet,' he answered. 'Give it another couple of hours, we might be in business. Things are so damn *slow* these days.'

Kiss fingered his chin thoughtfully. 'This war,' he said. 'Going to lead to anything, is it?'

'I do my best,' Philly replied. 'If you don't do your best, why bother to do anything at all?'

'I see. So it might be the start of something, well, big?'

'Fingers crossed.'

'Civilisation as we know it? Goodbye, Planet Earth?'

Philly smiled. 'Great oaks and little acorns, old son,' he said cheerfully. 'You never know.'

'Fine.' Kiss took a step forward. 'I hate to have to say this, but—'

'But you can't allow it?' Philly grinned at him. 'If I were you, I'd consider all aspects of the matter rather than relying on a snap judgement.'

'All aspects of global thermonuclear war are easily considered, Philly, and I don't hold with them. Cut it out, now.'

'Think,' Philly replied. 'Supposing the world is destroyed, right?'

'With you so far.'

'Well.' Philly Nine folded his arms. 'In that case, there's no way you'd have to marry that girl. Off the hook, you'd be, and absolutely nothing anybody could do about it. Just consider that for a moment, will you?'

There was a long moment of silence.

'Now you'll tell me,' Philly went on, 'that I'm contemplating something of a hammer-and-nut situation here. On the other hand, I can think of one hell of a lot of married men who'd say this was a classic case of omelettes and eggs. No disrespect intended, Kiss, old son, and I'm sure she's a charming girl, but when you actually stop and think it through . . .'

Kiss froze, his lips parted to speak in contradiction. Deep inside him, in the cubbyhole in his soul where his true identity lived (knee-deep in washing up and dirty laundry, overflowing ashtrays and discarded styrofoam pizza trays) a little voice piped up and said, *You know, he's got a point there, over.*

Balls, replied the rest of him. This is the temptation of the foul fiend. Rule One, don't listen to foul fiends. Any pillock knows that, over.

Yes, but think about it, will you? Not having to stop being a genie. To thine own self be true. Love means not being allowed to take your socks off in the living room. You would do well to consider all the pertinent aspects of the matter before committing yourself to any course of action, over.

Bugger off, over.

Yes, well, don't say I didn't warn you. Over and out.

'I hear what you say,' Kiss said, 'But no thanks, all the same. I reckon that if I can't sort out my domestic problems without conniving at Armageddon it'd be a pretty poor show – and besides, I live here. And you know what a drag it is finding somewhere decent to live these days. Carbon-based life forms don't grow on trees, you know.'

'Suit yourself, then,' Philly replied, and hit him with a thunderbolt.

'G'day.'

Asaf spun on his heel, missed his footing on the wet deck and sprawled against the mast, barking his shin.

'You again,' he snapped. 'I thought I'd seen the last of you.'

The Dragon King, hovering in a cloud of purple smoke, looked offended. 'Lighten up, cobber,' he replied. 'I'm a dragon, remember? And dragons don't bludge on their mates. She'll be right, you'll see.'

'What the hell are you talking about, you insufferable reptile?'

'Look, mate.' The Dragon King contracted his formidable eyebrows, until he looked for all the world like a bejewelled privet hedge. 'No offence, but I reckon I've had about enough of your whingeing for one adventure, thank you very much.' He nodded towards the sky. 'That sheila,' he continued. 'She's on her way.'

Asaf blinked. 'The rich one?' he asked.

The King nodded. 'Too right,' he replied. 'In fact, she should be along any minute now. So let's have a bit less of the complaints, right?'

'Right.' Asaf frowned. 'You're sure about that?' he queried. 'I mean, we are in the middle of the sea. I don't really see where she's going to . . .'

WHOOSH.

The carpet zagged down like a turbocharged pigeon, braked in mid-air and hovered. God knows how it managed it, but it somehow gave the impression that it had an invisible meter, and that it was running.

Jane opened her eyes. If the truth be told, she wasn't one hundred per cent taken with what she saw.

She appeared to have come to rest half-way through a dragon; in fact she was wearing the bloody thing round her neck, like a horse collar.

Now that, she said to herself, really is uncalled for. God knows, I've tried to be reasonable throughout this whole nightmarish business, nobody can say I haven't given it my best shot, but this really is . . .

The dragon was floating about ten feet above the deck of the ship; as was the carpet, which appeared to have come to rest half in and half out of the dragon's right shoulder. Seen close to, the dragon looked as solid as a Welsh full-back, but Jane couldn't feel anything there. Probably, she decided, just as well.

The dragon's head pivoted slowly on its long, elegant neck and turned towards her.

'G'day,' it said. 'Asaf, this is Jane. Jane, Asaf.'

Jane glanced down and saw that there was indeed a human being on the deck of the ship – a youngish man with a mop of black hair and a prominent nose, wearing a green anorak. He seemed to be staring at her in, well, disbelief.

'You're joking,' he said.

The dragon appeared disconcerted at this. 'No, mate, straight up. Get stuck in.' It winked a round blue eye.

'No way,' the man said angrily. 'If you think I've come all this way . . .'

'Don't you come the raw prawn with me, mate,' the dragon replied irritably. 'Jeez, what's a bloke got to do before you're satisfied?' He scowled, and mouthed the words *Loads of money* . . . The man shook his head.

'Money,' he said firmly, 'isn't everything. Look, is there some sort of ombudsman I can take this up with, because—'

'Excuse me,' said Jane.

'Ombudsman!' growled the dragon. 'You take the flamin' biscuit, you do. When I think of some of the stringy old dogs—'

Yes, but just look, will you? There's absolutely no way—'

'Excuse me.'

'Scheherezade,' continued the dragon, 'had a face on her that'd curdle milk. You don't know when you're well-off, mate.'

'I am definitely going to complain to *someone* and when I've finished with you, you'll be lucky to get a job swimming round and round in a small glass bowl—'

'Excuse me,' said Jane, 'but I think your ship is sinking.'

'You keep out of this,' snapped Asaf. 'Now then, I don't propose wasting any more breath on you. I shall be seeking legal advice on this, and—'

'Stone the crows, mate, she's right. Hey, there's water coming up through the—'

'Don't change the subject. My brother happens to be an accountant and I reckon we're looking at breach of contract, breach of statutory duty, trespass to the person and a bloody great claim in respect of pain, suffering, inconvenience, loss of earnings . . .'

'Bugger me, she's about to split. You want to get out of there quick, I'm telling you . . .'

'. . . false imprisonment, failure to report an accident, fraud, dangerous flying . . .'

'Look . . .'

The ship sank.

Funny, the way some ships just go under all of a sudden. Others hang around for days, leaning over on one side and allowing the survivors plenty of time to choose their eight gramophone records from the ship's library. This one, however, just went glop! and fell through the surface of the water like a lead weight.

Sinbad the Sailor watched her go down from the comfort of the one lifeboat, and shrugged. On the one hand she had been his ship, in which he had crossed all the oceans of the world, and inevitably a part of his soul went down with her. On the other hand, he had just renewed his insurance.

The cramped living quarters, he thought. The smell of stale bilgewater. The rats. The ship's biscuits, some of which were hard enough to polish diamonds with. The crew.

As he watched the last few bubbles rise and fade, therefore, his feelings were mixed. About 40 per cent happiness, and the remaining 60 per cent pure unalloyed pleasure.

Kiss picked himself up off the clouds and snarled.

To every cloud, the wiseacres say, a silver lining. Be that as it may; this one, as far as Kiss could judge, was lined with big lumpy chunks of rock, half-bricks and the like. In his list of My All-Time Favourite Things To Land On, it didn't score highly compared with, say, feather mattresses or trampoline cushions. It was also soggy and full of water vapour.

All in all he was working up a pretty good head of aggression. And the healthiest way to vent off the perfectly natural and wholesome aggression which lies buried in all of us is, of course, to thump somebody. Ask any psychiatrist.

Fortunately, he didn't have far to look for someone to thump. Not far, and upwards.

Philly Nine looked down nervously. There was something about Kiss's demeanour, and the way the cloud he was lying on was turning into fizzing steam, that made him feel uncomfortable and uncertain about his immediate future. He decided to try diplomacy.

'Now then,' he said pleasantly, 'you don't want to be late for your date, do you?'

'Yes.'

'But think,' Philly reasoned, 'of that sweet little girl of yours, counting every second before you come swooping down to rescue her. Think of the grateful smile on her face, the words of praise, the—'

'Are we thinking of the same person?'

'What about your honour as a genie? Her wish is your command, remember.'

'When I catch you,' Kiss replied calmly, 'I'm going to rip your lungs out.'

'If you catch me,' Philly replied, and fled.

'Excuse me,' said Jane.

Asaf glanced up from the piece of driftwood he was clinging to and frowned. 'What?' he said.

'I said excuse me.'

The sea, fishermen say, is a cruel playfellow. Actually they tend to express themselves in earthier, more basic terms, but that's the gist of it. For his part, Asaf had never really come to terms with the being-surrounded-on-all-sides-by-water aspect of fishing, despite his best endeavours, and consequently wasn't really in the mood to make new friends. His tone, therefore, was abrupt.

'Piss off,' he said.

'Be like that,' Jane replied equably. 'All I was going to say was, if you wanted a lift to dry land, I can take you as far as the coast. Probably,' she added, for she was a realist.

Asaf glowered up at the carpet, hovering about three feet over the waves. 'I don't believe in you,' he growled. 'Go away.'

'Don't believe in me?'

'You heard me. You're some sort of fatuous mythical practical joke, like everything else that's been happening to me lately. On the other hand, I do believe in this piece of driftwood. It's not much, but right now it's all I've got. Sling your hook.'

'HELP!' observed Justin.

Asaf lifted his head; suddenly, he was interested. By force of circumstance he was rapidly becoming attuned to the finer nuances of adventures, and it occurred to him that not many false visions of magic carpets have shit-scared young men clinging to them yelling 'HELP!' A nice touch, he had to admit. Either that, or it wasn't a mirage after all.

'Your friend,' he said.

Jane looked round. 'Oh, him,' she said. 'Yes?'

'Is he real?'

'I think so.'

'Ask him.'

Jane shrugged. 'Excuse me,' she said.

'HELP!'

'Yes, but are you real? I mean, do you exist? Only the gentleman down there in the water . . .'

'HELP HELP HELP!'

Jane nodded and turned back again. 'I would take that as a Yes,' she said.

'I see.' A small wave partially dislodged Asaf's grip on the driftwood and he floundered for a moment. 'That puts rather a different complexion on it, don't you think?'

'Sorry?'

'I wasn't,' Asaf replied, 'talking to you.'

'Oh.'

The Dragon King, who had drifted back into existence a few inches above the wave-tops, wiped his mouth on the back of his paw and nodded. 'Too right, mate,' he said. 'Sorry, forgetting me manners. You fancy a cold one?'

'Not now.' Asaf gave him a cold stare. 'Look, for once be straight with me. Are those two for real?'

'You bet your life.'

'That,' Asaf replied, 'is what I'm rather hoping I won't have to do.'

'Yes,' said the King, 'they're real. And by the way,' he

added in a whisper, 'that's her.'

'We'll discuss that later. Now, how do I get on that thing without it tipping over?'

'She'll be right mate, no worries. Just take a jump at it, and . . .'

Splash.

'Thanks,' said Asaf.

'That's all right,' Jane replied, preoccupied. She was wondering how the hell she'd managed to get the carpet to swoop low over where Asaf had landed in the water and scoop him up with its front hem. Pretty snazzy rug-handling, by any standards. And she couldn't remember what it was that she'd done.

Asaf cleared his throat diffidently. 'You said something,' he mumbled, 'about dry land.'

'Yes.'

'Well, if it wouldn't be too much trouble . . .'

'It'd be a pleasure,' Jane replied. 'Any dry land in particular?'

Like a blue crack in the firmament, a long streak of lightning snaked its way across the sky and earthed itself savagely in Kiss's neck, hurling him seven miles through the air. There was a loathsome smell of singed flesh.

Thirty-fifteen.

Roaring with pain and fury, Kiss reached up into the air and grabbed a handful of cloud. As soon as it touched his hand the water vapour froze, until the genie was clutching the hardest, most fearsome snowball in history. He whirled round three times and let fly. On the other side of the horizon, hidden from sight by the curvature of the earth, someone howled.

Thirty-all.

'You as well?' Jane said.

Asaf was about to express surprise, but thought better of it. Think about it logically, he told himself. Perfectly normal seeming young woman and wimp, floating about on carpet above the Indian Ocean. Reasonable to assume that they were in the same sort of fix as he was.

'Me as well,' he replied. 'I've got this confounded bloody nuisance of a Dragon King who's giving me three wishes.'

'I've got a genie,' Jane said, making it sound like some sort of horrible illness. 'Wretched, isn't it?'

'Absolutely. My name's Asaf, by the way?'

'Jane. Pleased to meet you.'

Asaf settled himself rather more comfortably on the carpet. 'There I was,' he said, 'minding my own business . . .'

'I was about to kill myself, when this Thing jumped out of a bottle . . .'

'. . . Dragged me half-way across the bloody continent . . .'

'. . . His wish was my command, he said.'

'Really? Mine keeps saying that.'

Jane nodded. 'I think they all do. Not that it means anything.'

'Quite the opposite, in my experience,' Asaf agreed. 'So how long have you had yours?'

Jane frowned. 'I'm not quite sure,' she said, 'but it feels like absolutely for ever.'

Asaf shuddered. 'I know the feeling. And they're so damned smug about it, too.'

'Mine was supposed to rescue me,' Jane said, with a glint of anger in her voice. 'The one time I actually asked him to do something useful, and where is he?'

'To hear is to obey, I don't think,' Asaf agreed. 'Just who the hell do they think they are, anyway?'

Jane glanced at him sideways. A fellow sufferer, she thought. Nice to know I'm not the only one.

'So yours has been mucking you about, has he?' she asked.

'Don't ask.'

'We could start a victims' support group.'

Asaf thought for a moment. 'Pretty limited membership,' he said.

'Well, there's you, me and him for a start.'

'Him? Oh yes, him.'

Jane looked round at Justin, who had folded a corner of the carpet over his head and was lying very still. 'Are you all right in there?' she asked.

'Help,' Justin replied. 'I want to go home.'

'I think he's eligible for membership,' Asaf said. 'How did he get involved?'

'From what I can gather, it's his uncle's carpet.'

'Ah.' Asaf wrinkled his brow. 'Sorcerer's apprentice, you mean?'

Jane shrugged. 'I think he was just minding the store.'

'Typical.'

The mountain hung in the air for a moment, 800 feet above the ground. Then it fell.

For a fraction of a second before it hit the ground, there was a shrill scream of agony and rage. Then silence, except for the sound of Philly Nine brushing granite dust off his sleeves.

Deuce.

The dust settled. Birds began to sing again. The inhabitants of the nearby village poked their heads out of their windows, wondering why there was now a mountain in the middle of what had previously been a flat alluvial plain.

And then there was a faint humming sound a long way under the surface of the earth. It could conceivably have been a high-speed drill, or someone digging extremely fast with his bare hands.

Kiss broke through the surface like a missile launched from a submarine and soared into the air, spitting out boulders as he went. As he passed the mountain's peak, he stuck out a hand and grabbed. The mountain lifted.

'Look, grandad,' said a child in the village. 'You can see it from the window. A great big mountain, just like I said.'

Grandad, woken from his afternoon nap and not best pleased, rubbed his eyes and looked blearily through the window. 'Where?' he asked.

'Oh,' said the child. 'It was there a minute ago.'

'Hello, Bruce,' said one of Saheed's regulars. 'I thought you'd be out looking after your customer.'

The Dragon King of the South-East sneered into his glass. 'Got fed up with the whingeing little blighter and left him to get on with it,' he replied. 'I've done my bit. If the stupid bloody wowser can't find his own way to the happy ending from there, he doesn't deserve it. Fancy another?'

'Why not?'

'Mind you,' continued the King, clamping his offside rear talon firmly around the brass rail, 'I won't say it was easy. Took some doing, though I say so meself.'

'I bet.'

'There comes a time, mind,' the King went on, 'when a bloke's just got to turn round and walk away. You carry on spoon-feeding these bludgers and the next thing you know, you can't call your life your own.'

'Wretched, isn't it?'

The King nodded. 'Anyway,' he said, 'there we go. And it wasn't all crook, 'cos I was able to do a mate a favour along the way.'

'You don't say.'

The King grinned and nodded. 'Yeah. That sheila that Kiss was having so much strife with. Reckon I've offloaded her on me mark. Two birds with one stone, eh?'

'Clever.'

The King looked contentedly at the side elevation of his glass. 'Reckon so,' he said. 'Reckon he owes me a couple of cool ones next time he's in.'

'You reckon?'

'Yup.'

Advantage –

The voice hesitated. Being an ethereal spirit, with no real existence within any conventionally recognised dimension, it had no hands with which to turn the pages of the book of rules, and it couldn't quite remember the precise wording of Rule 74. A tricky one, in any event. A grey area.

In the red corner: let your mind's eye drift to a barren plateau in the very centre of the desperately bleak Nullarbor Plain, to where a huge basalt outcrop has suddenly appeared from nowhere. While the seismologists stare at each other in blank amazement, and the cartographers draw lots to see whose turn it is to go flogging out there to draw pictures of the bloody thing, a relatively tiny form whimpers and struggles directly underneath it, pinned to the deck like a butterfly to a board. That's Kiss.

In the blue corner: the equally godforsaken north-east corner of Iceland has suddenly sprouted a new and exceptionally virulent volcano, which is pumping out red-hot lava with the frantic enthusiasm of a Japanese factory on the Emperor's birthday. Up to his neck in the lava outflow is Philly Nine.

Advantage –

Excuse me . . .

YES?

Is it possible to have a draw?

SORRY?

A draw. Like, when both sides are hopelessly stalemated and it's obvious nobody's going to win. Is that allowed?

I DON'T KNOW, replied God. I'D HAVE TO LOOK THAT ONE UP.

Could you? Only I think the sooner I give a decision, the happier they'll be. It can't be much fun for either of them.

HAVE YOU TRIED TOSSING A COIN?

The voice hesitated. On the one hand, what the big guy says, goes. On the other hand, there's such a thing as professional integrity: being able to face your reflection in the shaving mirror each morning, although of course in the voice's case that was pretty much a non-starter anyway.

Actually, if you don't mind, I'd rather we went for an outright decision on this one. Or at least a draw. If that's all right by...

YOU'RE THE EXPERT. DO WHATEVER YOU THINK IS RIGHT.

OK, fine. In that case ...

JUST GIVE ME FIVE MINUTES, IF IT'S ALL THE SAME TO YOU.

Sure. Um – why?

BECAUSE IF I'M QUICK I SHOULD BE ABLE TO GET PRETTY GOOD ODDS ON A DRAW. THANKS FOR THE TIP.

Question, thought the voice. What sort of an idiot would take a bet from God? Answer: an idiot who didn't want to spend the next five million years at the bottom of the burning fiery pit, I suppose.

Um ... You're welcome.

Like a bat out of hell following a spurious short-cut, the carpet raced through the sky over Stoke-on-Trent.

'Where can I drop you?' Jane asked.

Asaf looked down. The hell with it, he said to himself, I've come this far.

'Wherever suits you,' he replied. 'I'm pretty much at a loose end at the moment, as it happens.'

'Ah,' said Jane. She bit her lip. 'Fancy a quick coffee?' she added.

Asaf considered the position and decided that, all things considered, what he hated doing most of all in all the world was deep-sea fishing.

'Sure,' he said. 'Why not?'

'What do you mean,' Kiss demanded angrily, 'she's gone?'

Sinbad the Sailor shrugged. 'I suppose she got tired of hanging about waiting for you to rescue her,' he replied. 'I mean, no disrespect, but you did take your time.'

'I got held up,' replied the genie stiffly, 'saving the world.'

'It can be a right bummer, saving the world,' Sinbad said, 'especially when nobody thanks you for it.'

'You're telling me.' The genie sighed, letting his eyes drift out across the broad ocean. 'There are times, you know, when I really wish I was still in the bottle.'

'Well, quite. You know where you are in a bottle.'

'Peaceful.'

'Nobody to tell you what to do.'

'No telephone.'

Sinbad hesitated for a moment. 'Not your old-fashioned style bottles, anyway. No Jehovah's Witnesses.'

'And no bloody women,' Kiss added. 'Here, you haven't got such a things as a bottle handy, have you?'

'Afraid not.' He blinked and looked away. 'Sorry to change the subject,' he went on, 'but about this saving the world thing you were doing.'

'Yes?'

Sinbad paused again, wondering how to put it tactfully. 'If you've saved the world,' he said cautiously, 'presumably it doesn't matter that the whole of this sea is swarming with bloody great big nuclear submarines.'

Kiss wrinkled his brow. 'Oh, shit,' he said, 'the war. I

knew I'd forgotten something.'

At the bottom of the sea, far below the parts where the divers go, even further down than the gloomy bits where the light never reaches and you get the fish that look like three-dimensional coathangers, there is a doorway. And a car park. And a garden, with benches and lanterns. And a big sign, with fairy lights:

THE LOCKER

it says; and in smaller letters:

David Rutherford Jones,
Licensed to sell wines, beers, spirits and tobacco for consumption
on or off the premises

and then, going back to the bigger type:

LINERS WELCOME

The eponymous Mr Jones was quietly changing the barrels in the cellar, reflecting on the recession and how improved computerised weather forecasting was eating the heart out of the deep-sea licensed victualling business, when he became aware of an unfamiliar noise far away overhead. He stopped what he was doing and listened.

A humming noise. Like possibly engines.

A grin fastened itself to his peculiar, barnacle-encrusted face, and he ran up the cellar steps to the bar.

'Sharon,' he yelled, 'Yvonne! Defrost the pizzas! We've got customers.'

Women, Kiss reflected as he soared Exocet-like through the darkening sky. I have had it up to here with bloody women.

And not just women, he conceded, as he swerved to avoid an airliner. Human beings generally. In fact, I'm sick to the back teeth of all the damned creepy-crawlies that hang around this poxy little dimension. Come to think of it, for two pins I'd wash my hands of the whole lot of them.

The thought had scarcely crossed his mind when he became aware of something tiny and sharp, folded into the palm of his left hand. Inspection confirmed his instinctive guess. Two pins . . .

'Shove it, Philly,' he snarled at the clouds above him. 'I'll deal with you later.'

Ah yes, the war.

No names, no pack drill. We will call the opposing parties A and B.

Army A had occupied all Europe as far east as the Bosphorus, only to find themselves stuck in a traffic jam that reached from Tashkent to Samarkand. Army B had swept up through Central Asia in the time-honoured manner and had broken through as far as Baghdad before realising they'd forgotten to switch off the gas and having to go back.

Fleet A and Fleet B were both pottering about in the Mediterranean, trying to keep out of each other's way until somebody had the courtesy to tell them what the hell was going on, exactly.

Air Force A was scrambled, on red alert, absolutely set and ready to go as soon as the rain subsided a bit. Air Force B was engaged in frantic high-level negotiations with the finance company which had repossessed its entire complement of fighter-bombers.

In other words, stalemate; at least as far as the conventional forces were concerned. Not, of course, that conventional forces count for very much these days –

In the bunker, with half a mile of rock and concrete between themselves and the surface, the Strategic First Strike Command Units of both sides were locked in a desperate struggle with forces which, they now realised, were rather beyond their abilities to manipulate

'Look,' said the controller at SFSCU/A, 'it's perfectly simple. A child could understand it. If you press this one here, while at the same time pressing this one and this one . . .'

The senior technical officer shook his head. 'That's the automatic failsafe, you idiot,' he said. 'I reckon it's got to be the little red button here. If you look at the manual . . .'

'All right, let's look at the goddamn manual. *Congratulations! You have just purchased—*'

'I think you can skip that bit.'

'Right, here we are. *To commence War press START followed by C and E. The word READY? should then appear on the monitor—*'

'There isn't a button marked START, for God's sake.'

'It must be the little red one here—'

'No, look at the diagram, that's just for when you want to set the timer . . .'

'Actually, I think that's only for the Model 2693. What *we've* got is the Model 8537 . . .'

'You could try giving it a bloody good thump. You'd be amazed how often that works.'

'How about ringing the other side? They'd probably know how to make the bloody thing work.'

'Well, actually, I think they've got the Model 9317, which has a double-disk RAM drive, so . . .'

'I wonder what this button here does?'

WHOOSH!

Lightning, they say, never strikes twice. This was true before the introduction of free collective bargaining. Nowadays, lightning tends to work to rule.

Cupid, however, is resigned to the fact that he often has to do the job on the same target several times. This doesn't bother him particularly, since he charges the same fee for a repeat and there's usually less preparatory work the second time around. In the final analysis, so long as he shoots somebody and gets paid for it, he isn't too bothered.

A long, silver-tipped round slid frictionlessly into the chamber of the Steyr-Mannlicher, and he folded down the bolt with the heel of his right hand. He centred the crosshairs of the sight, breathed fully in and half out, and . . .

Her again. God knows, he thought dispassionately as he squeezed the trigger, what they all see in her. Probably, he reflected as he ejected the spent case and chambered the next round, why they need me.

He raised the rifle and took aim. Deep breath in –

'G'day, mate. How's she coming?'

Startled, Cupid jerked involuntarily and the shot went high. A portrait of Abraham Lincoln, which for some unaccountable reason hung over the sofa in Jane's living-room, glanced down and thought, 'Gosh . . .'

'You idiot,' Cupid hissed. 'Now look what you've made me go and do.'

'Jeez, sorry, mate,' whispered the Dragon King. 'I only stopped by to see how you were making out. Didn't mean to make you jump.'

'Shut up and stay still,' Cupid snarled. He chambered the third round and tried to recover his composure.

'Always wanted to watch a top-flight pro like yourself at work,' the King continued. 'I think it's marvellous, the way you fellers—'

Cupid forced himself to relax. 'Look,' he said, 'if you don't shut up and keep still, the next one's for you. You got that?'

Since the only female in sight was Jane, the King froze as effectively as if he'd been carved from stone. Cupid closed his eyes, counted to five, and raised the rifle to his cheek.

Deep breath in. Centre the crosshairs. Half breath out, and – steady . . .

Bang.

'SWITCH THAT BLOODY THING OFF!'

The King looked suitably mortified. 'Sorry, chum, I really am, only they make me carry this damn bleeper thing, it's in case anybody needs to call me in a—'

Cupid breathed out through his nose. 'Thanks to you,' he said, 'and a freak ricochet, the microwave is now hopelessly in love with the sink unit, which in turn is besotted with the electric kettle. I hope you're satisfied.'

'I've switched it off now. Sorry.'

'You haven't got a digital watch that bleeps, have you?'

'No.'

'Ticklish throat? Feel a sneeze coming on?'

'Nope.'

'Splendid. Now, since I happen to have one shot left, perhaps we can get on with it.'

Chamber the round. Lift the rifle. Centre the crosshairs. Deep breath in. Half breath out. Cuddle the trigger, and –

'Nice one!' exclaimed the King. 'Right up the—'

'I was aiming,' Cupid sighed, 'for the heart. But it doesn't actually matter all that much, not in the long run.'

'That's all right then,' said the King happily. 'Now, will you take a cheque?'

What Cupid didn't realise was that one of his shots – the one that nailed Abe Lincoln, for what it's worth – rebounded off the edge of the frame and ended its journey in the carpet. *The* carpet.

Carpets, especially the sentient, magical variety, are no fools. The specimen in question had been dozing quietly in front of the fire, resting after an unusually taxing day, when it became aware that someone was shooting at it. It did what any sensible item of soft furnishing would have done in the circumstances, and got the hell out of there.

For the record, it still had Justin on it. The negative Gs generated in the descent from 40,000 feet had knocked him out cold, and Jane and Asaf had been too wrapped up in each other to pay him any mind.

The carpet, then, zoomed off into the empyrean and kept going. As it flew, however, it found itself reflecting on its life so far, with particular reference to its solitary nature and the lack, to date, of sympathetic female companionship.

(We use the term female in this context for convenience only. Technically, what the carpet was longing for was companionship of the inverse-weft variety; but for all practical purposes, it amounts to the same thing.)

It was just beginning to feel sad and moody when something whizzed past its hem, leaving behind a blurred memory of a sleek cylindrical body and a tantalising whiff of perfume.

'Cor!' thought the carpet. 'That was a bit of all right.'

It did a double flip and followed the object's vapour trail.

What it was in fact following was an M43 ballistic missile with a 700-megaton warhead, launched after half an hour of frantic debate in the B-team bunker when the assistant scientific officer rested his coffee cup on the instrument panel.

The carpet sped on through the sky, established visual contact and fell hopelessly in love.

'Hi,' it said, swooping down parallel with the missile and shooting its hems. 'My name's Vince. What's a gorgeous metallic tube like you doing in a place like this?'

The missile made no reply, but there was a twinkling of LED readouts on its console that might be equated with a fluttering of eyelashes.

'Like the tail-fins,' the carpet persevered. 'They suit you.'

The rocket slowed down, ever so slightly. A product of

ninth-generation missile technology, the M43 is officially classed as semi-intelligent, presumably so that it feels at home in the company of military personnel. It's intelligent enough, at least, to recognise a basic chat-up line when it hears one. When you're an instrument of mass destruction, however, you don't tend to get many offers. Public executioners, lawyers and people who work for the Revenue tend to have the same problem.

The rocket bleeped.

'Say,' said the carpet, as suavely as a piece of knotted wool can manage. 'How about you and me grabbing a bite to eat somewhere? I happen to know this little place . . .'

The other nuclear missile, fired by Side A, shot over Kiss's head, neatly parting his hair with its slipstream.

Pausing only to use profane language, the genie hurried after it, caught it with his left hand and disarmed it with his right. He did so deftly, confidently and with the minimum of fuss, because the very worst epitaph the Planet Earth could wish for would be 'Butterfingers!'

Having programmed it to carry on into a harmless orbit, he sat down on a sunbeam and recovered from the retrospective shakes. A sense of humour was one thing but this time, in his opinion, Philly Nine had gone too far.

'Want to make something of it?' Philly demanded, materialising directly over his left shoulder.

'Oh, come on,' Kiss replied wearily. 'We've been here already, remember? Beating the shit out of each other with mountains, chasing about across the sky, all that crap. I'm really not in the mood.'

'Tough,' replied Philly Nine. 'Because I am.'

Kiss frowned. 'You are, are you?'

Philly nodded. 'Because,' he amplified, 'you're starting to get on my nerves. Nothing personal, you understand.'

With exaggerated effort, Kiss stood up. 'Has it occurred

to you,' he said, 'that since we're both Force Twelve genies, there's absolutely no way either of us can beat the other?'

'Yes. I don't care.'

'You don't?'

'No.'

Kiss scratched his head. 'You wouldn't prefer to settle this by reference to some sort of game of chance, thereby introducing a potentially decisive random element?'

'Not really. Two reasons. One, you'd cheat. Two, I want to bash your head in, and drawing lots would deprive me of the opportunity.'

'I wouldn't cheat.'

'Says you.'

'When have I ever cheated at anything?'

'Hah! Can you spare half an hour?'

'I resent that.'

'You were supposed to.'

The light bulb beloved of cartoonists lit up in Kiss's head. 'It's no good trying to provoke me,' he said. 'Sticks and stones may break my bones . . .'

'Good, I'd like to try that.'

'You know what your trouble is, Philly? You're unregenerate.'

'That's probably the nicest thing anybody's ever said about me.'

'It needn't be drawing lots, you know. We could try cutting a pack of cards, or throwing dice. Or snakes and ladders. Best of five games. Wouldn't that be more fun than scurrying round trying to nut each other with granite outcrops?'

'No.'

'Sure?'

'Positive.'

Kiss grinned. Blessed, he'd read on the back of a cornflake packet once, are the peacemakers, and he'd done his best. That, he felt, qualified him for the moral high ground; and the nice thing about the moral high ground was being able to chuck rocks off it on to the heads of the unregenerate bastards down below.

'In that case . . .' he said.

'You're not going to believe it,' muttered a technician in Bunker A, 'but one of our missiles has gone off.'

'What?' The Controller swivelled round in his chair. 'And I missed it?'

'Presumably. You can't remember pressing anything marked FIRE, can you?'

'Just my bloody luck,' grumbled the Controller. 'We start World War Three, and I miss it. That's a real bummer, that is. It would have been something to tell my grandchildr . . .'

He tailed off as the inherent contradiction hit him. The other inhabitants of the bunker shrugged.

'Never mind,' said the wireless operator. 'We've got plenty more where that one came from. Now, try and remember what it was that you did, exactly.'

'More wine,' breathed the carpet heavily. 'Go on, let's finish off the bottle.'

The atomic bomb shook its warhead. Nuclear weapons aren't accustomed to intoxicating liquor, and it was starting to see double. All it wanted right now was to go home and sleep it off.

'A brandy, then? Coffee? We could go back to my place and have a coffee.'

It occurred to the bomb that if it showed up back at the silo with its exhaust residues smelling of drink, it would have some explaining to do. It nodded, and lurched against the table for support. Suddenly it didn't feel too well.

'Waiter,' said the carpet, 'the bill, please.'

The waiter was there instantly, assuring the carpet that

this one was on the house, and could it please take its friend somewhere else quickly, because . . .

The bomb hiccuped. Geiger counters on three continents danced a tarantella. The waiter threw himself under the table and started to pray.

Cautiously, the bomb got up and promptly fell over. Fortunately for generations of cartographers yet unborn, it fell into the carpet, which lifted gracefully into the air and flew away.

Justin chose that particular moment to wake up.

He opened his eyes. Next to him, he noticed, there was a big black cylindrical thing, like a cross between a sea-lion and a fire extinguisher. There was stencilled writing on its side: THIS WAY UP and HANDLE LIKE EGGS and DANGER! The casing was warm.

The shop! He remembered about the shop. He glanced at his watch; Uncle would be home by now, and he'd be absolutely livid. He had to get back to the shop as quickly as possible.

'Excuse me,' he said.

The carpet frowned at him; that is to say, some of the more intricate woven motifs seemed to crowd more closely together.

'Not now,' it hissed. 'Can't you see I've got company?'

'We've got to get back to the shop,' Julian said. 'Now.'

'That's all right,' the carpet replied in a loud whisper. 'That's exactly where we're going right now. Be there in about five minutes.'

Julian breathed a sigh of relief and snuggled up closer to the warm flank of the ICBM, which had started to tick.

'That's all right, then,' he said.

TWELVE

Never in the history of superhuman conflict have two Force Twelves ever tried to fight it out to the bitter end.

Generally speaking, they've got more sense. They know that it's next best thing to impossible – nothing is definitively impossible in an infinite Universe, but there's such a thing as so nearly completely impossible that even an insurance company would bet on it never happening – for either participant to kill the other, or even put him out of action for more than a minute or so. It's a simple fact that, in this dimension at least, genies can't be killed or injured, although they can of course do a hell of a lot of damage to anything else in the vicinity. Think of a bar-room brawl in a John Wayne Western, and you get the general idea.

They can, however, feel pain; and so they do their level best to avoid fighting each other in any meaningful sense. A direct hit from a mountain hurts, and is best avoided for that very reason.

The battle between Kiss and Philly Nine was, therefore, something rather special; and when word reached the back bar of Saheed's, there was a sudden and undignified scramble for the exit. This was going to be something to see.

'GO ON, YOU BLOODY FAIRY, RIP HIS EARS OFF!' shouted a small Force Two, who had climbed a lamp-post to get a better view.

'Which one are you cheering for?' asked a colleague.

The Force Two shrugged.

'Both of them,' he replied. 'I mean, it's bound to be a draw, so ... COME ON, PUT THE BOOT IN! STOP FARTING AROUND AND BREAK SOMETHING!'

'But if neither of them's going to win, what's the point in cheering at all?'

The Force Two shrugged. 'It's a poor heart that never rejoices,' he replied. 'CALL THAT A RABBIT PUNCH? MY GRANNY HITS HARDER THAN THAT.'

'As I recall,' commented the other genie, 'your granny was Cyclone Mavis. Wasn't she the one that pulled that coral island off Sumatra right up by the roots and plonked it down again fifty miles to the east?'

'So I'm being factually correct. Where's the harm in that?'

Half an hour later, the two combatants paused for a breather.

'It's only a small point,' panted Kiss, picking shards of splintered basalt out of his knees, 'but what are we going to do about paying for the breakages?'

'Split 'em between us, I suppose,' Philly replied, lifting a small Alp off his ankle and discarding it. 'That's probably simpler than trying to keep tabs as we go along.'

'Fair enough,' Kiss replied. 'Otherwise it'd be like trying to work out the bill in a restaurant. You know, who had what, I thought it was you that ordered the extra nan bread, that sort of thing.'

'Ready for some more?'

'Yeah, go on.'

'Or do you want to phone whatsername? She's probably wondering where you've got to.'

Kiss shook his head. 'More important things to do,' he replied wearily. 'I mean, she can't expect me to phone her if I'm fighting for my life against overwhelmingly superior demonic forces, can she?'

Philly rubbed his nose. 'I dunno,' he said. 'You know her better than I do.'

Kiss thought about it. 'Maybe I'd better just give her a quick call,' he said. 'I mean, she may have started dinner or something.'

Philly put his head on one side and gave Kiss a thoughtful look. 'That'd take priority over mortal combat with the prince of darkness, would it?'

'You haven't had much to do with women, I can tell.'

'I suffer from that disadvantage, yes.'

'Don't go away, I'll be right back.'

Easier said, Kiss discovered, than done. When eventually he found a public telephone (he was in the middle of the Mojave Desert at the time) he discovered that all his loose change had shaken out of his pockets during the fight, and his phonecard was bent and wouldn't go in the slot.

Easier, he realised, given that I'm capable of travelling at the speed of light, to nip round there in person. He gathered up his component molecules and jumped –

There is a perfectly reasonable scientific explanation of how genies manage to transport themselves from one side of the earth to the other apparently instantaneously; it's something to do with trans-dimensional shift error, and it is in fact wrong. The truth is that genies have this facility simply because Mother Nature knows better than to try and argue with beings who only partially exist and who have all the malevolent persistence and susceptibility to logical argument of the average two-year-old. Let them get on with it, she says; and if they suddenly find themselves stuck in a rift between opposing realities, then ha bloody ha.

– and, before the electrical impulses that made up the thought had finished trudging along his central nervous system, he had arrived. He felt in his pocket for his key.

And stopped. And sniffed. Fee-fi-fo-fum, he muttered

under his breath, I smell the blood of a Near Easterner somehow connected with fish. Or rather the socks. And the armpits. Not to mention the residual whiff of haddock which is so hard to lose, all the deodorants of Arabia notwithstanding.

Funny, he thought.

He opened the door and strolled in; to find Jane, his betrothed, apparently joined at the lips with a skinny dark-haired bloke in a salt-stained reefer jacket and grubby trainers.

It's at times like this that instinct takes over. An instinct is, by its very nature, impulsive. Instinct doesn't stand on one foot in the doorway thinking, 'Hey, this really lets me off the hook, you know?' before discreetly tiptoeing away to see if it's too late to get the deposit back on the wedding cake. Instinct jumps in, boot raised.

Three seconds or so later, therefore, Asaf was lying in a confused huddle in the corner of the room wondering how he had got there and why his ribs hurt so much. Jane was standing up, gesticulating eloquently with her right hand while trying to do her blouse up with her left; and Kiss was leaning on the arm of the sofa, listening to what Jane had to say and thinking, Shit, I think I've broken a bone in my toe.

And just what precisely, Jane was asking, did he think he was playing at? And what made him think he had the right—?

'Hold on,' Kiss interrupted. 'That bloke there. Are you trying to tell me he was *supposed* to be doing that?'

It wasn't a way of putting it that Jane had foreseen, and for a moment it checked the eloquence of her reproaches. 'Yes,' she said. 'And—'

'This, not to put too fine a point on it, *mortal*—'

'Here,' broke in Asaf, 'who are you calling a mortal?'

'You.'

Asaf fingered his ribs tentatively. 'Fair enough,' he said. 'Hey, are you another one?'

'Another what?'

'Another bloody genie. Because if you are . . .'

WHOOSH!

'G'day,' said the Dragon King, materialising next to the standard lamp and knocking over a coffee table. 'Perhaps it'd be a good idea if I explained . . .'

Somebody threw a glass decanter at him. Who it actually was we shall probably never know, but there were three obvious suspects. He ducked, looked round to see where the decanter had met the wall, and winced at the sight of good whisky gone to waste.

'Not you *again*,' Asaf said. 'Not on top of everything else. Haven't you people got anything better to do?'

Kiss froze. 'That reminds me,' he mumbled.

'Shut up!'

Asaf, Kiss and the Dragon King all stopped talking at the same moment. 'Thank you,' said Jane. 'Now listen.'

They listened.

'First,' she went on, 'you with the scales and the beer-belly. I don't know who you are or what you're doing in my front room, but if you leave now and never come back I might just be generous and pretend you were never here in the first place.'

'Well, cheerio then,' said the King; and vanished.

'Next,' Jane continued, turning to Kiss, 'you. I have had enough of you. First you clutter up my flat with lethal gadgets that fly people half-way across the world; then, when I send for you to come and rescue me, you're nowhere to be seen; and finally you come bursting in here like the bloody Customs and Excise and beat up my friends. This is your idea of hearing and obeying, is it?'

'But he was—'

'In fact,' Jane ground on, 'I'm beginning to get just a little bit sick of the sight of you. In fact, I wish you were back in your damned bottle, where you bel—'

WHOOSH.

'Excuse me,' said Asaf nervously, extracting himself painfully from the corner of the room, 'but what the hell happened to him?'

'Who cares?' Jane replied. 'Left in a huff, I expect. Now, where were we?'

HELP!

HELP!

HELP! LET ME OUT, YOU IDIOTS, I'VE GOT TO SAVE THE SODDING PLANET!

In an aspirin bottle, no one can hear you scream.

This business with bottles. It has perplexed some of the finest minds in the Universe, almost as much as the perennial enigma of why the cue ball sometimes screws back off the pack for no good reason and goes straight down the centre left-hand pocket.

Some say that bottles are the gateways to other universes (generally small, cramped universes with convex sides, smelling of stale retsina), and that a genie imprisoned in a bottle has stepped sideways into an alternative reality. It's all, they say, part and parcel of the wish syndrome, whereby each wish calls into being an alternative reality where the wish comes true, however improbable this may be.

Another school of thought holds that a genie embottled is only a tiny part of the totality of that genie. Genies exist simultaneously in innumerable different dimensions, and by bottling one all you do is shove most of him out of this dimension and into the others, leaving only a token presence behind.

The French say that bottling genies is something that should be done at the *château* of origin, or not at all.

The major petro-chemicals manufacturers say that putting genies in bottles is fine by them, but wouldn't it make more sense to use plastic non-returnable bottles with screw tops, which means you can keep them longer before they go flat?

Genies take the view that getting put in bottles is just one of those things that happens to a guy at some stage in his life, and if it wasn't that it'd be something else, and there are probably worse small, confined spaces to pass the odd millennium in, for instance coffins, so why worry? This goes some way to explain why genies have never ruled the Universe.

Force Twelve genies, however, are a cut above the general production-line standard, and therefore can't afford to be quite so laid back all the time. Some of them have responsibilities – planets to save, and so forth. This means that from time to time they find it hard to be philosophical about the cork going back in. Some Force Twelves, indeed the elite few who have more moral fibre than a square yard of coconut matting, even resent it.

'Women!' said Kiss aloud. The word echoed round inside the bottle and died away.

Never mind. If it's any consolation, when the planet gets blown up in a few minutes I expect the force of the blast will shatter the bottle and you'll be away clear. It's an odd thing, but in any significant explosion, glass is usually one of the first things to go.

Kiss looked up, and then down, and then from side to side. 'Do I know you?' he asked.

I'm the duty GA. I'm having a busy shift, actually, because I was talking to another guy in more or less the same fix as you not that long ago.

'Go away.'

Beg pardon?

'I said go away. I've got enough to put up with as it is.'

There was a pause.

Why is everybody so blasted hostile? I'm only doing my job.

'Take the day off. Go and spend some quality time with the family.'

It's a pity you feel you have to adopt that attitude, you know, because the GA service really does have a great deal to offer to people in your position. If you weren't so cramped in there, I could give you some leaflets which—

'No leaflets. Piss off.'

It's this crisis of confidence which is bringing the profession to its knees. Me, I blame franchising. Under the old system—

'I said—'

Under the old system, you see, I could have brought gentle subliminal influences to bear on that mouse . . .

'Piss . . . What mouse?'

The mouse presently scampering along the mantelpiece on which your fragile glass bottle is resting, three feet above a tiled fireplace. Like I was saying, I could have subtly suggested to that mouse that it might find it a good idea to run along this mantelpiece terribly fast, regardless of the risk of accidentally brushing up against your bottle and dislodging it.

'Ah.'

Whereupon the bottle would have fallen to the floor and smashed, and . . .

'Yes, thanks,' Kiss said. 'I think I was there way before you. Now, about this mouse . . .'

'Small for its species, sort of greyish-brown, whiskers, answers to the name of Keek. Unusually gullible, too, even for a mouse. The faintest suggestion that there's a small crumb of mozzarella just to the side of your bottle, and all your problems would have been over. Pity, really.

'Gosh.'

Yes. As it is, the voice continued sadly, *all I can do is offer moral support and axioms of an uplifting nature designed to help you to come to terms with the harsh reality of your situation without too much culture shock. For instance, 'It's a long road that has no turning.' 'It's always darkest before the dawn.' Actually, that's not quite true, because generally speaking just before dawn you get that rather attractive pastel-pink light just above the horizon, which always puts me in mind . . .*

'Excuse me . . .'

. . . of a strawberry milk-shake. Sorry, did you say something?

'The mouse. Now where is it?'

About eight inches to your immediate left. It seems to be eating a microscopic crumb of some sort, probably toasted crumpet.

'I wonder if you might possibly . . .'

No, it's gone again. Something must have disturbed it. That's a real shame, in my opinion. A good mouse is hard to find, I always think.

'Gone?'

'Fraid so, yes. Now then, where were we? Had I got on to 'If at first you don't succeed' yet?

Kiss slumped against the side of the bottle. True, in even the most spacious bottle slumping room is generally at a premium, but he managed quite nicely under the circumstances.

'Listen to me,' he said. 'Any minute now, the air is going to be blue with fucking great big nuclear bombs. Unless I do something about it, these bombs are going to blow up the planet. Now, can you do anything to help?'

That does put rather a different complexion on it, the voice admitted.

'I rather thought it might.'

Quite so. In that case, I think either, 'You can't make omelettes', or 'It's no use crying over spilt milk', would be rather more appropriate. Or possibly even, 'It is better to have loved and lost than . . .'

This, Kiss reflected, is what comes of getting involved. If

I was back in the bar right now, along with the rest of the lads, none of this would matter. True the planet would go pop, but so what, there's plenty of planets. Let's have another cup of coffee and another piece of pie. But as it is . . .

'I think I'll pass on all of those, thank you. So unless you've got anything actually positive to suggest . . .'

Try singing.

'Right, that does it,' Kiss snarled. 'Unless you're out of my head in a five seconds flat, I'm going to bash my brains out against the side of the bottle. One-Mississippi. Two-Mississippi. Three-Mississippi.'

He paused and listened. Nothing. Good.

Won't be long now. Time, ladies and gentlemen, please. Haven't you got afterlives to go to?

He waited.

Try singing. Try singing, for God's sake. Yes, of course! Now why the hell hadn't he thought of that for himself?

The bomb had fallen asleep.

Just, grumbled the carpet to itself, *my bloody rotten luck. First time I've been on a promise in God knows how long, and she goes and falls asleep on me. Marvellous.*

The carpet flew on regardless. It was, after all, a gentle carpet. Take her back to the shop, let her sleep it off there.

As if things weren't bad enough, it noticed as it flew, she snores. Or rather, she ticks loudly in her sleep. Amounts to the same thing, in the long run.

Question. Since it's such a painfully obvious solution, why hasn't anybody thought of doing it before?

Answer. Because genies are generally too bone-idle and pig-ignorant to try anything. Put a genie in a bottle and he'll stay there till somebody lets him out. After all, they have all the time in the world.

Kiss cleared his throat, swallowed, and sang.

'Do-rey-mi-fah-so-la-tee-*do*!'

Nothing. He tried again, an octave higher. Then an octave higher still. That was enough to make his eyes water and his teeth ache.

Excelsior.

'*Do-rey-mi-fah-so-la-tee-DO!*'

He paused to massage his throat and jaw. Come on, Kiss, if some fat lady in a blond wig and a hat with horns on can do it, so can you. Higher still.

'DO-REY-MI-FAH-SO-LA-TEE-DO!'

He broke off, coughing like a terminal tuberculosis case, and wiped his eyes on his sleeve. Reckon I'm just not cut out for this sort of work, he told himself.

Indeed. Very apt.

'*DO-REY-MI-FAH . . .*'

Success; and just in time, too. Another note higher and he'd have been in no fit state to save green shield stamps, let alone the world.

Subjected to a harmonic stress equivalent to seven fat elephants jumping up and down on it, the bottle flew into pieces. Kiss tumbled out, cutting himself to the bone on broken glass as he did so, hit the tiled floor of the fireplace, swore horribly and scrambled to his feet; all in one nice, fluid movement. All around him windows were falling out, decanters were splitting, light bulbs were popping. The mouse was curled up in a ball in the coal-scuttle, its paws jammed in its ears. Only the picture of Abraham Lincoln seemed not to mind, probably because its mind was on other things.

'Now then,' Kiss said aloud, as he aimed himself at the window. 'That was the easy bit.'

He jumped.

The sky, when he got there, was a bit like the Rome rush-hour. Nose to tail intercontinental ballistic missiles, all hopelessly snarled up, their proximity-actuated guidance systems completely up the pictures, all at a complete standstill; honking, swearing, waggling their fins in unconcealed fury, trying to nudge past on the inside, ignoring the traffic-light beacons helpfully shot up into orbit by Side A's mission control centre, and generally not improving the situation. Kiss crossed from Europe to Asia by walking across the backs of bottleneck bombs.

There is no need, Kiss realised, to save the world. Just sit back and let old Captain Balls-Up do it for you.

Nevertheless he was here now, he might as well make himself useful.

He rolled up his sleeves, materialised a whistle and a pair of white gloves, took his stand on a small wisp of cloud a few feet over the seething mass of bombs, and started to direct the traffic out of orbit in the general direction of Ursa Major. It took him about half an hour, during the course of which his ankles were lightly singed by overheating rocket motors and a Class 93 ran over his foot. Apart from that, it was a doddle.

That left just the one bomb, presently sleeping it off on a mattress improvised out of priceless Turkestan rugs in Justin's uncle's shop. Kiss didn't know about that one, of course. Nobody can know everything.

Right, he said to himself, done that. That was more of the easy bit. It was time he got on with the job in hand.

'So there you are,' said Philly Nine, whooshing into existence a foot or so above his head. 'Pretty long phone call, if you ask me.'

'I got held up,' Kiss admitted, 'but I'm back now.'

'Good. Shall we get on with it, then?'

'Only too pleased. Oh, by the way, I got rid of all those missiles.'

Philly looked at him. 'Oh,' he said. 'You did, did you?'

Kiss nodded. 'They were cluttering the place up a bit,' he said, 'so I shooed them away. Hope you don't mind.'

'Plenty more where those came from, I expect,' Philly replied. 'Production lines probably working double time right this very minute. Honestly, Kiss old thing, you are naïve.'

In his time, which was roughly coeval with the Universe, Kiss had been called a wide selection of things, but this was a new one. 'You think so?' he said.

Philly nodded. 'You honestly think you can save the world by getting rid of a few bombs? Dream on, chum, dream on. All they'll do is build some more. Idiots they may be, but what they lack in basic survival instinct they make up for in dogged persistence. And of course,' he added, 'I shall be there to offer whatever assistance they require.'

'Will you now?'

'I confidently predict that I will be.'

'We'll see about that.'

Leonardo da Vinci, had he been there, would have wept.

So would Shakespeare, and Goethe, and Tolstoy. And Beethoven and Mozart and Jelly Roll Morton, and Sophocles and Flaubert and Rubens and Molière and Wordsworth and Brahms and Petrarch and Diaghilev and Jane Austen and Tintoretto and probably Virgil, Buddy Holly and Sir Arthur Conan Doyle.

All these people laboured, in their separate ways, to entertain and amuse the human race. But what the human race really wants to watch, in the final analysis, is a good, dirty fight.

Ernest Hemingway, on the other hand, would have loved it. Sir Thomas Malory would have been taking notes. Homer would have been sitting somewhere on a balcony wearing a straw hat and saying, 'Ah yes, but you should have seen Hercules back in '86, he had a copybook cover drive off the back foot that would have put these young whippersnappers to shame.' Chaucer would have missed the fight itself, since he'd have been tearing round the deserted streets trying to find an open betting shop.

It was a good fight, by any standards. Most fighters are inhibited by the fear that, unless they exercise at least some degree of circumspection, they may end up getting permanently damaged. Since Kiss and Philly Nine had no such worries, they were able to give their full attention to trying to beat the crap out of the opposing party.

Genies, for whom poetry inevitably begins with the words 'There was a young lady of . . .', and in whose world-view painting is something involving scaffolding, long brushes, ladders and being indentured to someone whose windowsills need doing, are connoisseurs of the fight beautiful, and as far as they're concerned the Marquess of Queensberry is a pub in Camden Passage. For the first time ever, Saheed's was deserted, except for a small knot of spectators peering out through the skylight.

'Strewth,' observed the Dragon King of the South-East. 'I never thought that was even possible.'

'Well, now you know,' replied a Force Six who had money invested. 'Wouldn't like to try it myself, mind.'

'You could do yourself an injury,' agreed a Force Three, who had the binoculars.

'Anybody know,' asked a small Force Two, whose view was obstructed by about ten larger genies and a few cardboard boxes, 'what the fight is about, exactly?'

There was a thoughtful silence.

'Good and evil?' suggested the Six.

'All violence is a symptom of the underlying malaise in carbon-based society,' said the Three.

'They do that,' agreed the Two. 'They lurk in among the rubber trees and jump out on people with big curly knives.'

'You what?'

'And in Sumatra and parts of Burma, too. I think it's something to do with the heat.'

A large chunk of rock, part of a mountain that had been pressed into service as a knuckleduster, hurtled down from the sky. The genies ducked.

'It's all right,' said the Three, looking up. 'Landed on Daras. Are they allowed to use weapons? I thought this was strictly a bare-knuckle job.'

'You want to go up there and remind them, be my guest.'

'Fight fair, yer rotten bludger!' shouted the Dragon King. The others looked at him.

'Yes, well,' he said, shamefaced. 'I mean, fair crack of the whip, lads. One of them is trying to save the world.'

'So?'

'Would you mind moving your bloody great elbow? You're blocking my view.'

'I think,' said a tall, thin Force Eight, 'it's something to do with a girl.'

'What is?'

'The fight. I think it's about some girl or other.'

'Surely not?'

'It's as good a reason as any. I mean, the fight's got to be about *something*. All fights are about *something*.'

'Oh.'

THIRTEEN

The fight was getting bogged down. It had, in fact, reached something of a stalemate.

'All right,' suggested Philly Nine, 'try this. You let go of my throat, and then if I simultaneously take my teeth out of your left ankle . . .'

'I don't think that'll work,' Kiss mumbled after a moment's thought. 'All that'll happen is we'll fall over.'

Philly, who was turning purple, clicked his tongue. 'Well,' he said, 'we'd better think of something, unless we want to stay locked together like this for ever and ever.'

'Agreed. The sooner the better, as far as I'm concerned.'

'How about if—?'

Whatever Philly's suggestion was, it never got a hearing; because before he could make it both genies were knocked spinning by a long-range intercontinental ballistic missile.

'Shit,' gasped Philly, who'd been winded, 'what the hell was that?'

Kiss floundered his way out of the soft cloud-bank into which he had fortuitously tumbled. 'Don't ask me,' he replied. 'It was long and metallic and—'

He broke off and ducked as a large and colourful carpet, flapping its edges frantically like a manta ray in a hurry, shot past, calling out, 'Stop! I didn't mean it!' at the top of a voice which Kiss only heard in the back of his brain. The two genies dusted themselves off and floated level with each other.

'One of yours?' Kiss asked.

'Never seen it before in my life.'

'Well, it's solved one problem for us.'

'True. Shall we carry on, then?'

'Might as well.'

'Where were we, exactly?'

'Hmm.' Kiss stroked his chin. 'Well, as I recall, you had me in a scissor lock and were trying to bite my leg off, and I—'

'Not a scissor lock,' Philly interrupted. 'More of a Polynesian death-grip, surely?'

'No, you're wrong there. Isn't that the one where the left knee comes up under the opponent's armpit?'

'You're thinking of the Mandalay wrench.'

'No, that's the one where—'

This time the bomb hit Kiss in the small of the back, catapulting him neatly into orbit. Philly had the presence of mind to duck, only to be swatted flying by the bunch of roses the carpet was frenziedly waving. He had just recovered his balance from that when a tall, thin apprentice carpet salesman landed around his neck, jarring his spinal column and sending him spiralling towards the ground. He couldn't have been more than ten feet off the ground, and travelling at a fair pace, when he managed to break the spin and pull out of it.

He landed and shrugged off the apprentice carpet salesman, who landed in a gooseberry bush and lay still, making faint whimpering noises. Philly looked down at him.

'Are you all right?' he asked.

'Heeeeeeeeeeeeeelp!'

Philly considered for a moment. 'Yes,' he said, 'you're all right. Don't go away, now.'

'Have they gone?' Kiss asked, when they were once more face to face.

'I think so,' Philly replied cautiously. 'Can't see them, at any rate.'

'You got any idea what they're playing at?'

'Not really, no. Looks like the rug's got the hots for the bomb, if I'm any judge.'

'How can a rug be in love with a bomb?'

'Dunno. Still, one of them's colourful and flat and the other one's dull grey and round, and they do say opposites attract.'

Kiss bit his lip. 'I ought,' he said, 'to go and defuse that bomb before it does any damage.'

'It'll keep. Looks like the rug's doing a pretty good job, anyhow.'

The genies shook their heads, as if to say that they wouldn't mind fighting to the death over the destiny of the world if only the world would show a little respect.

'Right,' Philly said at last, 'back to the job in hand. What say we start again from scratch?'

Kiss raised an eyebrow. 'You sure?' he asked. 'I had you ahead on points.'

'Did you?'

'Sure.' Kiss nodded. 'I was giving you six for the head-butt, nine for the savage blow to the left temple with the giant redwood and seven for the combined half-nelson and stranglehold on the windpipe.'

'OK,' Philly replied dubiously, 'but I wasn't counting that because of the nutcracker hold you had on my right elbow at the same time.'

'I don't remember that.'

'Maybe you had other things on your mind. Anyhow, I put us more or less dead level, so . . .'

'That's very sporting of you, Philly.'

'Don't mention it.'

They drifted a little way apart, each looking for an opening. Somehow the aggro seemed to have gone out of the whole thing, and both genies started to feel just a trifle sheepish.

'This is the point,' suggested Kiss, putting the mutual feeling into words, 'where one of us should say, "This is silly, there must be a better way of settling things".'

'Doesn't that come later?'

'Could do. Or we could do it now.'

'Get it over with, you mean?'

'We could skip it if you like,' Kiss replied accommodatingly. 'After all, you're trying to destroy the planet, I'm trying to save it, so there's not all that much scope for creative bargaining. On the other hand . . .'

Something, Philly noticed, had gone in his back. He winced. 'Quite,' he said.

'I mean, it's a bit daft when you think about it.'

'Two intelligent beings . . .'

'Two supernatural beings . . .'

'And not just your average thing that goes bump in the night,' Philly added. 'I mean, Force Twelves, not many of them to the pound avoirdupois, if you get my meaning.'

'Better things to do with our time, wouldn't you say?'

'Exactly.'

Philly looked down at the world beneath him. From the vertiginous height they were presently occupying, he could see all the kingdoms of the Earth spread out before him like a giant map. Hmmm, he thought. Bloody untidy, with all those green and brown splodges and the blue stuff just slopping about anyhow. Not a straight line to be seen anywhere. On the other hand . . .

Kiss looked down at the world beneath him and thought of bottles, and all the time he'd had to spend in them over the years. No more earth, he thought, no more bottles. No more women. No more having to fetch and carry after snot-nosed mortals who happen to unscrew a cap.

'How about,' suggested Philly, picking his words carefully, 'I just destroy a bit of it?'

'Which bit had you in mind?'

'Well . . .' Philly peered down through the swirling clouds. 'How about Australia?' he said. 'I mean, nobody's going to miss Australia, are they?'

'Not immediately, certainly,' Kiss conceded. 'But it's a big place, Australia. And somebody's got to be fond of it,' he added doubtfully.

'All right, then,' said Philly. 'What would you say if I left you Queensland?'

Kiss pursed his lips. 'Don't know if that'd work, actually,' he said. 'I mean, geography's not my strong point. Could be that the other bits are holding it up or something.'

'All right then,' Philly replied. 'How about Tasmania? That's just an island, for pity's sake.'

Kiss remembered something he'd heard once. 'No man is an island,' he said sagely.

'Well, of course not,' Philly responded. 'I don't know about you, but I can count on the fingers of one hand the number of flat people with frilly edges entirely surrounded by water that I know to speak to.'

'I didn't mean it literally,' Kiss replied. 'What I was getting at is, you can't really go knocking off hundreds of thousands of people, even if they are Australians. I think it's something to do with divine justice.'

'Divine justice!' Philly sneered. 'Don't you give me divine justice. Fifty talents they fined me, and I was only doing ninety-five, top whack. And they made me blow into a little bag.'

Kiss frowned. 'I'm not saying I hold with it,' he said. 'All I'm saying is, it's there. And—'

'And what?'

Kiss shrugged. 'I'm not sure, really. Only it's probably a good idea. On balance. In the long run. I mean, I think things tend to come out in the wash, in the fullness of time.'

'I see. And because of that, you'd begrudge me Tasmania?'

'Look, Philly, if it was up to me you could have Tasmania in a paper bag with salt, vinegar and a lemon-scented napkin. But you've got to face facts. Destroying Tasmania would be . . .'

'Would be what?'

'. . . antisocial.' Kiss scooped up a handful of cloud and began picking at it. 'Not a very nice thing to do. A bit unnecessary.'

Philly sighed. 'All right,' he said. 'Tell you what I'll do. Scrub round Tasmania, how'd it be if I just destroyed a bit nobody wanted at all? Some desert or something? Now nobody could object to that, could they?'

Kiss scented a chink in the argument. 'In that case,' he said quickly, 'why bother at all? I mean, if nobody's going to mind? Like, if it's a desert anyway, surely you'd be wasting your time. And how could anyone tell the difference once you'd finished?'

Philly frowned. 'I would,' he replied. 'It's a matter of principle, really. Something I promised myself a long time ago.'

Kiss stared. 'A matter of *principle?*' he repeated incredulously.

'Yeah. What's so funny about that?'

'Genies can't have principles. If they could, what'd be the point of having humans?'

'To be honest with you, Kiss, old mate,' Philly said, with a slow smile, 'I never could see the point in having humans. That's why I decided, a long time ago, to do something about it.'

There was a long silence.

'Well,' said Kiss at last, 'I suppose we'd better carry on with the fight, then.'

'Reckon so.'

'Pity, though.'

'It always is,' said Philly, and hit him with a railway station.

'Sorry to interrupt,' said Asaf, 'but there's something going on.'

'Hmm?'

The interruption, Asaf admitted to himself, was not entirely unwelcome, because he was starting to lose the sensation in his lower lip. He untangled himself from Jane, got up and walked over to the window.

'Not to worry,' he said, having looked. 'It's only two genies fighting.'

Jane scowled and started to button up her blouse. 'They're starting,' she said, 'to get on my nerves.'

'Who?'

'The genies,' Jane replied. 'I think it's time I did something about it.'

The word 'You?' froze on Asaf's lips. True, his experience of female facial expressions was limited, since where he came from they tended to go around with curtains over their faces (and no bad thing too, he remembered, calling to mind some of the blind dates his brothers had fixed him up with in times gone by. Actually, the blind ones hadn't been so bad; it was some of the deaf-mutes who made him cringe with embarrassment, even now); there is, however, a basic defence mechanism built into the male psyche that reacts quickly to flashing eyes and deep frowns, and sends men of all races and creeds dashing out of the house in search of an all-night florist.

'Absolutely,' he said, therefore. 'If you don't mind, though, I'll just—'

'Get your coat, it's turned cold.'

It occurred to Asaf, as he scuttled after Jane down the stairs, that he still had an indentured genie of his own on the payroll, with at least one ungranted wish still in reserve. 'I wish,' he muttered to himself, 'she wouldn't go dashing off getting us both involved in things.'

Sorry, mate. This time you're on your own. G'day.

'In that case,' he said aloud, 'you'd better give us a lift.'

Jane stopped at the foot of the staircase, looking impatient. 'Come on,' she said. 'We haven't got all day, you know.'

'Sorry. I was just arranging us some transport.'

'Transport?'

'G'day.'

The Dragon King materialised, filling the stairwell and substantial parts of the up and down stairs as well. Huge, Asaf noted, magnificent, brutal and stuck. Probably better off with a taxi.

'Good idea,' said Jane briskly. 'You.'

The Dragon King winced. 'G'day, miss. What can I do you for?'

'That fight. I need to stop it now. Take us there.'

'Um.' The dragon looked at her, mentally comparing the respective risks of going within a hundred miles of a fight between two crazed Force Twelves and refusing a direct order from Jane. 'Straight away, miss,' he said. 'No worries.'

They scrambled on to his back. A moment later, the stairway was empty.

A long time ago, when God created the world –

A feature common to all building sites is the presence of many, many long pieces of timber with nails stuck in them. Nobody knows where they come from, or what they're designed to achieve. What they actually do is wait until the grass has grown up round them and then spring out on passing builders, preferably when they're carrying precarious loads of fragile objects. When the building is completed they are sometimes ritually burned, but as often as not they stay, forgotten and untouched.

It was just such a piece of timber, undisturbed since the Fourth Day (on which He dug out the footings and poured the concrete) that Philly Nine was using to batter Kiss about the head. Given the origin of the thing, it was not surprising that the bent, rusty nails were in fact made from extruded amethyst. This didn't stop them hurting.

Kiss wasn't taking this lying down. More sort of crouched on one knee, cleverly managing to ward off most of the blows from his body with his head, and groping with his left hand for a large chunk of rock (Malta) he'd noticed out of the corner of his eye a while back.

'Hey, you!'

Philly paused, club upraised, and looked round.

'You talking to me, chum?' he said to the Dragon King of the South-East, who was hovering sheepishly over his left shoulder.

The King shook his head vigorously. In Wisconsin, they thought the result was snow.

'Didn't say a word, mate, straight up,' he said, smiling meekly.

'I thought you just spoke to me.'

'Nah. Try the sheila between me shoulder-blades.'

'What she . . . oh, her. What does she want?'

'*Hey!*'

Philly glanced down, lowering the club a degree or so. 'Do I know you?' he asked. 'Not that it matters much, but if we are acquainted, I shall send a wreath to your funeral. That's,' he added, 'always assuming they find enough of you to fill a coffin. Being realistic, though, a doggy bag might be more suitable.'

'Oh, shut up, Jane replied. 'And put down that silly stick before you put someone's eye out.'

Philly frowned and lashed out with the club. What with residual particles of self-doubt and guilt, combined with extreme irritation at not being able to make much impression on Kiss's head with one of the nastiest blunt instruments in the cosmos, he had just about reached the stopper of his bottle (genies don't have tethers), with the result that his sense of chivalry was down there with the Polly Peck shares. Fortunately, the King's nose came between Jane and the plank.

'Missed,' Jane called out. 'You want to saw that thing in half.'

'Do I? Why's that?'

'Then you'd have two short planks. Company for you.'

'Very droll.' He tried the reverse sweep, but this time the King ducked and suffered no more than a slight scratch to his right ear from one of the nails. With a sigh, Philly swept round on his heel and belted Kiss again, knocking him back off his feet.

'Missed again,' said Jane smugly.

'Third time lucky.' Philly swung the plank, feinting high and then changing tack in mid-blow. The resulting impact missed Asaf's head by a few thousandths of an inch and found its mark on the King's back.

'Fair go, mate,' the King squealed. 'What harm have I ever done you?'

'Call it pre-emptive revenge,' Philly replied. 'In the meantime, could you try and hold still? It's harder than it looks, swatting something that small.'

Jane bristled and turned to Asaf, giving him what used to be known as an old-fashioned look.

'Well?' she said. 'Don't just sit there. Do something.'

The bomb was confused.

It was dizzy, sick, miles and miles off-course and beginning to see spots in front if its eyes. Furthermore, it had the feeling that running away from an amorous carpet wasn't really the sort of thing self-respecting atomic bombs are supposed to do.

It slowed down and activated its rear-view sensors. The carpet was nowhere to be seen.

Bombs are nothing if not logical. This goes with the territory. A fat lot of good an emotional, sensitive, caring bomb would be to anybody. Probably cry all over its own fuse.

The logical argument was this:

* I do not want to be chased about any more by this frigging carpet.
* If I go off, everything within five hundred miles will be turned into little grey wisps of curly ash.
* Including the carpet.

It sniggered, and armed itself.

'What,' Asaf asked, 'did you have in mind?'

By way of reply, Jane just looked at him.

'Right,' he said, 'fine. Just leave it to me.'

Kiss, meanwhile, had dragged himself back up to cloud level, having collected on the way a massive charge of static electricity which someone had left lying about in the bottom of a cloud he'd passed through. Observing that Philly was preoccupied with trying to brain the Dragon King with his oversize telegraph pole, he took the opportunity to connect his new plaything up to the inside of Philly's knee.

The results were quite entertaining.

Doctors, he recalled, as he watched Philly soar steadily upwards, use a similar technique to test their patients' reflexes. Nothing wrong with Philly's reflexes, as far as he could make out.

He waited where he was for a moment or so, on the offchance that gravity might have something to say about Philly's movements. He counted to twelve. Probably safe to assume that gravity knew when to leave well alone.

'Hello,' he said.

'Where the hell were you?' Jane replied.

'I—' He checked himself. Oh woman, he murmured to himself, in our hours of ease uncertain, coy and hard to please; when pain and anguish rack the brow, an even greater nuisance thou. 'Sorry,' he said.

'And you just sat there,' Jane continued, 'while that great oaf tried to hit me.'

'Yes.'

'And you call yourself a genie!'

'I tend to exaggerate.'

'Aren't you going after him?'

'No.'

'You mean you're afraid.'

'Naturally. I do also have a nuclear missile to see to, but that's only a flimsy excuse. Really it's because I'm a coward.'

'You haven't heard the last of this.'

'I should think not. Excuse me. 'Bye.'

'I haven't finished with you yet!' Jane called after him, as he dwindled away into a tiny dot on the horizon. 'Honestly!' she summarised.

Beside her, Asaf made a vague oh-well-never-mind noise. 'Any how,' he said, 'that's sorted that out. Can we go home now, please?'

Jane looked around and noticed, as if for the first time, that she was sitting between the wings of a dragon thousands of feet above the surface of the earth. 'Gosh, yes,' she said. 'Let's do that right away.'

'I was hoping you'd say that.'

'Well, go on, then. It's your stupid dragon.'

'Sorry, yes. Now then, I wish—'

As he said the words, he chanced to look up; and the terms of his wish changed slightly. In its amended form, which he didn't actually vocalise, it consisted of, *I wish the other genie, the one who got hit by the electric shock and jumped up miles into the air, wasn't coming back.*

Unfortunately, as the Dragon King hastened to point out to him, that one was asking a bit too much.

'Here, bomb,' Kiss called. 'Here, nice bomb. Bommy-bommybommybommy.'

No reply. And no sign of the poxy thing, as far as the eye (even his) could see. How do you attract bombs, exactly? Bomb-nip? Rattle an empty uranium canister?

'Oo vewwy naughty bomb,' He experimented. 'Oo come here *this minute*, or else no . . .'

He paused. What do bombs like best?

He squirmed. No prizes for guessing what bombs like best.

'If you don't come here *this very minute*,' he essayed, 'the nasty Peace Movement will get you.'

Of course, he rationalised as he swung low over San Francisco, it might just be that he was looking in the wrong place. But he didn't think so, somehow; he could smell bomb – a strong, not very pleasant smell drifting back from the possible future – and it was definitely coming from this direction.

'Come out with your fins up,' he shouted (but it turned into a whimper somewhere between his larynx and the atmosphere). 'I have this planet surrounded.'

He heard a click. It was a tiny sound, no louder than, say, a safety-catch being thumbed forward or a life-support machine being switched off. But he heard it, because it was the sound he'd been listening for.

'Now then,' he wailed, 'there's no need to take that attitude.'

Think, you fool, think. Somewhere out there is a bomb, armed and dangerous – a small, functional intelligence, probably scared and confused, trying to know what's the right thing to do.

Get real, Kiss told himself, this is a fucking *bomb* we're

talking about here. Bombs aren't like that. When was the last time you heard of a three-hundred-megaton warhead being talked down off a twelfth-storey parapet by highly trained social workers?

There it was, a little high-pitched whining of artificial brainwaves, like a gnat in a sandstorm. And what was it saying?

It was saying, *Nothing personal.*

Swearing under his breath, Kiss did a back somersault that would have ripped the wings off even the latest generation of jet fighter and doubled back, head, down, in the direction of Oakland.

Thirty seconds, and counting.

'You're too late,' Jane said, arms folded, face a study in defiant satisficiton. 'He's gone to catch the bomb, and he'll defuse it. You've—'

'Did you just hear something?' Philly interrupted.

'No. What?'

'Sounded to me like a faint click.'

'That'll be Kiss,' said Jane, smugly, 'defusing the bomb.'

Nine seconds, and counting.

Mortals, who tend to think of their lives as the shortest distance between the two points Birth and Death, have a bad attitude towards Time. They accuse it of being inflexible, doctrinaire, officious. In the collective imagination of the human race, Time wears a peaked cap and carries a thick wad of parking tickets.

This is unfair. Time does, in fact, have a considerable degree of discretion. True, it rarely exercises it in favour of mortals (because of their bad attitude), but even so, most of us will have experienced moments when Time has seemed to slow down or stop altogether. The tragedy is that in those moments we're usually sailing through the air, staring at an oncoming car on our side of the road, or realising with a feeling of sick horror that the sound of key in lock means that our spouse has come home earlier than anticipated. We therefore lack the leisure and the objectivity to give Time its due.

Nine seconds and counting. Kiss, being a genie (and having done Time an enormous favour years ago in a rather shabby incident involving yogurt, rubber tubing and a goat) kept his head and called in, so to speak, his marker.

Sniff, sniff, sniff. The smell of bomb was overpowering, but still he couldn't see the bloody . . .

Gotcha! Big steel tube, leaning nonchalantly against a row of other steel tubes, which Kiss identified as liquid nitrogen canisters propped up against the wall of some factory or other. He braked sharply, leaving pale grey skidmarks on the sky, and swooped down.

The bomb saw him and flinched.

'There, there,' he said, 'it's all right, I'm not going to hurt you.'

That, replied the bomb, *must be the stupidest remark I've ever heard.*

Kiss blinked, and then realised that what he was hearing was his own brain's instantaneous translation of the subtext of the bomb's computer intelligence's extraneous drive-chatter; the equivalent of the dead-cat-dragged-over-velvet noise you get when you switch on the tape deck to full volume with a blank tape in it. Gosh, he said to himself, I'm so much cleverer than I ever realised.

'OK,' he replied, 'point taken, let's approach this from a different angle. What harm have we ever done you?'

I'm sorry?

'Us. Sentient life forms. What harm have we ever . . .?'

Let me see. You made me, for a start; that involved being hacked out of the living rock and run through heavy rollers and then heated in a blast furnace until I melted and then poured into a mould like I was jelly or something and then shoved through more rollers and then punched full of sodding great rivets and drilled full of holes with a drill that makes your dentists' drills seem like feather dusters and then packed full of horrible ticklish uranium and shoved down a long, dark tube in a submarine hundreds of feet under the sea and then shot out again, which feels like being farted out of God's arse, let me add, and a fat lot you care about my vertigo and then . . .

This, Kiss realised, is starting to get a bit counter-productive. 'Fine,' he said, 'you've got real grievances, I admit, but is this really the best way to settle them? I mean, really?'

The bomb's sensors treated him to a withering stare. *I'm a bomb, for fuck's sake, this is what I'm supposed to do. Why don't you creeps make up your damn minds?*

'Ah,' Kiss replied quickly. 'The I-was-only-obeying-orders defence. That won't wash, you know.'

So what? I'm about to be blown into my constituent atoms, right? And you're suggesting that something bad *might happen to me afterwards? Grow up.*

Eight seconds and counting. More like seven and four-fifths. Fortunately, Kiss's pores didn't have enough time to start sweating, or he'd have been drenched.

'How would you feel,' he asked, 'about bribery?'

There was a tiny flicker of interest in the readout patterns. *How do you mean, bribery?*

'We pay you, anything you like, if you don't blow up. How does that grab you?'

Like I said, I'm a bomb. What the hell is there that I could possibly want?

Kiss turned up the gain in his brain. 'I'm sure we could think of something,' he said. 'Anything you like, anything at all. A velvet-lined silo. Raspberry-flavoured rocket fuel. A nice little land-mine to cuddle up to in the evenings?'

What's raspberry?

'You see?' Kiss shouted, waving his arms. 'A whole Universe packed with scintillatingly thrilling sensations, and you haven't experienced any of them. You haven't *lived*. But think how different it could all be, if you'd only—'

Of course I haven't lived, I'm a bomb. And how the blazes am I supposed to experience all these wonderful sensations of yours? All I'm built to do is fly and go bang.

'We can fit you with new sensors, of course,' Kiss replied. 'Audio, visual, sensory, you name it. Just think of it. Ice cream, music, the scent of primroses after a heavy shower, the sunset over the Loire valley . . .'

I could experience all that?

'No problem. And that's just the start of it. If you'd just use your imagination, there's no end to what we could show you.'

Fuck.

Kiss blinked. 'What?' he said.

I said fuck. It'd have been really nice, I bet. Too late now, of course.

'Too late?'

Use your common sense. I'm armed and about to blow. You don't think there's anything I can do to stop it, do you?

'But—'

You honestly believe I can switch myself off? Get real. As far as bombs are concerned, free will is a lawyer's marketing gimmick. God, I wish you hadn't said all that stuff about what I could have had. You've really upset me now.

Five seconds and counting. Time was doing its best, but there are limits. At the back of his cosmic awareness, Kiss could feel the world tapping its foot and saying, Come on, *do* something.

Do what?

Anything. Anything is better than nothing.

Nothing. Generally defined as an absence of anything, nothing is usually produced by some catastrophically traumatic event; an atomic bomb, say, going off in a confined space. Such as a galaxy.

Kiss thought, and something came. If he'd been a cartoon, a bubble with a light bulb in it would have appeared above his head.

Sugar and spice and all things nice, that's what supernatural beings are made of. Among other things; including a pretty substantial amount of pure, crude energy. Kiss had never bothered to learn the physics (he'd spent physics lessons practising simple levitation on the underwear of the girl sitting next to him) but he had an idea that what he was mostly made of was raw power. Which accounted for his being able to fly and materialise physical objects, not to mention the chronic indigestion.

And to every action, there is an equal and opposite reaction; which he had only been able to understand in terms of a very fast car hitting a very solid lamp-post.

Indeed.

The trouble was, if he used himself as the lamp-post, he was likely to get seriously bent.

Omelettes and eggs. Three seconds and counting. Yes, he screamed in his mind, the complaint of every poor fool since time began who'd suddenly found out he's been cast to play the hero, but why me? And the inevitable answer: because you're here, and there's nobody else. Because we didn't think you'd mind. You don't mind, do you?

Kiss moved.

Here, protested the bomb, *what the devil do you think you're playing at? It was bad enough with that goddamn nymphomaniac carpet* . . .

'Shut up,' Kiss replied. He wrapped his arms tight around the bomb, and closed his eyes.

No seconds, and counting.

FOURTEEN

I expect you're right,' said Philly Nine wearily. 'No doubt he's disarmed the bomb in the very nick of time, and all my hours of hard work gone straight down the pan. Which only leaves me,' he added, taking one step forward, 'the consoling thought of what I'm now going to do to you.'

Jane's eyebrows shot up like Wall Street after a Republican landslide. 'Me?' she snapped. 'What on earth have I got to do with it?'

'A whole lot,' Philly replied, flexing his fingers purposefully. 'If it hadn't been for you, he'd never have thought to interfere. All this is your fault.'

'Rubbish.'

'Your fault,' Philly repeated, pale with anger. 'Your god-damned meddling can't-mind-your-own-business fault. Well, you can take it from me, it's the last time you'll—'

'Excuse me,' said Asaf.

The shock stopped Philly Nine dead in his tracks. The feeling was hard to describe, but it was something along the lines of the way you'd feel if you were sitting in, say, the roughest dockside bar in San Francisco and a four-foot-six eighty-year-old missionary tottered in on a zimmer frame and offered to fight any man in the place.

'What?'

'Please,' said Asaf, standing up, 'don't talk to the lady like that. You'll upset her.'

'You *what*?'

'And if you upset her,' Asaf continued, 'you'll upset me. So please, cut it out. OK?'

The Dragon King, who had been trying to look unobtrusive to the point of virtual translucence, suddenly snapped out of existence. He rematerialised as a vague presence at the back of Asaf's mind, hammering on the door of the Instincts Section, Self-Preservation department, which appeared to be locked.

Cripes, mate, are you out of your tiny mind? This bastard'll have you for flamin' breakfast.

'I know what I'm doing,' Asaf replied. 'You go away and leave this to me.'

Don't say I didn't warn you.

Philly Nine narrowed his eyes. 'Are you serious?' he said.

'Yes.'

'*You* are threatening *me*?'

'If you choose to look at it that way, I suppose I am.'

It had been a long day, and Philly had had enough. 'You're dead,' he said softly. 'Dead and buried. Now then ...'

And then he stopped. In fairness, he tried to back away and run for it, but somehow he couldn't. Rabbits who go foraging for food in the middle lane of a motorway often experience the same effect.

'Please ...' he said, and then his tongue packed up, immobilised like the rest of him.

'I really don't want to do this,' Asaf said, 'but you leave me no choice.'

He was holding a bottle. To be precise, it was one of those small screw-top plastic bottles they sell fizzy drinks in nowadays. Slowly, his body language broadcasting determination and regret in equal proportions, he advanced.

Philly's tongue came back on line just before the neck of the bottle touched him. 'You can't make me get in there,' he hissed. 'Absolutely no way. There is literally no power on earth ...'

'In you get.'

'I steadfastly and categorically refuse to—'

'In.'

Wildly, Philly stepped backwards and groped behind him for something to cling on to. Try as he might, he couldn't take his eyes off the neck of the bottle; it seemed to summon him.

'As you can see,' Asaf said gently, 'this is no ordinary bottle.'

'You're lying. It's just a bog standard pop bottle, and I'll be damned if I—'

Asaf's face creased in a smile that had nothing whatsoever to do with humour. He levelled the bottle as if it were a gun, and beckoned.

COME

'Shan't!'

COME.

'Good Lord,' Philly gibbered, both arms linked round a granite outcrop, 'you didn't honestly think I was serious about destroying the world, did you? It was just a joke, honest. I mean, why on earth would I possibly want—'

WHOOSH.

Asaf shook his head sadly, screwed on the cap and held the bottle up to the light. It was transparent plastic; but there was nothing to be seen inside the bottle except the usual few beads of condensation clinging to the sides. And they had been there before.

'Gosh,' said Jane.

With a sigh, Asaf swung his arm back and threw the bottle up into the air. There was a sudden terrifying clap of thunder, a streak of lightning that made Jane think the sky had finally come unzipped, and then nothing.

'A pity,' Asaf said. 'But there it is.'

There was a flutter of air and the Dragon King hove back into existence, hovering a few feet above the ground. He was shaking slightly, and his wings were creased.

'Stone the flaming crows,' he said. 'I never seen the like in all my . . .'

Asaf nodded to him. 'Thanks,' he said.

'You're welcome, mate, no worries. Any time.'

Jane looked from one to the other, and made a sort of feeble questioning gesture with her left hand. She couldn't think of anything to say.

'It was his bottle, you see,' Asaf said, in a matter-of-fact tone of voice. 'I guess he must have been carrying it around for years. Boy, how he must have hated himself.'

'*His* bottle . . .'

Asaf nodded. 'Fell out of his pocket or his scrip or whatever genies have, when that other genie hit him with the thunderbolt. I guessed it might come in handy, so I picked it up. It was the dragon who drew my attention to it.'

'Pleased to be of service,' mumbled the King.

'It was the way the dragon jumped up in the air and made a little screaming noise when he saw it that put me on the right lines,' Asaf continued. 'And while you two were having your slanging match, it suddenly occurred to me. Why would a genie, of all things, carry a *bottle* around with him? Particularly the sort of bottle he could never ever escape from. Shatterproof, you see. And non-biodegradable.'

Jane waited for a moment, and then said, 'Well?'

'Simple.' Asaf sat down and opened a roll of peppermints. 'Because he wanted to be put in it. Subconsciously, I guess. I mean, that ties in with all the rest of it. The wanting to destroy the world, and that stuff. What he really wanted to destroy was himself.'

Jane's mental eyebrow rose sharply. This all sounded a bit too glib, too Lesson Three, Psychology For Beginners for her liking. Any minute now and he'd start talking about sublimated urges, cries for help and traumatic potty-training in early childhood. However, she held her peace.

'Added to which,' Asaf went on, 'there's the simple logic of the thing. All those chances he had to destroy the world, and he couldn't actually do it. Bearing in mind what he was, that could only mean he didn't want to do it. You do see that, don't you?'

Jane frowned. 'I don't quite …'

'Well,' Asaf replied through a mouth full of peppermint debris, 'it really does stand to reason. If you're a genie and you want to destroy the world, you don't muck about, you just get on with it.'

'Unless,' Jane interrupted, 'somebody stops you.'

Asaf shook his head. 'A genie who wanted to destroy the world wouldn't have gone about it in a way that would have given anybody any opportunity to stop him. Isn't that right? he asked the King, who nodded.

'Fair dinkum,' he said. 'Five-minute job. Melt an ice-cap, release a plague virus, anything like that. All this pissing about with flowers and ants …' He shook his head in sage contempt.

'All self-delusion on his part,' Asaf went on. 'Really, it was basically just a cry for help—'

Ah, thought Jane. Thank you.

'– because, deep down, he couldn't stand being him. Thinking about it, you can see his point.'

'And when it came right down to it,' the King joined in, 'when the chips were down and push came to shove and he actually could have destroyed the world if he wanted to, he just—'

'Lost his bottle?'

'You could,' Asaf said, frowning, 'put it that way. If you had less taste than the average works canteen Yorkshire pudding, that is.'

Jane drew in a deep breath and looked at the sky. It was still, she noticed with relief and approval, there. As were all the other necessary odds and ends: the ground, for example, and the hills and the sea. Whatever the hell had been going on, it had stopped. Which was probably just as well.

'That's that, then, is it?' she said.

'That's that.'

'Good.' She turned round and beckoned to the carpet. 'Let's go home.'

The shop door opened.

'Justin,' called the proprietor, 'I'm back. Anything happen while I was away?'

'Not really, Uncle.'

'Anybody buy anything?'

'No, Uncle.'

The proprietor glanced round. 'Just a second,' he said. 'Where's the big Isfahan that was in the corner there? You know, the one with the goats.'

Justin swallowed. 'A customer,' he said, 'sort of borrowed it.'

'Borrowed it?'

'On approval,' Justin said.

'I see. Leave a deposit?'

Justin reached under the counter and produced the big, fat, heavy sack he'd discovered in his hand when he'd woken up and found himself back in the shop. As it touched down on the desk, it chinked; and there is only one substance in the whole of the periodic table that chinks. Two clues: it's yellow, and before the development of specialist dental plastics they used to make false teeth out of it.

'I guess so,' he said.

Think what the sea can do to a coastline in thirty million

years. The shock wave from the blast had the same effect on Kiss's body in about a fifth of a second.

Souvenir hunters would have been disappointed. Not even the characteristic black silhouette etched on the glazed earth; just nothing at all to show that Kiss had ever existed.

He was disappointed. Optimist that he was, right up till the very last moment he'd somehow believed that when the smoke cleared he'd still be there; a bit singed, perhaps, and threadbare, like a character in a Loony-Tunes cartoon, but nevertheless basically in one piece. The stern reality that faced him when he came round, however, was that he was now in more pieces than the mind could possibly conceive.

Gosh, he said to himself (or rather, selves), so these are smithereens.

On the other hand, he reflected, it's not use moping. It's times like these when you just have to pull yourself together and . . .

Pull yourself together. Easier said then done.

He considered himself, hung in suspension above the surface of the planet like one aspirin dissolved in twenty million gallons of water. Spreading yourself a bit thin these days, Kiss, old son, he reflected. On the other hand . . .

Yes, he noticed, that's interesting. He realised that every single atom of his former body still had the consciousness of the whole, so that instead of there being just one Kiss, there were now several billion. A shrewd operator, he reflected, could turn this situation to his own advantage.

A gust of high-level wind reminded him of the downside. True, there were billions of him, but each one on its own was about as ineffective as the average civil rights charter. It's molecules united who can never be defeated. A solitary atom on its own, with nothing except the moral support of its fellows, is effectively dead in the water.

And likely to stay that way. Think of all the aggravation it takes to get together a mere twenty or so people for a school reunion, and then multiply that by ten billion.

Another aspect of the matter that he had to admit he didn't like much was the fact that each individual consciousness seemed to be fading rapidly. How long since the blast – one second, maybe two – and already he was starting to sound in his mind's ear like a cassette recorder with flat batteries.

There was, he recalled, a technical term for all this. What was it again? Ah, yes. Death.

Now there's a thought. If I die, I'll get to collect on my insurance policy.

(For he had indeed, many years ago and when under the influence of curdled whey, taken out a life policy with the most senior underwriter of them all. He had regretted it ever since, because (a) in the normal course of things he was immortal, and (b) he had nobody to leave the proceeds to even if he collected.)

Proviso B was still as valid as ever, but that was pretty well beside the point. So anxious was he to find a silver lining for the mushroom cloud that he was prepared to overlook the pointlessness of the exercise. Accordingly, he summoned up what energy he still had, and put a call through.

This wasn't, in fact, difficult; since bits of him had been dispersed to every nook and cranny of the planet, it wasn't surprising that one stray atom had lodged in the Chief Underwriter's ear. This made notifying the claim fairly simple.

'Hi,' he said, 'my name is Kiss, policy number 6590865098765. I'm dead, and I want to make—'

YOU CAN'T.

The particle buzzed softly, confused. 'How do you mean, I can't?' he demanded. 'If you want the policy document, it's in a tin box under a flat stone in a crater in the Sea of Tranquillity. I can draw you a map if you like.'

YOU CAN'T CLAIM. SORRY.

'Well, of all the ...' He would have expanded on this theme, but one of the seraphim who sit on the right hand of the Chief Underwriter pointed to the burning sword lying across its knees and made a pretty unambiguous gesture with it, implying that taking that tone with the Boss would result in extreme loss of privileges. The Kiss-particle subsided a little.

'Something in the small print?' he enquired. 'Some sort of all-purpose cow-catching exclusion clause?'

NOT AS SUCH, NO. THE CLAIM WOULD BE PER-FECTLY VALID. IT'S MORE A MATTER OF FEASI-BILITY, REALLY.

'Ah.' The batteries were very nearly flat now, and it was taking him all his strength just to stay awake. Nevertheless, he was intrigued. 'In what way?' he asked, as politely as he could.

SIMPLE. THE TERMS OF THE POLICY. I'M SURE YOU SEE WHAT I MEAN.

'I'm sorry, I don't think I quite ... Oh. Oh yes, I see. Yes. Quite.'

A particle can't grin, but the bit of Kiss in question came very close to succeeding. The Chief Underwriter's ear began to itch.

'It's just as well you reminded me of that,' he chirruped. 'Left to myself, I'd never have seen it that way.'

SHIT.

An insurer's nightmare.

There's a strong argument for saying that paying out any money to anybody under any circumstances whatsoever produces the same effect on your average insurer that two pounds of mature Cheddar eaten as a bedtime snack has on other people. But by any standards, the problem facing the Chief Underwriter as the bits of Kiss embarked on their final decay into oblivion was a honey.

The policy promised to pay Kiss, on his demise, the sum of ten thousand celestial dollars.

(There was a lot of other guff about with profit and provisions in the event of surrender prior to the contractual maturity date, but we can skip all that. Not germane to the issue in hand.)

Let's just pass that concept round the room and see what we come up with.

When Kiss dies, he gets ten grand. It can also be construed as saying that each time Kiss dies, he gets ten grand. Nothing at all in the small print about this being a one-off payment.

As noted above, there are currently tens of thousands of millions of Kisses (each one with the same consciousness, the same self-awareness, the memory, the persona, however you like to put it; at this point the vocabulary tends to get a bit fancy, but the idea is clear enough), all of them scheduled to die at precisely the same moment. Each one entitled to claim under the terms of the policy.

Now that's an awful lot of lettuce.

Which is not to say that the Chief Underwriter can't afford it. Somewhere buried in a cave in Galilee, or deep in some unexcavated catacomb in Rome, or maybe stashed away in a secret chamber under a Crusader castle somewhere, there's a tablet of stone in a cedarwood box that says, This guy's cheque will not bounce.

There is, however, more to it than that. In a word, inflation. More precisely, a desperately overheated money supply, leading to an inevitable devaluation, with knock-on effects on the divine economy which would throw countless angels on the dole and spell ruin for all those saints that from their labours rest who have to make ends meet on a celestial pension. Put it another way, things could hardly be worse if God suddenly fell off his yacht and drowned.

As the Chief Underwriter realised, a fraction of a second

before his unwonted lapse into vulgarity, there's only one thing that can save Heaven at this point.

A miracle.

HAVE A SEAT, said the Chief Underwriter. *AND A CIGAR. I THINK WE CAN COME TO SOME SORT OF AN AGREEMENT.*

Wherever it was that Philly Nine actually went to, when he got there he found a table and a plastic bucket.

Inside the bucket were hundreds and hundreds of brightly coloured little plastic bricks.

Philly stood for a long time, staring at the bricks and thinking 'What the ...?' Probably his mind wandered during this time, because the next thing he knew was that he had taken two bricks out and slotted them together. Each brick had little knobs on the top and little holes on the bottom that the knobs fitted into; and some of them were square and some of them were rectangular, and there were a lot of other excitingly different shapes and sizes.

Without really thinking what he was doing, he pulled the bucket towards him, sat down on the floor and began to build.

And in the evening, he looked upon everything that he had built, and saw that it was good.

And the evening and the morning were the first day.

'Thanks,' Kiss called out as he ran down the steps.

DON'T MENTION IT. ANY TIME.

A satisfactory outcome, all told. The simple task which all the king's horses and all the king's men had so conspicuously failed to do for Humpty-Dumpty had taken the Chief Underwriter's staff about seven minutes. And there had been time to suggest a few subtle design improvements along the way.

True, Kiss reflected as he strolled back down the sky, he'd had to agree to forgo a quite bewilderingly large sum of money to which he was, strictly speaking, contractually entitled; but he wasn't too bothered about that. It wasn't, he decided, that you couldn't take it with you, because you could. It was just that there wasn't exactly a superfluity of things you could spend it on once you'd got there.

Right. What shall I do now?

Well, I could pop into Saheed's for a milk sour and a game of pool. Or I could put a girdle around the earth in twenty minutes. Or I could check out the thermals. Heaps of things I could do. The rest of Time's my own.

Or I could go and see if Jane . . .

He stopped dead in his tracks, and swore. It's a basic ground rule of genie life that you don't allow yourself to get involved with mortals, and he should by now know that better than anyone. And if there was one mortal in particular who merited complete avoidance . . .

Because of her, he reflected, I've been humiliated, threatened with imminent loss of divine status, involved in a series of horrible fights with a fellow Force Twelve and finally blown to bits. By any standards, that's taking the old wish/command nexus to its absolute limits.

The sequence of thoughts reminded him of something, and he closed his eyes and listened. Nothing. He knew without having to enquire further that as far as this dimension was concerned, Philly Nine no longer existed. The threat to the world was over. Another tick on the list of Things To Do.

Well, that milk sour surely does sound inviting. I think I might just as well . . .

He looked down. He had arrived, doubtless through sheer force of habit, a few feet above the block of flats where Jane lived. That bloody woman. Hah!

There could be no doubt whatsoever, he reflected as he

walked in through the front door of the building and summoned the lift, that as far as his indentures were concerned, he was free and clear. She'd had far and away more than her bottle-top's worth out of him. Under no obligation whatsoever.

Nevertheless, he rationalised as he rang the doorbell, it'd be a shame to part on bad terms, and their previous parting hadn't exactly been cordial. Besides, he never had given her the obligatory bottomless purse, and he felt conscientious about that. Like the little silver inkstand-cum-paperweight you get given when you're knocked out of a TV game show after the very first round, the bottomless purse wasn't optional. It came with the territory.

Rather to his surprise, the door was opened by the Dragon King of the South-East.

'G'day, mate,' said the King. 'I was just leaving. Done me stint on this job.'

'Me too.'

The King shook his head. 'Right bunch of wowsers if you ask me,' he muttered, 'the lot of 'em. Glad to be through with 'em at last.'

'Quite.'

'That bloody sheila . . .'

'Indeed.'

'Well.' The King hesitated for a moment, as if considering whether some gesture of solidarity – a slapped back, perhaps, or a matey hand on the shoulder – would be more likely to result in the offer of a cool one down at Saheed's or an instinctive left hook to the jaw. He must have been a pessimist at heart because he smiled, shook his head and trotted off down the stairs. In human form this time, naturally. Eventually, even Dragon Kings learn by their mistakes.

Kiss stood for a few minutes, a hand on the half-open door. I don't really need to say goodbye, he told himself.

The more usual form of ending a mortal/genie relationship was a string of vulgar abuse and a puff of evil-smelling green smoke. Nevertheless. Trends are there to be bucked, and fashions led. He pushed the door open and walked in.

About fifteen seconds later he came out again, moving fast and a sort of deep scarlet colour from the hairline to the collar-bone.

It only goes to show, he muttered to his immortal soul as he bolted down the stairs, humans and genies are on different wavelengths altogether, and probably for the best. As a genie, he hadn't thought twice about strolling in unannounced on two mortals of different sexes who were just embarking on the traditional living happily together ever after. Exactly what went on under such circumstances was, he realised, not something he'd ever given much thought to, in the same way that the bricklayers don't generally hang around to see what colour carpets eventually go into the house they've just built. By the time the happy ending was properly under way, he was usually long gone and starting on another job.

Well, now he knew; and, from what he'd seen, he was well out of it. For one thing, it looked so damn undignified. Not to mention uncomfortable. Cramp would be the least of your problems.

Each to their own idea of a good time. Compared to, say, a good game of pool, however, he was amazed that it had lasted as long as it had.

A good game of pool. And a quart or two of natural yoghurt with the lads, a really hot curry and so to bed. What could, in all honesty, be better?

Jane stirred, brushed aside the heavy residue of sleep and reached out towards the pillow beside her.

Nothing.

Or rather, a note. With a frown like gathering thunder-clouds, she picked it up.

BACK ABOUT SIX-THIRTY

she read; and underneath, obviously added as an after-thought,

GONE FISHIN'

'An' another thing.'

The other regulars propping up Saheed's back bar bestowed on him the look of good-natured contempt that relatively sober people reserve especially for those of their fellows who've had more natural yoghurt than is good for them. One of them said, 'Yes?'

'Humans,' said Kiss, 'have no sense of proportion.'

'Really?'

'Really.'

'You mean, their heads are too big for their bodies, that sort of thing?'

Kiss shook his head, a courageous act under the circumstances. 'You're thinking,' he said, 'of perspective. They're quite good at perspective, actually, give the buggers their due. Used not to be, of course. Anyway, where was I?'

'Proportion. Lack of sense of, prevalence of among the more ephemeral species. You were pontificating.'

'Yeah. 'Specially women. Women have no sense of proportion,' Kiss said, swilling the dregs of cream round in his virtually empty mug, 'whatsoever. All they care about is—'

'Yes?'

'Carpets. And curtains. And loose covers. And what colour the bloody things should be. I mean, I ask you.'

'What?'

'Sorry?'

'What do you ask us?'

Kiss blinked. 'I ask you,' he continued, after a moment's regrouping, 'what the hell difference the colour makes to a cushion. I mean, are red cushions softer than blue ones, or what?'

'I think they like things to look nice. After all, they're the ones who spend all their time at home, so I suppose it's—'

'Balls,' said Kiss, with grandeur. 'I mean, can you tell me without looking what colour your trousers are?'

'As a matter of fact, I can. They're a sort of pale beige, with a faint—'

'All right, then, all right. Can you tell me what colour your bathroom curtains are? Go on, you can't.'

'True, but since I'm a river-spirit I don't actually have a bathroom. The rest of my place is done out in blues, greens and browns, and that's in the lease.'

Kiss scowled. 'You know what I mean,' he said. 'All women care about is fripperies. Stupid, pointless things which—'

'And I suppose,' interrupted the river spirit, 'that we devote all our time to higher issues. Like darts.'

'Applied ballistic research,' someone broke in. 'Very important study.'

'Betting on horse-races.'

'Advanced probability mathematics.'

'Combined with equestrian genetics.'

'And meteorology, don't forget. Depending whether the going is hard or soft.'

'I thought that was flying rocks and stuff.'

'Look,' Kiss broke in, 'all right, we may not exactly cram each something minute with sixty seconds of whatsit, but in our case it doesn't matter. Only matters if you're gonna die some day. Ruddy women, now, they're all going to go to their graves and nothing to show for it except a load of soft furnishings. Absolutely futile, if you ask me.'

The river spirit shrugged. 'So?' he said. 'What of it? Mortals are mortals and we're us.' He grinned. 'Vive la difference,' he added.

'Yeah, well . . .'

'Fancy a game of dominoes?'

'Now you're talking.'

After leaving Saheed's, Kiss wandered slowly up through the clouds and perched for a moment between the upper and the lower air. It was just after sunrise, and the big red splodge was beginning to give way to the first blue notes of a new day. From where he sat, Kiss could see the whole of the daylight side of the planet. He shaded his eyes with his hand and had a good look; something, he realised, that he hadn't done for a long time.

There was a lot to look at. All over the surface, and particularly in the yellow sandy bits, the armies who had failed to get to the war on time were slouching listlessly at home, trying to remember as they did so what the hell all the fuss had been about. There now, Kiss told himself, if it hadn't been for me . . .

So? What of it? Mortals are mortals and we're us. If ever they do blow up this planet, we can just move to another one. Who gives at toss, anyway?

As he watched, the Earth turned. Night retreated to the right and advanced to the left. One step forwards, balanced for ever by one step back. How it ought to be, of course. Except that if you got together say a hundred genies, and by dint of some miracle you persuaded them all to work together, you could get them to haul another star in from another solar system and so position it that it could be day on both sides of the planet simultaneously. Sure, you'd have to make some adjustments to the mechanism, so that the seas didn't dry up and that sort of thing; but it could be done. All manner of things could be done.

Probably just as well, Kiss told himself, that they aren't.

On an impulse, he spread his arms wide and drifted down to the surface. He wasn't aiming for anywhere in particular, and he ended up hovering a few feet above the water, somewhere in the middle of the sea.

There was nothing except water for miles in every direction; nothing to be seen except the regiments of waves, marching in perfect formation in accordance with the orders of the moon. Nothing, except a tiny speck, so small that he couldn't even tell how far away it was.

For genies, though, thinking is doing, and without a conscious decision he found himself hovering directly over the speck, which turned out to be the neck of a floating bottle.

That rings a bell.

Mortals, Kiss recalled, when cast away on desert islands, sometimes write messages and put them in bottles, in the hope that somehow, at some time, somebody will find them and do something: notify the next of kin, or the coastguard, or more likely the insurance company. And although it might be considered a futile gesture to launch so tiny and frail a communication into so much savagely indifferent water, you had to admit it showed a bit of class. A random particle of optimism fired blindly into infinity in the hope of hitting the bull, of achieving something worthwhile. The fact of death and the promise of hope; between the two of them mortals had a rough time of it, and they coped remarkably well.

Through the opaque green glass, Kiss could see a scrap of paper neatly folded and tucked in underneath the cork. His heart unaccountably high, he dived and picked the bottle out of the water as neatly as a Japanese fisherman's cormorant. Pop went the cork (not whoosh, this time) and he unfolded the message, which said:

NO MILK TODAY
signed
D. JONES

'Marvellous,' said Kiss disgustedly; and he was reflecting bitterly on the nature of anticlimax when an idea struck him.

A message in a bottle. Yes, why not?

Without giving himself time to think, he jumped down through the neck of the bottle and dragged the cork in tight after him. Then he leaned back, smiling contentedly, waiting to see what would happen next.

GRAILBLAZERS

Tom Holt

THE HOLY GRAIL AND THE WHOLLY INEPT ...

Fifteen hundred years have passed and the Grail is still missing, presumed ineffable; the Knights have dumped the Quest and now deliver pizzas; the sinister financial services industry of the lost kingdom of Atlantis threatens the universe with fiscal Armageddon; while in the background lurks the dark, brooding, red-caped presence of Father Christmas.

In other words, Grailmate. Has Prince Boamund of Northgales (Snotty to friends) woken from his enchanted sleep in time to snatch back the Apron of Invincibility, overthrow the dark power of the Lord of the Reindeer and find out exactly what a Grail is? And just who did do the washing-up after the Last Supper?

Take a thrilling Grailhound bus ride into the wildly improbable with Tom Holt.

Faust Among Equals

Tom Holt

WELL I'LL BE DAMNED ...

The management buy-out of Hell wasn't going quite as well as planned. For a start, there had been that nasty business with the perjurors, and then came the news that the Most Wanted Man in History had escaped, and all just as the plans for the new theme park, Eurobosch, were under way.

But Kurt 'Mad Dog' Lundqvist, the foremost bounty hunter of all time, is on the case, and he can usually be relied upon to get his man - even when that man is Lucky George Faustus ...

Exuberant, Hell-raising comedy from Tom Holt at his inventive best.

ODDS AND GODS

Tom Holt

IT'S A GOD'S LIFE ...

... at the Sunnyvoyde Residential Home for retired
deities. Everlasting life can be a real drag when all
you've got to look forward to is cauliflower cheese
on Wednesdays. And even though few things go
unnoticed under the steely gaze and iron fist of
Mrs Henderson, all is not well.

For a start, there's a major technical problem with the
thousand-year-old traction engine which has been
lovingly restored by those almighty duffers Thor,
Odin and Frey ... the damn thing actually goes.

And then there's Osiris, pushed one tapioca too far by a
power-crazy godson with friends in very smelly places,
and forced to set out on a quest which will test his
wheelchair to the very limits.

Only one thing might save the world from an eternity of
chaos ... dentures. It's true. Honest to god.

MAIL ORDER - BOOKS BY POST

All Orbit books are available through mail order or from your local bookshop or newsagent.

☐	Expecting Someone Taller	Tom Holt	£4.99
☐	Who's Afraid of Beowulf?	Tom Holt	£4.99
☐	Flying Dutch	Tom Holt	£4.99
☐	Ye Gods!	Tom Holt	£4.99
☐	Overtime	Tom Holt	£5.99
☐	Here Comes the Sun	Tom Holt	£4.99
☐	Grailblazers	Tom Holt	£4.99
☐	Faust Among Equals	Tom Holt	£4.99
☐	Odds and Gods	Tom Holt	£4.99
☐	My Hero	Tom Holt	£15.99

Please send cheque, eurocheque, or postal order (sterling only), or complete details for Access/Visa/Mastercard:

☐☐☐☐☐☐☐☐☐☐☐☐☐☐☐☐☐☐

Expiry Date: _____ Signature: _____
UK Customers: Add £0.75 per book for post and packing.
Overseas Customers: Add £1.00 per book for post and packing.

All orders to:
Little, Brown
Special Sales Department
Brettenham House
Lancaster Place
London WC2E 7EN

ORBIT

or fax 0171 911 8100

Name: _____
Address: _____
_____
_____

Please allow 28 days for delivery.
Prices and availability are subject to change without notice.
Please tick box if you do not wish to receive any
additional information.   ☐

interzone

SCIENCE FICTION AND FANTASY

Monthly   £2.25

- *Interzone* is the leading British magazine which specializes in SF and new fantastic writing. We have published:

BRIAN ALDISS	GARRY KILWORTH
J.G. BALLARD	DAVID LANGFORD
IAIN BANKS	MICHAEL MOORCOCK
BARRINGTON BAYLEY	RACHEL POLLACK
GREGORY BENFORD	KEITH ROBERTS
MICHAEL BISHOP	GEOFF RYMAN
DAVID BRIN	JOSEPHINE SAXTON
RAMSEY CAMPBELL	BOB SHAW
ANGELA CARTER	JOHN SHIRLEY
RICHARD COWPER	JOHN SLADEK
JOHN CROWLEY	BRIAN STABLEFORD
PHILIP K. DICK	BRUCE STERLING
THOMAS M. DISCH	LISA TUTTLE
MARY GENTLE	IAN WATSON
WILLIAM GIBSON	CHERRY WILDER
M. JOHN HARRISON	GENE WOLFE

- *Interzone* has also introduced many excellent new writers; illustrations, articles, interviews, film and book reviews, news, etc.

- *Interzone* is available from good bookshops, or by subscription. For six issues, send £14 (outside UK, £17). For twelve issues send £26, (outside UK, £32). Single copies: £2.50 inc. p&p (outside UK, £2.80).

- American subscribers may send $27 for six issues, or $52 for twelve issues. All US copies will be despatched by Air Saver (accelerated surface mail).

- -

To: **interzone** 217 Preston Drove, Brighton, BN1 6FL, UK.

Please send me six/twelve issues of *Interzone*, beginning with the current issue. I enclose a cheque / p.o. / international money order, made payable to *Interzone* (Delete as applicable.)

Name _____

Address _____

_____